Fracture

Amanda K. Byrne

ISBN: 09860990-1-5
ISBN-13: 978-0-9860990-1-4

Fracture

ACKNOWLEDGMENTS

Fracture never would have made it out into the world if it hadn't been for Liv Rancourt's absolute faith that this story needed to be heard. So thank you, Liv, for your feedback and your unwavering support, even when I went all whiny and self-doubty.

To my editors, Rhonda Helms and Rebecca Weston, for helping me turn this into a gem of a book. You've both made me a better writer, and I loved working with you.

Whitney Fletcher, for your valuable feedback and your cheerleading—I'm so glad to have you as a friend and CP. Shannon O'Brien—you rock. Thanks for coming up with a fab title and for being an awesome friend.

And finally, thank you to my friends and family for cheering me on as I slogged through the process of putting out this first book. And to the world's greatest BF, Aaron, your support means the world to me. I love you!

CHAPTER ONE

SARAJEVO, BOSNIA-HERZEGOVENA
PRESENT DAY

My heart stops.

The nightmare plays out in the wet and muddy street, air filling with the sickening noises of bones breaking, flesh striking flesh, horrible, nasty words uttered in gravelly voices. Yes yes yes it's happening again. Ryan, curled up like a potato bug. Ryan screaming as his spine is broken. Ryan gasping for air, the skies opening up and drowning us both.

I blink the memory away, and it's no longer Ryan. It's someone else entirely. Government soldiers aim their steel-toed boots at the man's stomach, his head, his back. I have two choices: slink away or try to get them to stop.

Because that worked so well the last time.

Except last time I wasn't prepared. Last time I held my ideals and hopes and prayers out for anyone to take.

I need a distraction. Something fiery. Something like the Molotov cocktails Ismael thought to store in a crevice in the wall. Smart man, Ismael, predicting our corner of Sarajevo might be one of the next neighborhoods to fall. Hopefully the fuse hasn't gotten wet.

Where'd he put the lighter?

Fire licks up the rag, forcing me to throw the bottle before

I have a chance to rethink my decision. It lands away from the group in the street. Flames dance over the gasoline puddled on the cement, inching closer to the car I'd aimed for. I'm sure Mrs. Vukic won't care about losing it. The fuel rationing has become so extreme almost no one can afford it any longer.

A *whoosh*, a second of suspended silence, and the gas tank catches fire. I cover my head and brace for the explosion. Metal and rubber shrapnel litter the pavement, and just as I'd hoped, the soldiers abandon their victim and draw their weapons, fanning out, searching for the culprit.

My alley is merely a crack between buildings. Skinny enough it will go unnoticed, and perfect for hiding in. The soldiers have spread out around the car, heads down against the encroaching smoke, which means I have very little time, and no plan for getting the injured man out of the middle of the street.

Fuck. I should have walked away. I should have pretended I didn't see a thing.

I can't let him die out there. Not like Ryan.

Curled up as he is, I can't judge his height, if he's slim or muscled, still conscious or a dead weight. Fire crackles and sends black smoke spewing into the air. It's disgusting, a thick, nauseating cloud that wants to settle in my chest. Before long it'll make visibility nil.

I'm running out of time. If I'm going to continue to play hero, I have to move. Now.

I can't.

I have to.

Darting forward, I keep an eye on the soldiers, or what I can see of them. The smoke's doing a decent job of creating chaos in addition to a distraction.

His hair is black. At least, it looks black. Broad shoulders. His jaw looks intact, but his nose is definitely broken. One arm is cradled to his chest. Two fingers are out of joint. His coat is torn and bloody and covered in mud. His jeans are in slightly better shape than his coat, and I can't tell if there's any damage to his legs.

His moan of pain is followed by a jerk of his leg, but his eyes remain shut as I feel my way down his thigh, over his knee, along his shin. The moan comes again as I prod his shin. Possible break. Great. Outstanding. He has the use of one leg. Maybe. Leaving him here is starting to sound like a much better idea. Save my own ass.

And they'll come back and finish what they started. Tears sting my eyes—from the smoke, from the thought of another person suffering the same fate as Ryan—and I blink furiously to keep them from falling.

Sticking my hands under his shoulders means scraping them along the damp pavement below, and I can't stop the hiss of pain. "Get up. I need you to get up, because it's the only way you'll get off this street."

"Can't," he gasps.

"*Can't* won't work right now. Get up. I don't care if you have to crawl, but I can't lift you." I push at his shoulders, attempting to shove the man into a sitting position and only succeeding in pulling a harsh groan from him.

"Get help." I hadn't thought it was possible to infuse that much pain into two words.

"No time. You can't walk—I think your leg's broken—so get on your knees, we're going to try crawling." Please move. Please let this horror show end. I can't leave you. I can't leave you behind, whoever you are.

After an eternity, he rolls onto his stomach, his legs twitching as he bends them, working them under him. He flops down again when his good arm gives way. A few more attempts, my heart breaking a little more each time, and he remains up. Not standing, but in a mobile position.

I drop to my knees beside him so he'll be able to see me better. The smoke's thick enough it's getting hard to breathe, and sight became a thing of the past several minutes ago. They're out there, waiting, circling, trained to pounce, and I've got nothing left. Crawling over the pavement is hell on my knees. I grit my teeth as I stick to the man's side.

By some miracle, we reach the sidewalk. "Almost there."

"Almost where? The entrance to hell?" Under the pain coloring his voice is an accent I can't place. Not Slavic. A mystery that will remain a mystery. My goal now is to get him into the alley and go for Doctor Gudelj.

"Pretty much. Keep moving."

The alley entrance has never looked so inviting, dark with shadows and shrouded in smoke, smelling of burning rubber and damp. I push to my feet and dash inside, waiting impatiently for him to follow.

He collapses as soon as he's through the opening, the toes of his shoes sticking out into the street. Not good enough. With the smoke clearing and the shouts of the soldiers coming closer, our reprieve has ended.

I try not to think of all the bacteria swimming in the puddle he's landed in as I work my hands under him. A few more feet. Grunting, I dig into his armpits and heave.

He moves about three inches.

Again and again and again, until sweat slicks my spine and my back screams in protest, but his feet are clear of the entrance. By a solid distance, too. It'll do. He needs help, attention I can't give him.

I stumble and catch myself as a hand closes around my ankle. "Thanks," he rasps.

I strip off my coat and fold it up, shoving it under his head. "Don't thank me yet. I've got to go get you some help."

"'Kay." The word is faint and buried in the fabric. He'll live. He's not as bad as Ryan was. There's no babbling, no pleas for death. No mercy. No desperate *I love you.*

Still, I hesitate. He needs medical attention and strong arms. Neither of which I can provide. I can wait until the soldiers leave, or I can go now. If he's bleeding internally, those minutes, however long they may be, could make all the difference.

I race down the alley, Ryan's ghost hard at my heels.

* * *

"He is where?" Dr. Gudelj's accent gets thicker when he's excited, and right now is no exception. I'm asking him to run into a hot zone. Anyone's pulse would race.

"The alley. Well, the sort of alley. Right across from where Mrs. Vukic parks her car? The car's not there anymore," I add. "I blew it up."

To his credit, the good doctor doesn't look surprised, merely continues rushing to and fro as he collects the various implements he'll need. So disorganized. I'm surprised he can find them so quickly, given how cluttered his flat is. They should all be packed away in his bag, cleaned and ready for use. Pointing this out is a waste of time; Doctor Gudelj is one of the few medical personnel in the neighborhood who'll willingly treat almost anyone and is even less likely to request payment.

"Run downstairs and get Murat and Ismael."

I race for the stairwell, slowing slightly so I won't trip on my way down. In any other city, I'm sure the frantic banging and shouting would have drawn the neighbors' attention, but nobody sticks a head out to investigate. No one will. Not anymore. Mind your own business is the new mantra of this city.

The door swings open, and Ismael squints at me, his dark hair in drooping spikes. "Nora. Too early. Come back later."

I stick my foot in the door before he can shut it. "I need you and Murat to come with me. Government soldiers attacked a civilian, busted his leg and a few other things. He can't stand on his own."

The change from sleepy to alert is instantaneous, and Ismael nods once before shutting the door in my face. Typical Ismael. I'm only allowed inside if I come bearing alcohol or if Murat takes pity on me.

"You tell them to come?" Doctor Gudelj jogs down the stairs, his face already red with exertion.

The door opens again, revealing Ismael, followed by Murat. "You ready, old man?" Murat asks the doctor before flashing me a grin, blue eyes alight with excitement. The guys love this. Running on the edge between the rebel faction and the government soldiers keeps them on their toes.

The four of us hurry to where I'd left my charge, and at a

head jerk from Murat, I dash off ahead. I'm not as fast as they are, but I'm smaller and it's easier for me to blend into the shadows. I've spent the last two years perfecting it.

He's still there. Still quiet. Unmoving. Fear and pain freeze my blood, numbing my limbs, and if I don't move soon I won't be able to tell Murat it's safe to come around the front, onto the street.

Move. It's not Ryan. It's someone else, someone I don't know, someone I can see to safety.

Hugging the side of the building, I edge past his prone form and peek around the corner. Fire flickers over the twisted, groaning frame of the car, fitful plumes of smoke drifting upward every so often. The cold air is mostly clear, a fine layer of ash and dirt and shrapnel on the sidewalks and the street.

I creep out, staying low, staying close to the building. Nothing. It's empty. No civilians. The soldiers have moved on. I hurry down the street to the corner. Murat's waiting at the end of the block. I wave him over, and he jogs toward me, nodding when he passes. They'll take the man to the clinic, provided it hasn't been boarded over and locked tight by one faction or the other. It should still be safe. It was a few days ago.

"Nora?"

Murat's waiting at the alley entrance, the question clear in his voice. Am I coming? This is my find. My responsibility to see it through to the end. To find his family or his friends, to return him to his keepers.

Dread weighs me down as I trudge toward Murat. I should have left the man in the street when I had the chance.

But the ghosts would have never left me alone.

Doctor Gudelj looks up as I stick my head in through the entrance. "Go. Open the clinic and start some water boiling. The first room should be clear. We will put him in there." He digs for his keys and tosses them to me.

Grateful to have an excuse to leave, I shove them into my pocket and take off, keeping to the shadows as much as possible. It's not hard to do in this city, full as it is of broken buildings and souls. The skirmish the outside world thought would end quickly has gone on for two years now, with no end in sight. Word is it's spread to the countryside, but with the city's borders closed, no one can say for certain if that's true.

The soldiers have deserted this sector for the time being. A buzz, a snap, and the lights flicker on, casting light over a facility edging toward nonuse. The front windows are long since busted out and covered in plywood and whatever else we could find. Cupboards and drawers stand open, papers fluttering listlessly in the breeze blowing through the cracks. The place is chilly, and I blow on my hands to warm them. I grab the one large pot that hasn't been stolen and fill it with water, begging the spluttering tap to give me just enough to cover the doctor's tools. It can shut off after if it wants. Not before.

They'll be here soon. I can reassure myself the man will be fine and slip away, go back to hiding from everyone. I set the pot on the hot plate one of the nurses brought in, leaving it to boil while I pull out supplies.

Rebels and soldiers alike have ransacked the place for everything of use. Except for what they can't find. What they can't find is hidden, covered by a panel, then a shelf, and the shelf scrapes over the floor in a grating, nails-on-chalkboard sound. Behind the panel is the neighborhood's dwindling supply of bandages, antiseptic, and precious, precious drugs. Antibiotics, painkillers. The inhalers were the first to go. With the constant smoke and soot, the incidence of breathing problems increased, and the nebulizers, both the pocket-sized and the larger machines, are gone.

Bandages. Antiseptic. A packet of antibiotics. What's left looks so forlorn and abandoned. He'll need an ultrasound or something to check for internal bleeding. Crutches. A sling. Plaster if his leg is broken. The rebels took the ultrasound machine and the government appropriated the crutches.

Someone's here. The scuffling coming from the front entry is too loud to be rats. Murat and Ismael, the doctor and the

7

patient. Faster than I'd anticipated.

Sure enough, Ismael and Murat shove their way through the door, the injured man hanging between them, his face twisted in pain. Agony, really. He'd probably appreciate it if he could just pass the fuck out.

"Is the water ready?" The doctor raises a brow and I scurry off to check. I know the drill. Ladling a portion into a small bowl, I bring it in and the doctor's metal implements to be sterilized. They clank against the sides of the pot. The autoclave crapped out a long time ago, back around the start of the skirmish. Replacement medical equipment is even harder to come by than replenishing medical supplies. Hopefully whatever incisions need to be made are minimal.

A moan. Thrashing. A yell, followed by babbling. It's worse. So much worse than sitting in the street, watching the life drain from Ryan. This man is trying, and maybe failing, to live. My ears wish he'd give up.

"Nora." Ismael appears in the doorway. "Gudelj needs you."

The scalpel and tongs haven't sat in the water long enough, not by the doctor's exacting standards, but it'll have to do if he's calling for them already. Scooping them from the water, I wrap them in a towel and hurry across the hall to the exam room.

Sweat's popped out on the man's forehead, his skin grey in the dull lights. "Bandages, yes? We have some?" the doctor asks.

"I left them in the other room." Ismael slips out to get them, leaving Murat standing at the man's head, holding him down by one shoulder. I shift my attention to Doctor Gudelj. "You still need me?"

"Yes."

This is not from the doctor or Murat, but the man lying on the table. It's a hoarse, dirty rasp, one that makes me cringe. His hand flails around, groping for something. Someone. Me? "You. You should have left me. You didn't."

Oh god, he needs to stop talking. Fierce stabs of grief slice

8

through my stomach, tearing me open with every tiny word. "Shh." Without thinking, I take his flopping hand in both of mine. "Calm down," I whisper. Please calm down. Please stop talking.

"There. That is better," says Doctor Gudelj. Murat's hold loosens and the doctor resumes cutting away the man's jeans. "Tell me, what is your name?"

I don't want to know his name.

"Declan."

Definitely not Slavic.

"Yours. Tell me yours." His eyes slit open and all I see is black—dark pupils bleeding into irises, eclipsing them. His hand tightens in mine as pain twists his mouth.

I have to go. The past wants to swallow me whole, make me drown, swamp me cover me kill me. He won't let go of my hand, those slitted eyes holding me hostage.

"Nora. My name is Nora."

CHAPTER TWO

"Fuck! Bloody fucking hell!"

Declan's refusing to surrender to the pain, which means he's fully conscious of having his leg set, his shoulder shoved back into its socket, his torso palpated and a myriad of other necessary tasks while Doctor Gudelj tries to get a complete assessment of the damage.

I *know* the doctor's got a syringe. I saw it earlier. A syringe of sanity-saving bliss, something that may not knock Declan out but will take away some of the pain, make him let go of my hand, allow me to escape. My part here is done.

Declan won't let go.

His hair's matted now, thin rivulets of sweat running down his temples like tears. Stray locks flop over his forehead, the dark strands stark against the sickening pallor of his skin. My free hand moves unbidden, pushes them up and off. The bruises are coming into their own, showing their full range of purples, yellows, reds, and an angry, ominous grey. He curses again as his fingers are wrenched back into place and taped together. No splints. Those went almost as quickly as the inhalers.

"There. I think we are done." The doctor rolls his stool away from the bed. "Now, Declan, you have family here? Friends?"

"No," he mumbles.

"No? You are alone here?" Ismael, leaning against the doorjamb, frowns at the thought. It's not so unusual to be completely alone in this city. I am. I am completely alone in this city.

"No," Declan answers, the word a little firmer than it was before. "There is no one."

"Surely, there is someone. You will need help for the first few weeks while you heal."

Declan winces as he turns his head toward me. "She can help me."

No way in four hells am I helping him. I'm not a nurse.

His slits for eyes latch on to mine, and though there's so little that I can see, what I do is challenging me. "She can help me," he repeats, even as my head shakes no.

"Ah. Yes. Nora can help you. Nora, this is okay, yes?"

Not okay. Not okay at all.

He's tugging on my hand. Tug tug tug, his hand working its way up my arm to my shoulder. Along the curve, to the back of my neck, the pressure of his fingers insubstantial after the crushing blows he's dealt to my hand. "A few days." The words come out through gritted teeth, his breathing labored. "A few days, then you'll be rid of me."

Painful words, words I don't have defenses against.

"Good! It is settled. Murat and Ismael will help you get him to his flat." The doctor bustles around, tossing his tools into his bag without care.

"No."

"No?" What the hell does he mean, no? "You can't stay here."

The hand on my neck tightens. "I can't go back to me flat."

And I'm not taking him to mine. My haven. My sanctuary. Where no one can find me and I hide for days. The solitude is the only thing that makes this war bearable, knowing the people out there dying aren't people I care for. Selfish, yes, but it keeps me sane.

"You must go somewhere." Murat pulls out his

intimidating face, but it doesn't work on Declan. "The clinic is not safe. You will not return to your flat? We take you to Nora's."

"No!" The hold on my neck breaks as I surge up. "N-n-no, he can't. I can't have him there."

The room quiets, everyone's eyes on me. Staring. Waiting.

There's one place I can take him. It's likely cold and dusty and stale-smelling, but no one will find him there.

I push the air from my lungs. "If you're worried people will come looking for you, I know where you can stay."

* * *

I'm right. It's cold and dusty and stale-smelling. Full of ghosts. Haunting laughter and sighs, and harsher, sharper sobs. Echoes of a dying and dead relationship. It wasn't my fault. It wasn't his. It was *theirs*. The rebels and their stupid war took my fiancé from me. All I've got left are these shreds that I'm forever trying to pull into a whole.

"Wow. This place has not been used in a while, huh?" Murat helps Declan across the small room to the even smaller bedroom.

I shrug. "Wasn't any reason to." Not after Ryan died. This place was supposed to be nothing more than a weigh station. I'd never imagined it would be the mausoleum to our dream. "Bedroom's through there. The blankets are probably in terrible shape."

The three men make their way into the darkened room, Declan muttering in pain. The guys were probably maneuvering him onto the bed. He'll need food. Water. Clean clothes and soap. Towels and better blankets that aren't dusty and possibly moldy. "Hey, Murat?"

He sticks his head out, wincing as Declan curses. "Yes?"

"I need to go out, grab some stuff. Can one of you stay with him until I get back?"

He narrows his eyes. "Maybe I should come with you. Ismael can stay here."

His concern is touching, if misplaced, considering I've been running around this city mostly unseen for almost two years.

"I'll be fine."

"That's not what I'm talking about."

Oh. "I'm going to come back. I promise."

"Do. Or no vodka for you."

I flip him the bird. "Get his address for me. I'll grab some of his stuff while I'm out."

Murat disappears into the gloom, the low rumbles of conversation rising to frantic shouts. "Where is she? She can't go!"

Sighing, I walk into the room, squinting as my eyes adjust to the shadows. "Someone has to. There're no supplies here, and someone's got to go get them. If you want clean clothes, you give me your address."

"So send one of them." His accent's more pronounced now that he's not wheezing with pain every three seconds.

"I could." But they can't blend like I can. They'll attract attention. I don't. Or, at least, not much.

No one speaks. It's an audio version of a Mexican standoff, but I have no stakes in the outcome. If Declan wants to spend days sitting around in his dirty, torn clothes, he's free to do so.

"Dolac Malta," he says at last.

Dolac Malta's some distance from here. How he ended up in our streets is something most people would be curious about, but asking questions only leads to more questions and conversations I'd rather not have. I've learned to keep my mouth shut.

"I'll be a while, then." An age, if I can. Being in the flat is making me twitchy, and the less time I spend in it, the better. The weight of all those memories is suffocating. Coming here was a terrible idea.

A few days. Until the worst of the pain passes and he can move about more freely. Or as freely as you can with a broken leg, a multitude of bruises, a dislocated shoulder, a sprained wrist, and several broken ribs. Oh, and let's not forget the possible concussion.

Maybe more than a few days. Dammit.

Murat and Ismael are used to my coming and going without

so much as a word, and I swing out of the flat, down to the street, planning my route. The encroaching twilight will both help conceal me but make the trek more dangerous. Shutting down my thoughts, I draw in a frosty breath and focus on the route that will take me to my flat. Two blocks down. Through the alley. Three blocks over, a block back, another five blocks down. A crack-like alley. A passageway between buildings, cross the street, a block back. All so I'm invisible. All so I can't be found. Ridiculous, at first, then necessary when Cristian found me. Now I have a reason not to be followed.

Being followed means he can find me whenever he wants. I hold all the cards so far by being unreachable, and I intend to keep it that way.

My flat is cooling and dark by the time I reach it. I can't take much. Too heavy a load cuts down on the response time, and with bullets flying out of nowhere, a half-second is the difference between living and dying.

Clean sheets, an extra blanket. A change of clothes for myself. Food. Water. Another blanket. The sweatshirt I swore I'd left in Murat and Ismael's flat and they claimed they didn't have.

I have too much stuff. The growing bundle is heavier than I'd like, and I'll need to move quickly to get to Dolac Malta before it gets too late. It'll have to stay here for the time being. I'll pick up Declan's clothes and come back for the blankets.

Inefficient. But necessary. Declan's choices are grubby clothes or going naked, and I'd rather not have to deal with a naked Declan. Or any naked man, for that matter. So clothing. Nice, clean clothing.

His shoulders are so broad. How had they managed to take him down, take him by surprise? The dark hair should have allowed him to blend in, as long as he kept his mouth shut. Irish. He must be Irish, with a name like Declan. Declan of the broad shoulders and pain-roughened voice.

My swirling thoughts are the only excuse I have for why I run right into Murat the second I open the door. "Jesus!"

"I thought you might need help. Declan would not shut up

until one of us went after you." He peers around me into the flat. "You are not close, are you? And you walk home in the dark, after the vodka." The scowl on his face shouldn't be comforting, but it is. "Nora. No more. You drink, you sleep on our couch. Or we take you home."

The wall around my stinking well of emotions has too many cracks and patches in it. His words threaten to undo me because, as mean and chastising as they sound, it means he cares. It means they both care, and I can't have people caring for me.

Murat's a big guy, and his hands make my arms look like matchsticks as he clasps them, moving me to the side and scooping up the bundle I've dropped by the door. "Let's go. And you will tell me why you led me on a duck chase."

"You mean goose chase. It's so I won't be followed." Because he's here, I clatter down the stairs instead of slink, not bothering to muffle my footsteps. It's not hard to do; just contract your leg muscles and hold everything stiff. "Obviously I need a different route."

"But why do you do it in the first place?" He pushes open the door to the street.

Because if I don't, Cristian will find me. I'll never know peace again. "There are—" A pause. "—people who think I'd be useful. And they refuse to accept I'm of no use to anyone." It's true. I'll never be a spy. A thief, a runner, a broken human, a shell of the girl I was, but never a spy. Never for *him*, no matter how enticing his promise of a way out of the country is.

Murat stops me with a hand on my shoulder, and again there's the sensation I could be snapped into tiny pieces. I've seen Ismael in full temper, chasing off rebels and soldiers alike, driving them from the neighborhood, but never Murat. Ismael's buddy is the friendlier of the two, though just as fierce in a fight. "You are in trouble? You need help?"

I can't help it. I stiffen. "No." His hand drops away at the ice in the word.

The streets are quieter than I'd like, a distant rat-a-tat-tat warning us of a firefight some streets over. Too faint to be close enough we'll run into it, loud enough for nerves to kick in my belly. My feet are itchy and my hands twitch along with my shoulders and my hips. We're moving too slow.

"Nora?"

"Faster," I whisper. We need to get off the streets, out of the way, grab the clothes and be back soon. Now. Soonnow.

Declan's block has all the streetlights shot out. The dark covers everything, turning the buildings into fuzzy outlines. It's as close to utter silence as you can get in the middle of a city in the middle of a war zone, and it's got me closer to the edge than being weighed down with Murat's presence.

I don't need to tell him to walk softly. The pair of us creep up the steps side by side. The landing is clear. So's the hallway.

The door to the flat is wide open, beckoning a sinister welcome.

Setting the bundle of blankets down, Murat jerks his head to the door, holding up his hand for me to wait. That's fine. I'm perfectly content to wait out here, in the dark hallway that is probably clear of anyone wanting to get into some shenanigans. A few tense minutes later, he motions for me to come inside and eases the door shut behind me.

Somehow the war outside made its way into Declan's flat. Books and papers, food cartons, broken plates, ripped pillows and cushions with the stuffing spilling out like entrails. Clothing and shoes and paper, so much more paper than one would expect. Bending down, I pick up a scrap. Glossy. Smooth and glossy, like a photograph.

Torn pictures, littering every surface.

Murat disappears into the bedroom in search of intact clothes, leaving me to scout out perishables. I can't stop picking up the pieces of the photos. They're a puzzle I need to figure out, only Murat's reappeared and I don't have time. The paper falls from my hands, useless.

Murat doesn't question me when I take the lead, zigging and zagging our way home, doubling back, circling, edging around corners and darting through glass-strewn streets.

Ismael's grumbling is loud enough to be heard on the steps.

"Soon. He will keep her safe." The relief in his eyes doesn't quite cancel out the impatience as we walk through the door. "See? She is back now."

"I can't fuckin' well see. I can't get off the bed." Declan's disembodied voice holds even more pain than it did before. My stomach knots at the sound. I can't do this. And I really don't want to take the syringe Ismael's holding out.

Why couldn't the doctor have given him the shot earlier?

"He would not let me stick him until you got back," Ismael says as I stare at the needle.

"He's incapacitated. You could have dosed him anyway."

"Nora?" Declan, calling from the bedroom.

Nora, the way it sounds, even with his ravaged voice. Something dark and sinful and lovely. My name never sounded as sweet when Ryan said it. An unfamiliar feeling wells. Guilt. I nudge it aside.

Snatching the syringe, I stalk into the bedroom. "Sheets and blankets need to be changed first. Guess it's a good thing you're still conscious." The brothers shift him off the bed and prop him against the wall, stripping the sheets and blankets aside, smoothing on the clean ones. "Why were you waiting until I got back?"

Declan's eyes are still swollen, but there's a gleam of blue in them, the cracks wide enough for me to see the irises. "You're a tiny thing, and you went out there alone. You'd already risked your life for me once today. Keep doing it and I'll be further in debt. I hate owing people."

Sheets changed, he's helped onto the bed again, and he growls until they leave. "I hate being at your mercy almost as much, lass." Lass? Lass is Scottish. Maybe he's Scottish. "Go ahead." He holds out his good arm.

The man is in a tremendous amount of pain, and he waited until I returned before allowing anyone to dose him. For what? Because he feared I wouldn't come back, that I'd leave him helpless? "Don't you think you'd be more comfortable if your clothes weren't all bloody and soaked?"

One side of his mouth pulls up in a smirk. His lips are

17

unblemished, full and firm. "Gonna undress me?"

It's been so long. The guilt rises again, spreading sticky little tendrils through my chest.

"Hey."

Ryan's gone. I have no reason to feel guilty.

"Nora." He tries to snap his fingers and grimaces. "I'm foolin' with you. And yes, if you could get me boots off, that'll do for now."

Foolin'. Turning away, I head for the kitchen, ignoring his protests, and find the scissors exactly where I knew they'd be, in the second drawer to the left of the sink.

Declan's eyes widen as much as they can as I give them a testing snap. "Now—"

"Oh, hush. It'll be easier to cut them off you." Easier said than done, too, the denim stiff with blood and dirt. Half of one leg is already ripped, thank god, from the cast. He's motionless as I snip away, only daring to move when I ask him to lift his hips. I cut away his sweater, a beautiful heavy blue wool I hate ruining. The boots come off, and I tug the covers over him before I have a chance to see him, really see him, stretched out before me dressed in nothing but boxer briefs, a cast, an Ace bandage, and medical tape and cotton pads.

"Can you move onto your side a little?" He does, and I slide the needle in, depressing the plunger. "Now shut up and get some rest. I'll wake you in an hour."

"Yes, Nurse Ratched," he mumbles.

Without waiting to see if he sleeps, I hurry out of the room.

CHAPTER THREE

He's awake.

Shuffles and muffled whimpers drift out of the bedroom. Crap. I was supposed to have checked on him several hours ago, and I forgot, too wrapped up in my own thoughts and half-baked plans to remember his concussion. Now it's early morning, early enough it still looks like night, and Declan's awake.

Something thunks, followed by a streak of blue words. The crash followed by another thunk sends me into the bedroom.

He curses again when I flip on the overhead light. The lamp's on the floor, and his fingers are doing their best to dig into the fake wood of the bedside table. "What are you doing?"

"Dancing a jig," he growls. Someone doesn't wake up pleasant. "Bathroom through there?" He jerks his head toward the door in the wall.

Nodding, I start forward, jerking to a stop when he growls again. "G'won. I've got it." His eyes are still mostly swollen, but there's no mistaking the glare. Fine. If he wants to stumble around and hurt himself even more, he's welcome to do so.

More thunks, more cursing, another crash. Shaking my head, I make my way to the tiny kitchen and hope there's something that can be used as an icepack. The swelling on his face looks horrid.

The electricity hasn't been cut on this block, and the fridge cooled off quickly once it was plugged back in. The ice in the trays is cloudy and dirt-encrusted. It's frozen. That's what matters. It pops out with a crack.

I need a towel. A washcloth. Some kind of cloth.

The flat looks the same as it did when I abandoned it two years ago, if a little shabbier with age. The kitchen towels should be in the same place. Wary of spiders and other nasty things, I stick my hand in the drawer and pull one out. I dump the ice into the middle of a towel and wad it up.

Declan's managed to navigate his way back from the bathroom, though he's balancing on one foot next to the bed. The scowl he shoots me speaks for itself; he can't quite lower his body to the bed without causing himself immense pain or falling over. Placing the towel full of ice on the bedside table, a grunt escapes me as I take most of his weight. He hisses and flops inelegantly onto the bed, sheets and blankets bunched under him. "Thanks," he grumbles.

"Here." I pass him the towel. "It's for your face. Help with the swelling."

He doesn't say anything, just presses it over his eyes, groaning as the cold seeps through to his skin. It's not long before the chill of the flat pricks goose bumps on his skin. I'm terrible at this nursing thing. If I'd been thinking, I'd have moved the covers out of the way before he got back into bed. "Lift your hips."

He doesn't.

"Declan. You want to freeze?"

"Not particularly."

"Then lift your hips, you ass. The blankets are all bunched up under you." With a grunt, he does, abs contracting with the effort, the light throwing his bruises and scrapes into stark relief.

It always hits when I least expect it and never at a convenient time. I'm not sure there's ever a convenient time for a panic attack. It's a rising wave of greasy, oily black, suffocating and intense. I'm pulling the blankets up, fingers brushing his shoulder, and the miniscule contact rushes through me. A vise tightens its grip on my lungs. Ryan's in the street, broken and still. The ground is wobbly and someone's speaking. I think. I can't hear too well.

Then there's a wall of sound, Ryan's whimpers and hisses, the agonized screams, grunts and taunts in a language I can't understand. A grip so tight on my wrist I'll have bruises, and the sound stops and it's just Declan, but he's so far away. Tiny, tiny, growing smaller by the minute until there's nothing more than black sucking me in.

* * *

A soft buzzing wakes me, my name, over and over. *Nora. Nora. Nora.* It's starting to lose meaning.

I'm heavy. My limbs won't move, and I can't feel my feet any longer. Opening my eyes takes what little energy I have.

"Nora."

There's my name again.

"Nora. Lass. Fuck. Get up."

Up. Right. Up. Up? Oh. I'm on the floor, next to the bed. How did I end up on the floor? "Why am I on the floor?"

"You fainted. Or something. Surprised you didn't land on me or hit your head on the table on the way down."

Unreasonably irritated at his lack of concern, I manage to prop myself up with my hands and immediately regret it, blood surging and swirling, black edging my vision once more. I suck in a breath, let it whistle through my teeth, and wait for the sensation to pass.

I move slowly, arms and legs still half-asleep. My eyes are gritty from the lack of it. I've never passed out from a panic attack before. My stomach clenches with a vicious twist, and I try to remember when I ate last. Probably yesterday morning. Maybe that was why. "How long was I out?"

The skin around his eyes is a sickening greyish purple, the faint gleam of blue visible through the cracks of his lids. "A minute, maybe. Hard to tell." He narrows his eyes further, if that's even possible. "You need some sleep." With his good arm, he gestures to the other side of the bed. "Get in. Or get

21

on."

"I'm fine." I will be, anyway, once Declan drops it.

"You're not."

"I'm not getting in the bed. Or on it. You done with the ice?" The towel's next to his head on the pillow. His hand closes around my wrist. I yank it free. "Don't *touch* me." Not now. Not when my skin is fragile and easily scarred. I stalk out of the room.

I wipe off the dusty countertops and eat some crackers I'd found in Declan's apartment, wasting time in the dark and wondering how I'm going to continue caring for my uninvited guest. Better than thinking about the fainting spell and what brought it on. Better than acknowledging *again*, that I can't move past Ryan's death. I don't know how. I'm trapped here, surrounded by reminders of how he died. As long as I am, the nightmare won't end.

The sounds coming from the bedroom are too restless for Declan to have fallen back asleep. Dawn is still a few hours away, not that it matters. I have nothing to do other than play caretaker to a stranger.

A shower will pass a few minutes.

Locating the change of clothing I brought with me, I hunt down a towel and some soap. It's dish soap, abrasive, but it'll do the job. Hopefully the water will heat.

The towel's over his eyes when I enter the bedroom. "Think you could turn off the overhead light now?"

I bite my tongue at his carelessly dismissive tone. While not exactly helpless, he's certainly not mobile. I replace the lamp first and switch it on before flipping off the light. "Thanks," he mumbles.

The bathroom is tiny. Ryan and I would squish ourselves together in the shower on occasion, water trickling into the cracks between our bodies, slicking skin and steaming away. Close, close sex, the kind that's only possible when movement is limited and lust drives your actions.

I'm used to the ache—it's a constant companion—but it always gets worse after a panic attack. Tears are pointless. That doesn't stop them from running down my cheeks, mingling with the pitiful spray from the showerhead. The water's lukewarm, growing colder, and still I stand under it until I shiver. Penance. For not being strong enough to put this behind me. For choosing to wallow in the darkness, to shut everyone out.

The water does its job. I've numbed myself, and I'm wide awake. Wide awake with nothing to do.

Declan doesn't make a sound when I step out of the bathroom. Asleep, hopefully. It's good for him, helps dull the pain, speeds healing. Moving as quietly as I can, I pad to the bedside table, fingers closing around the switch at the base of the lamp.

"Don't."

Okay. Not asleep.

"Is there more ice?" He moves the towel.

I take it from him. "I doubt it." Leaving the lamp burning, I head for the kitchen again. The ice trays are empty, nothing in the freezer that would be of use. I fill the trays and, in a fit of inspiration, soak some of the towels and fold them over, laying them flat in the freezer.

"No ice, but this'll help a little." I'm careful not to touch his bare skin again as I lay a cold, wet towel over his eyes. His jaw twitches. "Go back to sleep."

"Can't. Not tired. Need a distraction. I can't just keep lying here."

I huff out a breath. "If you think you can sit up without any pain, be my guest. I highly suggest you remain horizontal for a while longer. Your torso took a pretty brutal beating."

"Thanks for pointing out the obvious." But he stays on his back. "Talk. Or something."

Or something. Something to keep him entertained. "Be right back."

The bookshelf in the living room holds Ryan's textbooks and a handful of novels. The spines spark more memories, and I shove them aside, choosing a book at random. *The Master and Margarita*, one of the few Ryan didn't like and couldn't finish.

Carrying it back into the bedroom, I lower myself to the floor. "Ever read *The Master and Margarita?*"

"It's a favorite of mine." He sounds surprised. So am I. I'm always surprised to find others enjoy the same books I do. My taste is a bit...eclectic. "Are you on the floor again?" I ignore him and open the book. I've barely made it through the first paragraph when he interrupts me. "Get up. I'm in no condition to pull anything if you're worried about your virtue."

My virtue is the last thing I'm worried about. I'm scared if I touch him it'll send me into the spiral.

I should have just brought him to my flat instead of here. I'll never last a day, much less weeks. Doctor Gudelj says he should move his shoulder to keep the muscles from locking up. His sprained wrist and broken leg still make him incapable of doing much for himself until the worst of the damage begins to heal. With every object, every inch possessing a memory that wants to crash down and take me under, I'm useless.

The bruises and bandages on Declan only make it worse. He could have been Ryan. Ryan could have been him.

"You getting up?" I rise, circle the bed and edge onto the mattress next to him. "Good. Keep going," he says. Settling a pillow behind my back, I open the book and resume my place.

Page after page, my voice loud in the unnatural quiet of false dawn. No firefights tonight. I wonder which neighborhood they're stalking through now. I read until my voice goes raspy and grey light fades to the bright white of day, another overcast sky devoid of rain. I read until the words blur on the page and my throat protests. I read through the death of Berlioz and the doubts of the MASSOLIT, excited to get to Woland's magic show.

And Declan is still awake. He's removed the cloth, tossing it on the floor some time ago. His eyes find mine at odd moments, breaks I'd give myself to swallow. They're still so swollen, the irises barely visible.

We've made it a quarter of the way through the book when he stretches out his hand and closes it around my knee. His hand is huge, large enough to cover my kneecap and wrap around to the back if he wants. "Stop."

I mark my place and set the book aside. "You want to sleep?"

"You should. Sleep," he clarifies. He squeezes hard when I start to protest. "Sleep."

It's a command, a siren's call to my body, finally aware of the aches and small pains I'd been oblivious to from crawling and dragging and holding myself so rigid with fear that I'd end up watching another brutal murder. Sliding down on the bed, my mind goes blank.

Maybe if I'm lucky I can avoid the nightmares.

CHAPTER FOUR

Golden brown eyes, filled with agony and love and sorrow. Full of all the things we've lost. A sob threatens to choke me, my throat closing up, clenching tight. Then they're blue, still full of pain, but no love, no sorrow. Only pain and a fierce determination to understand why this is happening. They change again, golden brown once more opening wide. Watching them go blank shatters the world around me, and there's no sound save the high, keening wail coming from nowhere and everywhere.

"Nora."

I bolt upright. Sweat skates down my spine, and I can't seem to get enough air into my lungs. The dream's still fresh, the images playing before me whether my eyes are open or closed. I shut them anyway. It takes a few minutes, but my heart finally slows down.

"Now that you're awake, think you could get me some more ice?"

Oh, for— Declan's staring at me expectantly. Like I'm supposed to jump at his command. The raised brow on the swollen mess of his face somehow manages to come off as imperialistic. His "Well?" does the job, setting my temper at a slow burn. Ice. Ice because the patient can't get out of bed just yet and get it for himself. I slide off the bed and stalk out of the room, slamming open drawers and twisting the ice tray with unwarranted viciousness. I fill a glass with water before carrying it and the ice pack into the bedroom

But the temper and his treatment help. Most people would have moved to soothe, seeing someone shoot out of a horror like that. Declan chose to ignore it. My anger drains and leaves me feeling beholden to him in a whole new way. I don't like it.

He must be tired of lying on his back. I pause in the doorway. The covers are rumpled and strewn about, his left arm strapped to his chest in a makeshift sling, his right wrist encased in a bandage. Blues and dusky purples and reds mar his chest, bloom along one side of his jaw, mask his eyes.

I wonder what he looks like without the bruises.

"You just gonna stand there?"

"No." *Yes*. Staring at him, imagining what he looks like when he's whole is appealing, and disturbing that it's appealing. The groan escaping his throat when I lay the ice across his face carries a note of pleasure that zips right through me.

I join him on the other side of the bed, and we sit in silence for a while. His wrapped right hand gropes over the bed until it finds my hand. He laces his fingers with mine. Comfort. Comfort after the storm, waiting for the heat of it to pass.

The gesture sluices away the dregs of the nightmare still taunting me, the anger, the fatigue. I've no idea how long we sit in silence, our hands entwined, ice melting over his eyes. My water is long gone by the time I shift to remove the towel. I set it on the table so I can check the swelling.

He doesn't hiss in pain as I press the ridges of his eyes sockets, the bridge of his nose. "You'll probably be able to open your eyes fully soon."

"Yeah, well, not sure how much of an improvement that'll be." He has a point. With the broken leg and a bum shoulder, he won't have much mobility for a few days, and even after that, without crutches he won't be able to get around until the cast comes off.

A few days. I can handle a few more days. Then I'll see about moving him to Murat and Ismael's apartment. They're stronger than me. If he falls, they can lift him. I can't.

My fingers drift over the line of his cheekbones, down to

his jaw. "You want to take a shower?"

"No sponge bath?" His eyes slit open.

"They cover that in advanced nursing. I took the remedial class," I quip. "Doctor Gudelj should be coming around later to check on you. Something about exercises for your shoulder." Climbing off the bed, I retrieve the soaked towel and take it to the kitchen, hanging it over the lip of the sink. "You want a shower or not?"

"Yes," he calls back.

I hunt down a plastic bag big enough to cover the cast, uncovering a few more books, a sweater I'd forgotten about, and enough dust to fill a small sandbox. Motes catch the dim light filtering through the blinds, drifting like sneeze-inducing snowflakes.

"Here," I say. He's pushed back the blankets and sat up, legs hanging over the side of the bed. He waits while I unhook the sling, rotating his shoulder and grimacing while I unwrap the bandage around his wrist. "Watch your fingers." Bending down, I fit the bag around the cast.

"You really are small. I thought I was imagining things."

His eyes are open, scrutinizing every inch. Or every inch he can see. Hunched over as I am, trying to secure the bag so his cast doesn't get wet, I'm even smaller. Throw in a skinny build and dark hair I keep as short as a boy's, and I don't look like much. "Elfin" is a word that gets tossed around a lot. Ryan used to tease me with it, knowing it irked me. "And?"

Confusion clouds his face. "And what? It's an observation. I could snap you in two." With a wince, he pushes up on his good foot, hand on the bedside table for balance. "Fuck," he mutters and begins hopping slowly across the small distance between the bed and the bathroom.

Trusting he'll be able to get out of his boxers and into the shower on his own, I turn away and straighten the blankets.

"Shit! Bloody hell." A thump, followed by more curses. "Aye, fuck me."

Quiet. It lengthens, and I'm about to leave the bedroom, take stock of what else might be needed for a few days, when

28

he breaks it. "Nora?"

I'm not going to like this. I just know it. "Yeah?"

"I need—" More muttering. Another thump. "Fuck!" He yanks the door open. "I need some help."

One brow goes up. "Help doing what? I'm not giving you a sponge bath."

"Ha ha." His face is grim. "I think I can get in the shower okay. It's these —" He waves a hand at his shorts. "—that I can't seem to get rid of. I think if I try to bend over far enough to take them off I won't be able to stand back up."

Oh dear god. It's bad enough I have to deal with him being charming and then growly, mostly naked and morose because he's so dependent, but now I have to take off his boxers for him?

Suck it up, Nora.

"Turn around," I say briskly.

After a moment's hesitation, he obliges, bracing a hand on the sink. Without giving myself the chance to build up to it, I grasp the waistband and yank. Sure enough, they catch at the top of his cast. I crouch down, keeping my eyes trained on the cast. Not on his ass. Or between his legs. Just the cast. Seconds slip by as I tug the boxers carefully over the plaster.

As soon as they're off, I rise and turn around, cheeks burning as I step out of the bathroom, shutting the door behind me.

I'm human. I'm not immune to hormones, and ones I thought were long dead are waking and starting to mutter. It's horrible, because it's only temporary. He'll leave soon enough because *he* hasn't been branded a terrorist.

Reality wipes away those soft, squishy thoughts, leaving behind a cold, harsh truth that's never far from my mind. I am alone. I'm alone, abandoned by my country, forced to stay because I have nowhere else to go.

The air in the apartment's too close. Too stale. I grab the sweatshirt I dropped on the floor earlier and head for the door.

I steal down the stairs, trying to remember which ones squeak. The back door opens onto an alley, the front door to the quiet side street we'd chosen for its distance from the university. I check both doors for soldiers. The alley is clear, and I hurry down it, hugging the building as I turn onto the next street, weaving through the blocks, away from the center of the neighborhood.

Cristian likes to wander the blocks, searching for me if it's been more than a week, and it's going on two. He'll be making a push for my help soon. Sidling through the courtyard of a nearby building, I check the street before I step out.

"Nora?"

Months of Cristian getting the drop on me has taught me not to jump when he sneaks up behind me. He's good. Better than me, yet he only caught me once. Once was enough. He thought I was a child, stealing food, when what I was really going for was the packet of pills on the other side of the apples. He handed one to me but I swiped the packet when he turned away, and I became a better thief after that.

"Hi."

He busses my cheek, a gesture I'm used to by now, then frowns. "I have not seen you here before."

My old flat isn't close to where I live now, not that Cristian would know. I've gone out of my way to ensure no one knows where I live. "Checking out the neighborhood."

He scrutinizes me a moment longer. "How is my favorite thief? You are not eating again. Here." He thrusts a small plastic bag at me, and I peek inside. I allow him to see my grin of delight. Nectarines. Fresh vegetables are hard to come by, but fresh fruit? Almost impossible.

"Thank you. And yes, I have been eating. Just had a difficult night last night, that's all." He crowds me into a doorway, away from any curious eyes. "Ah, the firefight." He nods.

Firefight? "Yes." The lie rolls off my tongue. "It sounded close."

His expression turns grave. "Two blocks from here. My apologies for keeping you up. It took a while for my unit to push the rebels back."

Shit. I've been lucky so far, the fighting limited to seconds-long skirmishes in the blocks surrounding the flat I moved to after Ryan's death, the lengthier fights taking place farther away. But I've seen what happens when those skirmishes turn to brawls. Bricks crumble, buildings ignite, and innocent people stream onto the streets, caught in the fight to keep communism from overtaking the country again.

"You should come in. I'll keep you safe." His touch no longer makes me flinch, but it isn't welcome, either. The fingers trailing along my jaw make my skin want to drop off my bones and run away.

I make a noncommittal noise. "You know how I feel about that. I'd be taking advantage of you." Convincing Cristian I'd be a terrible spy so he'll leave me alone hasn't gone well, not from the start, though he keeps at it. I think he likes the challenge. Just because I can get into places I shouldn't without being seen doesn't mean I'm cut out for snooping.

"So sweet, *pile moje*," he murmurs, his hand dropping to my shoulder. "It's getting more dangerous, though."

"How so? Seems like it's been pretty calm for a while now." The main reason I don't try harder to avoid Cristian at all costs is because he gives me information unknowingly. I've heard about medical supply shipments, food shipments, communications embargos being placed and lifted. I knew when the cell towers were knocked out to prevent the rebels from communicating, same as they'd tried to knock out the phone lines.

He shakes his head. "No. They've moved in on this neighborhood. We've managed to keep them on the fringe, but it's taking more force than we'd anticipated."

Oh, not good. Not good at all. I need to move, and soon. Now.

What the hell am I going to do with Declan? I can't take him to my new flat, though it's certainly safer and more secure than the one we're in now. From the state of his own place, he won't want to go there. The neighbors I'm friendly with—Murat and Ismael, Mrs. Vucik, Mila, Dr. Gudelj—are stressed enough as it is.

"I need to get home," I mumble, mind racing, trying to piece together a plan.

A burst of gunfire has Cristian pressing me farther into the doorway, shielding me with his body. In the ensuing silence, he leans back and sticks his head out, turning this way and that as he checks the street. "It's not near—"

More shots. An explosion. Heartrending screams, shouts. The ear-shattering crack of bullets. Over and over, until the world is made of noise and nothing else. I'm surprised my ears aren't bleeding.

If this street is clear, I can head away from the noise, wind my way back to the flat. I visualize a possible route, strain to gauge the direction the fighting's coming from. Cristian's fingers tip my chin up, and I shake myself. "What?"

"I have to go. My unit is in the area, that's probably them. Stay here until it clears." He pushes me back into the corner and ducks out.

I can't stay here. What a stupid, *stupid* idea. There's no way to tell if the fighting will move, if I'll end up trapped. First rule of living in a war zone: don't get caught out in the open. A doorway counts as open. The door's probably locked but I try it anyway, cursing uselessly when I find it's true. My lock picks are in the jeans I wore yesterday. I'm screwed.

The fighting sounds like it's coming from all directions, so I pick one and pray I won't walk into a bullet. I jog to the corner and peek around it. The street's clear. For now. Now is my window. The soundtrack of war crashes over me as I dash from one block to the next.

I've done it before, raced through the streets as guns blaze hot one block over. It's not my favorite. But I've heard too many stories of people waiting in doorways, huddling in alleys, hoping for the best and getting caught in the crossfire because there weren't four walls and a roof over their heads. Shelter doesn't always equal safety, but it's better than none at all.

I'm so relieved to make it back to the flat in one piece I don't bother trying to be quiet as I climb the stairs to the second floor. Outside, the fighting's just as loud and fierce as it was when I made a break for it. The door swings open as my hand touches the doorknob.

The scowl gracing Declan's face is all the more imposing for the bruising on it. Add in his broad shoulders blocking out most of the light and his imposing height, and if I hadn't already seen his naked backside I'd be intimidated. "Where have you been?"

An explosion rocks the street outside, the windows rattling with the impact. I hold up the plastic bag I somehow managed to hang on to, my hands shaking along with the rest of me. "Nectarine?"

CHAPTER FIVE

His mouth shuts with a click of teeth. A muscle jumps in his jaw. "Could you try not to get yourself killed? I can't exactly run out after you."

"I don't need you to." Another *boom*, and a crack snakes its way up a living room window. A tremor shrills through my body. Breathing is difficult. I hate these moments. Hate how easily broken I am. "Bedroom. Please. Now. It's safer."

The flat's laid out so the bedroom faces an inner courtyard and the living room and kitchen face the street. Sliding an arm around Declan's waist, we make our limping way to the bedroom just as another explosion rocks the building.

He hops over to the bed while I shut the door behind us. "What were you thinking, going out alone?"

I was thinking I had to get away from him. I wrap my arms around my middle. "I've been doing it for the last two years. Haven't gotten so much as a scratch. And I had no way of knowing a firefight would start up after I'd left, or that it would be right outside."

"After the one earlier this morning, I could have told you it was a possibility." He flinches at the sound of glass breaking, the tinkling strangely musical over the harsh crack of guns firing. "Think you can help me out?"

That's when I notice that, while he managed to pull on a sweater, he's only wearing boxers. And one sock. He'd removed the plastic bag from his cast. "You're going to have to cut up a pair of pants. Or two."

"Fine."

I retrieve the scissors from the bedside table and go to work on a pair of jeans. "You could have done this yourself, you know. You got the boxers on."

"More fun to have you do it." The smile he flashes is wicked and charming and turns my stomach into one giant knot.

"Right." The forced intimacy of the situation is wreaking havoc on my brain. Too long avoiding extended, *meaningful* contact with people. Light catches the scissor blades, my hand jerking with each blast of gunfire. The cut in his jeans is jagged and uneven as a result. He tugs them on without further help from me and reaches for the bandage to rewrap his wrist.

The explosion happens right next to my ears. I'm airborne. There are shadows in front of my eyes, smoke in my nose, a ringing in my ears. A heavy weight presses me to the floor, warm, solid, and immobile. No amount of wriggling and shoving gives me room to move.

"*Stop it.*" Declan, his breath whispering against my skin. *He's* what's on top of me. We're on the floor on the opposite side of the bed. Pain glazes his eyes as his arms curve around my head.

Thud. Thud. Thud. My heart's been replaced by a subwoofer. Fingers curling into the soft wool of his sweater, I breathe in the scent of dish soap. It strikes me as hysterical, that we've been showering with dish soap, and the giggles bubble up and over. Tears leak out and become sobs, soaking his sweater.

The absolute certainty we're going to die isn't the balm I'd expected it to be.

The floor shakes under me, and Declan shifts, trying to keep me covered. Keep me safe. No one's held me safe in a while. It's always been me cowering in the corner farthest from the street, curled into a ball, arms aching with the effort to stop the trembles.

Each rapid patter of gunfire jolts me, hands curled around the wool so my fingers go numb. Fear skitters like bugs under my skin. My face burrows further and further into the crook of his neck. His arms eventually come around to cradle me, one hand at the back of my head, the other arm under my shoulders, and I want to sink into him, let him absorb me, let him hide me from the mayhem outside.

Another explosion, the floor shaking with the impact and it sounds like the door to the bedroom has come off its hinges and fallen on the floor.

The ensuing silence is entirely absent of sound. I've always wondered about deafening silence. Never thought I'd get to experience it. When Declan speaks, it's like being underwater, the words indistinguishable. His hold loosens, slow and careful, the hand at the back of my head falling away.

Then the weight of him is gone.

The rush of air has me scrambling for him again, clinging to his side, whimpering, the whole works. *Don't. Don't let go. Not yet.*

There's a new hesitation as I try to fuse myself to him, try to bring back the sliver of security I felt with his weight pinning me to the floor. This one was so much worse, this fight, longer and dirtier than the others I've been through. They sent me scurrying for cover but I'd find there was no structural damage. This time, I'm certain the living room of the flat's in shambles.

I've spent a lot of the last two years contemplating my own death. It seemed a fitting thing to do, given I couldn't re-enter the United States. I couldn't imagine staying in this hellhole, not after everything I'd gone through. But with my expired visa and my name on a watch list, I've effectively been immobilized. I don't exactly go out looking to get myself killed. I'm just not afraid of dying.

Seems today, at least, I've had a change of heart.

"We can't stay here."

I nod, clutching at Declan's sweater like a child. "Don't let go yet."

On a soft sigh, his arms tighten around me, the steady thump of his heart calming my racing one. "Is your flat in this neighborhood?" My head shoots up, and he levels his gaze at me. "Don't lie," he warns. "This place is something to you, but you don't live here anymore. Haven't for a while, I'm guessing?" I swallow hard instead of responding. "You've seen my flat. If you've got another place and it's not in the middle of a hot zone, we need to go there. At least for the time being."

The fact this completely logical argument is being delivered in a lilting accent muddles my brain for a minute. I'm about to agree before I bite the tip of my tongue. I've guarded my privacy like a wolf guards its den, but it's already been invaded. Murat following me was only the beginning.

I don't respond right away. "It's on the other side of the neighborhood. We'll probably be okay for a few days, but if the damage outside is bad, we should assume they'll keep pressing forward." Maršala tita isn't exactly a small neighborhood; the walk to my flat takes around twenty minutes if I'm not circling around willy-nilly like I do.

I sit up, surprised to find I'm reluctant to let him go. What would it be like to lay next to him, sprawled out all lazy? He hisses as he shifts to a sitting position himself. Needing something to do, I grope around until I locate the bandage for his wrist. "Hold out your arm." Pushing up the sleeve of his sweater, I focus on winding it around his wrist. "It's going to take a while to get there, since you don't have crutches. How's your shoulder feel?"

"Hurts like a bastard."

I tuck the end of the bandage in. "I'm going to check out the living room. If it doesn't look too bad, we can stay in here for a little longer. There's probably still some intermittent gunfire going on outside."

He grunts his assent, and I help him to his feet, making sure he's settled on the bed before I turn toward the door.

It *has* come off its hinges, but the thunking was it coming to rest at a slant on the wall. If the door's not where it's supposed to be, the living room must be worse.

Worse. Much, much worse. A huge hole in the wall, where a trio of windows once were. Crumbled plaster and bricks everywhere, a faint groan before a section of floor near the hole collapses. Screams and faint cries drift up from the first floor. Dust hits my nose, and I start sneezing and coughing, attempting to dislodge it.

The picture of Ryan and I, happy and laughing, days after we arrived in the city, perches on the desk Ryan would cover in papers and books and his laptop. Right at the edge of the hole.

I've always meant to go back for that picture. Eventually. If I ever reached a point where the fractures in my soul healed enough I could look at Ryan's pictures or his books or his favorite shirt without tumbling head over feet into darkness.

The floor creaks and groans as I creep toward the desk. More shouts from the street, the dust growing thicker. I see why the hole opened up—a huge chunk of the front wall in the unit below is missing. There's nothing to hold up the wall above it.

Almost ... there ...

Another round of shouts, feet pounding over pavement. The floor is unstable under my feet, no matter how lightly I tread. Stopping at the edge of the desk, I stretch across it, fingers brushing the frame.

Fists pound on the door. Startled, I sprawl across the desk. The floor buckles, jolting me as I snatch up the picture. A long moan, and the far end of the floor gives way.

The desk jerks and tilts. Scrambling for purchase isn't easy when you're holding something in your hands, but I can't let go. This is the last thing of our life together I *want*. Everything else can burn, split apart, disintegrate. I *need* this photo.

My feet touch the floor as the front door bangs open, frame splintering from the force. The desk tips down, Ryan's papers sliding along the surface and landing in the unit below.

"Nora!"

Legs weak and shaky, I ignore Murat and back away from the desk, stepping carefully, hoping the rest of the floor doesn't collapse without notice. It doesn't take long for the weight of the desk to launch it completely over the edge, and it lands with a splintering crash below. God, I hope no one was home.

Or maybe they're dead.

My stomach tightens at the thought, nausea slopping around. It's too much, imagining all those staring, sightless eyes, limbs bent in places they shouldn't be, dirt mixing with blood to create a mud no one wants to see. Bile rises, and still clutching the picture, I race back into the bedroom and straight into the bathroom.

It burns. I can't stop retching, long after my stomach is empty. I've been ridiculously lucky these last two years, the fighting on the outskirts, the carnage out of my line of vision. Sarajevo's a not huge city, but it's a slow-moving war. Almost boring at times. Weeks will go by without a peep out of either side, each waiting with tense shoulders for the other to let their guard down. Then the cycle begins again, and it drags its citizens back into the chaos. Just when we think things might be going back to normal, when we start to see the stores open again and the lines at the fuel pumps, someone goes and blows something up.

Never, until today, have I been in the line of fire. I'd rather not be in it again, thank you very much.

Empty, weak, and mortified at how quickly I broke, I get off my knees and slap on the tap. A trickle of water appears. Oh. Right. Plumbing's probably shot to shit. Cupping my hands, I throw a couple of handfuls on my face and rinse my mouth. I dry my face, straighten my clothes, and step out into the bedroom.

Murat's standing next to the bed, adjusting the sling trapping Declan's arm against his body. Both their heads snap toward me. I lift a hand to hold off their questions. "I take it we're leaving now?"

Murat won't let it go. "What were you thinking, getting that close?"

"Close to what?" Declan's gaze swings from me to Murat,

brow furrowed. It locks on the frame in my hands. "What is that?"

If I could push it into my body, I would. "Nothing. The living room floor's starting to crash. We can't stay here much longer or we won't be able to get to the door." Ignoring the furious looks from the two men, I slip the picture into Declan's bag, toss in the nectarines and *The Master and Margarita* for good measure, and skirt the edge of the living room, heading for the door. "Coming?"

The trek from Maršala tita to Grbavicka is slow and silent. Occasionally Murat or Declan will mumble something and the other will mumble right back, but they ignore me, for the most part.

We've been walking for a half hour, keeping to the shadows as much as possible, when Murat stops, Declan stumbling next to him. "We are going to your place, correct?"

I hadn't given it much thought. Or any thought, really. But Declan and I need a place to go—or, rather, *Declan* needs a place to go. "You can take him to your flat, right? One of you can sleep on the floor or something." I'm being bratty. I don't care.

"I have only been there once, but I am certain I can find your flat again." Murat's gaze burns with anger. What? Does he think having someone around will keep me from doing stupid things? As evidenced by the picture I rescued, that's not the case. "We will go there."

Since Murat's the one bearing most of Declan's weight and not me, I don't have much choice. We start moving again, and twenty minutes later we reach my building.

Murat deposits his burden on the old couch in my living room and stalks out of the flat, slamming the door behind him. Declan's face is impassive, his gaze sharp as he watches me drop the bag on the floor and pull out the nectarines, book, and the framed photo.

I can't have it out. Not yet. I'm not ready to see Ryan's smiling face every day. Opening an empty drawer in the kitchen, I slip it inside.

Declan, unsurprisingly, hasn't moved. "Think you can stay out of danger for the next few days? Or is it too much to ask that you wait until I'm rid of this sling?"

How is this Declan the same man who flung himself over me, who let me hold on and held on *to me* just a short while ago? He's even crueler than the man from this morning, and there's no trace of the charm he turns on and off at whim.

It makes him easier to deal with. With a shrug, I pick up the bag of nectarines. "Want one?"

He studies me, no, *scrutinizes* me for long, long moments. Finally, he nods. Then he slouches down, wincing at the movement, and tips his head back to rest against the couch. Lines of tension bracket his mouth, fan out from his eyes.

I should apologize. For running out on him this morning, for not stopping to think before I risked my life to retrieve a simple picture.

I head for the kitchen instead.

CHAPTER SIX

I've got to remember to thank Cristian the next time he finds me. The nectarines are delicious, plump and juicy and that perfect combination of tart and sweet. Inside my flat, it's silent save the slurping of nectarine juice.

It's strange, being here with someone else in the room. Since I moved in almost two years ago, no one has been inside. Certainly not the actual tenants. I suspect they've either left the city or are dead, which makes it easier on me. I won't have to explain why a stranger is living in the flat.

But Declan's continued silence means I feel obligated to make conversation. "Do you want something to read?" I wave my hand at the bookshelf. Books are crammed in every which way, stacked two deep, and when I ran out of room I used the floor.

He still says nothing, only continues eating his nectarine and watching me with cold, cold eyes. He stares for so long I start to squirm. Finally his gaze shifts to the shelf behind me. "Anyone ever tell you you've got a problem?"

"Ha ha." I know how it looks. I raided every English-language bookstore in the city. And by "raided," I mean *stole*. When you have very little money, you get desperate for entertainment.

Licking the last of the juice from my fingers, I wipe my hands on my jeans and stand, wandering over to the bookcase.

It's tall and wide, and the books cover every topic imaginable. Some of the books are Ryan's, those pieces of him that melded themselves to me and I couldn't let them go. I've thumbed through his copy of *The Art of War* so many times I can't open it any longer, for fear of it falling apart. Others are mine, ones I picked up later. *The End of Alice. A Tree Grows in Brooklyn. Night. Prisoner X. The Communist Manifesto.*

I'd never fully understood, nor paid much attention to, what Ryan's thesis was about. All I know is that socialist theory was a part of it. Socialist theory and the renewed interest in a Communist state in Russia, building off the fears we'd see a regenerated Communist bloc in our lifetime. Not something I would have expected the US government to be wary of, although they're so skittery these days, I wouldn't be surprised if they'd reconvened the House Un-American Activities Committee.

After Ryan's death, needing a distraction from all the desperate calls and letters and emails home, I started reading everything I could get my hands on regarding communism and socialist theory. It's an endless source of fascination to me, and I thought—still do—that the more I knew about the subject that was barring me from American soil, the better off I'd be. Forewarned is forearmed, and all that shit. What if I somehow made it out of Bosnia and wasn't allowed refugee status? I could end up in the hands of American forces and thrown in prison. If I ever had to explain Ryan's thesis in an attempt to wiggle my way out of trouble, I didn't want to make an even bigger mess of it.

Whether this theory is correct is another question. I haven't had much opportunity to pursue it, spending my time stealing medical supplies and avoiding grenades. Mostly it just makes me feel closer to him.

"Anything catch your fancy?" I glance over my shoulder. He's gone back to studying me, like I'm a puzzle he needs to solve. I shrug, covering my discomfort. "Or not." My palms are starting to itch. I rub them over my thighs, the tingling growing until it's almost painful. It happens when I'm nervous.

"I need to go back out, get more food."

"No." The answer is harsh and immediate. He struggles to his feet and hops over to me, pain etched on his face. "You've already proven your stupidity. You don't need to keep proving it."

Why? Why does he care? Why would it *matter* to him what I do? He has a roof over his head and apparently the determination to get around on his own, broken leg and all. Murat, Ismael, and the doctor all know where he is now, and they'd be around to check on him regardless of what happens to me.

"I've got a conscience," he continues. "I'd rather not have your death on it, lass."

"We still need more food, though. I don't have enough to feed two people." I barely have enough to feed myself sometimes. "And we've no guarantee how long we'll be safe here. I need to find a place to move to. You're not exactly mobile. I am."

His entire body goes rigid, then relaxes. "Fine." The look he gives me is blank, devoid of everything, coldness included. He turns and limps back to the couch, lowering himself with the care of a beaten man, old before his time.

There's too much pain on his face. "Sure you don't want a book or something? I can see if I've got some painkillers. Don't know how much good they'll do, but it'd be something." Without waiting for an answer, I duck into the kitchen, rummaging through the cabinets until I locate the ibuprofen.

"Here." Sitting onto the couch next to him, I shove a glass of water into his hand and shake out a couple of pills.

He balances the glass on the arm of the couch before holding out his hand for the pills. Tossing them back, he chases them with water, draining the glass. A fat drop clings to his lower lip, disappearing when his tongue swipes over it. "Can you get this sling off?"

"You're supposed to keep it immobile except when—"

"Except when I'm doing the exercises. I know. I've dislocated my shoulder before. It hurts like a motherfucker. I'll live." I help him unhook the sling. He jerks his head toward the book I set on a nearby table. "Keep reading. It's a good distraction."

He's probably right. We could both use distraction at the moment. I retrieve the book and settle into the corner of the couch, the space familiar in its ability to cocoon me. I locate the bookmark and start reading.

It's not as one-sided as last time. Declan interrupts on occasion, asking questions or musing on a particular point, the discussion and reading eating up the minutes. After about an hour, my already abused throat on fire from continuing to talk, I glance up from the page and see he's asleep. His chest rises and falls in steady, even movements, the lines on his face faded.

It's the perfect time to get up, to leave, to go about all the tasks I need to accomplish. But the terror of the day has drained me as well, and I curl up in my corner and shut my eyes. Just for a little while.

* * *

I'm trapped by something warm and solid. Warm, solid, and smelling faintly of dish soap.

Dish soap?

My eyes snap open as a hand brushes over my arm. "Declan?"

The hand on my arm stills. "Yeah."

Oh. His chest rumbles under my ear, his sleep-rasped voice with that lovely lilt slinking under my skin. Tilting my head back, I meet his gaze. Sleepy, yes, edged with discomfort. His arm. He's got me pressed to his side, caging me with the arm he dislocated. "*Declan.*"

"Shh. You were cold. Shaking with it. You don't remember moving over here?"

I shake my head. "I don't understand you," I blurt.

His lips tip up in a wicked little smile. "I'm not that complicated."

I scowl, which only makes him smile wider. "Why do all men say that? 'I'm not that complicated.' Right."

"It's the truth." He tugs me back down, and because he's warm and the flat is cool and growing cooler, I let him. "Being laid up, forced to sit around while you cluck over my injuries—"

"I do not cluck!"

"Yes, you do, although you're trying not to. I can't go out and get the food for you, and I can't find a new place to stay. I don't like the thought of you wandering around out there on your own, no matter how capable you are, because it's not smart. I don't like having to take care of someone else."

"How is that not complicated?"

"It's contradictory," he says, nudging me a little closer. "Not complicated."

"Why don't you let me up so I can get us a couple of blankets? Or dinner?"

"Because I tend to go with what feels good, and having you right there feels good."

I snort, his words making no sense but sending a shiver down my spine all the same. "I'm lying on your injured ribs and your shoulder must be killing you."

"The ribs are on the other side." He doesn't say anything about his shoulder. Giving in, I settle my head on his chest, draping a leg over his thigh in an attempt to get more comfortable. It's the closest I've gotten to a full body embrace in ages, and my skin sings at the contact, begs for more.

This is enough for now.

"Where are you from?"

He chuckles again, and the vibrations hum through me. "The accent and the name didn't give me away? Ireland. Galway."

Galway. Wild and open on the coast. Can he see the water from his house? Smell the ocean? "I wasn't sure. *Lass* isn't exactly Irish."

"Isn't it? You look like a lass to me."

"Hmph." I trail my fingers over the cabled ridges of his sweater. "How'd you end up in this godforsaken city? Why didn't you leave when all the foreigners were evacuated?"

"Not all the foreigners. There are pockets here and there. It's an assignment. Got here a few weeks ago. I'm a photographer." His hand comes to rest at my hip. "You? You're an American?"

His warmth is intoxicating. I'm drunk on touch. "Yeah. Pittsburgh. In Pennsylvania."

"I know where Pittsburgh is."

A giggle escapes. "Yeah, well, that's where I'm from." God, I haven't felt this good since Ryan...

Since before he died. Before he was beaten to death in front of me, while I stood by and didn't do anything other than scream and struggle against the arms holding me back.

The heat's unbearable and Declan's touch suddenly heavy and unwelcome, but I'm careful not jostle him too much as I struggle to sit up. He resists, the two of us in a tug of war, and he lets me win, his hand dropping away. A part of me protests at the loss, the slight, possessive pressure a ghost fading with each second. "I should see about dinner."

I escape into the kitchen just as my legs start to shake. I grip the counter. Food. I came in here for food. Opening the fridge, I locate a package of chicken breasts and check the date. Over a week old. Using a knife to slit open the plastic, I examine them, sniff them, grimace at the slimy texture. But they seem okay. Or they will be, once they're cooked. "Chicken okay?" I call out.

"Yes."

The familiar rhythms of cooking blanks my mind, though the preparation doesn't take nearly long enough. All too soon I'm dishing up the chicken and rice and carrying the plates into the living room.

We eat in silence, utensils scraping along ceramic filling the void of conversation. More silence as I clean up the dishes. I take my time, wiping the counter aimlessly. Nerves rumble in my belly. I don't like what he's doing to me, making me remember, making me *forget*. He's giving me thoughts and ideas I'm not ready to entertain.

Steeling myself, I poke my head out. He's staring into

space. "Tired?"

He startles. "What? No."

"Bored?"

One side of his mouth tips up. "Getting there."

I wander over to the couch and plop down in my spot. "How's your wrist?"

He rotates it, the bandage hampering the movement, but he still winces. "Stiff."

I can't stand this, seeing him so uncomfortable, his body protesting and trying to drag itself back together. I gesture to his wrist. He holds it out, and I unwrap it, running my fingers over the bones. Swollen and, as I press down, his mouth thinning, likely tender. I keep the pressure light, working the tiny muscles and ligaments.

"Think you can do that for my shoulder?"

I nod and withdraw my hands. His sweater comes up, inch by inch, revealing his stomach, his chest, his shoulders. Angry splotches of purple and red, the edges a sickening yellow, cover a lot of it, his flesh a grotesque canvas.

It hurts to look at him, to see injuries so similar to what Ryan must have suffered, yet Declan's alive and Ryan is not. Sucking in a breath, I lift my gaze to his face.

There's no trace of emotion. Utterly flat. And there's comfort in that. "Scoot forward." I stand up, and he complies, propping his broken leg up on the coffee table. He's given me a few inches of space.

I kneel behind him, thighs pushed up against his back. He groans as my fingers dig into his shoulder, and my breath catches. "Too hard?"

"No," he rasps. "Keep going." I do, working my way up his back and over, the heat of his skin burning through my jeans, through my sweater. His head tilts to rest against my breasts. The massage gets softer, becomes faint circles over his pectoral, hands brushing along the line of his shoulder. I could do it. I could lower my mouth to his, slide around and straddle him, and the temptation of it shocks me and makes me want to whimper with needs long buried.

He shifts away abruptly and grabs his sweater, pulling it on. Well. That tells me. I climb off the couch and resume my usual spot, avoiding his gaze.

Awkward. Very, very awkward. The silence grows more and more strained the longer it drags on. He breaks it by picking up the book and flipping it open to the bookmark.

Oh, dear sweet baby Jesus. Listening to Declan read one of my favorite books is a sinful, sinful pleasure. He has the perfect voice for it, gravelly and unexpected. Pages fly by, but it's not long before I'm starting to shiver with cold.

"Can we stop for a minute?" I want a blanket and maybe some tea. No. Tea's too cozy.

He closes the book and levers himself off the couch. "Bathroom?"

I point to the far door. "Through the bedroom."

I grab a couple of blankets and settle back on the couch, an old wool blanket wrapped around my shoulders. There's cursing, and I tense, waiting for him to call my name. He doesn't, and a minute later, he reappears. He lowers himself to the couch, jaw clenched, knuckles white as they grip the back.

"Want a blanket? The heat doesn't work very well in here."

He suddenly looks exhausted. "Nora."

"What?"

He squirms around so much I get off the couch. He lifts his arm, the one with the dislocated shoulder, and jerks his head toward it. "Come here."

No. Oh, no. I'm not doing this again.

"You need it. It's not uncommon for people who've lived through traumatic experiences to take comfort from one another. Now. Come here." He glares at me, and I glare right back. We've done this already, our impromptu nap, but I can't deny I need more. So much more than he knows.

Careful of his cast and the bruises on his legs I *know* must be bothering him, I climb over and stretch out against his side, spreading the blanket over the two of us. I *feel* him sigh, feel the tension drain from his body. Then he picks up the book as his arm settles around me, hand worming under the blanket to splay over my hip.

It's late when he lays the book on the table. He reaches above his head and flicks off the lamp, then slides down on the couch. He should move to the bed. More comfortable. Warmer. His hand slips under the blanket and gropes around, curling around my thigh and pulling it over his.

One hand on my hip, the other on my thigh, I'm surrounded by Declan, his broken body protecting mine from whatever approaches in the dark. Tomorrow he might back away, or I will. But I think he needs this, and I can give this to him.

Tonight, I'll take what he's offering.

CHAPTER SEVEN

"Baby, where'd you put the soap?" Ryan never put it where it belonged.

He slipped his arms around me from behind, tracing kisses along my neck. "Where you'll never be able to find it. Leave the dishes. Come to bed."

Tempting, very, very tempting. I leaned into him and shut my eyes, body absorbing the delicious shocks as his hands roamed under my t-shirt. "Someone's gotta do them," I murmured.

I gasped as he tweaked a nipple. "Later. Right now I need you." He spun me around, lifting me so I was balanced on the edge of the counter. "Mine."

"Yours, huh? Didn't you learn how to share in kindergarten?" His hands cupped my breasts. His blue eyes were hard and possessive. "No."

That wasn't right. Ryan's eyes weren't blue. I blinked, and they were Ryan's again, the golden brown gleaming with desire and love. "All mine," he whispered, dipping his head, his lips hot on my jaw. "All mine forever. Beautiful Nora."

All his. Forever. Yes. Forever Ryan's.

"Nora."

I burrow further under the blankets. It's too damn early to get up, too warm, too comfortable.

"Nora. Get up."

On a whimper, I open my eyes. Grey light streams through the living room window. Living room? Did Ryan and I fall asleep on the couch again? Bad habit. I thought we'd broken it.

His shoulders are all wrong. Too broad. His scent is wrong, too. Not Ryan. Ryan's gone, and Declan is not. I'm plastered against him. At his request, I remember, sleep clearing from my brain. For comfort, he'd said. Lifting my head, I try to focus on his face. The swelling's gone down some more, the bruising around his eyes a gruesome yellow mask tinged with red. I trail my fingers over the bruising on his jaw. He doesn't flinch, the hard gleam in his eyes not dissipating in the least. Such a difficult man to understand, Ryan's opposite in every way. Yet here I am, molded to him like this is where I belong and I have no desire to leave.

"Fuck," he mutters. Heedless of his sprained wrist, he slides his hands under my arms and jerks me up, his mouth closing over mine before I realize what's happening.

The contact is a lightning bolt, piercing the last of the dream and the sleep haze and scattering it like mice before a cat. It leaves no room for doubt that this is exactly what he means to do, kiss me, no, *ravage* my mouth, his tongue slipping past my defenses when I part my lips unconsciously. His mouth moves with the confidence of a man who has been kissing women for a long, long time, kissing them and getting kissed in return. There is no *asking* in this kiss. He tells me with his lips, his teeth, his wicked tongue that we're doing this, and we're doing it *now*, so I'd better hang on. My mind threatens to blank as my body takes over, reveling in the increasing heat.

Our noses bump, and he hisses, breaking the kiss. Shit. I'd forgotten about his injuries, the broken ribs and nose, the deep, throbbing bruises along his torso and thighs. A lapse. A side trip into insanity. Two people who've been thrown together by circumstance and nothing more, warm bodies to draw from. That's all it is.

I guess Declan's not done being crazy because he grips my hips, positions them over his groin, and pushes up. I can't stop the moan from escaping. My body's completely taken over. It wants what's between my legs and covered in layers of fabric.

I dive for his mouth again, craving more. Needing more.

He gives it to me, tongues thrusting and parrying in a primitive dance echoed by the rocking of our hips. One hand curves around my nape, his teeth nipping into my top lip as his other hand grips my hip, further encouraging their movement. It's the sweetest, darkest kind of madness. I want to drown in it. I want it to sink me, sate me, whip me into a frenzy I haven't felt in years.

And as abruptly as it starts, it stops, Declan's face impassive, his ragged breathing and the hard bulge under me betraying him. He shifts me to the side and sits up, pushing to his foot and hopping into the bedroom. He pauses in the doorway. "Who's Ryan?"

The mention of Ryan's name drains the desire from me in long pulls, chilling me from the inside out. The dream floods me with images, guilt right on its heels. A vise squeezes the air from my lungs, pressure building behind my eyes. I will *not* cry. I curl my hand into a tight fist, nails biting into my palm as I push the memories back into their box.

When Ryan and I first arrived in the city, we'd been engaged four months. Four blissful, amazing months, our future set, bright and full of promise. Our relationship had always been passionate, but those first few days in a strange city, before the responsibilities of his course work took precedence, we went to bed early and stayed in it until late in the morning.

I can't give him Ryan. I can't let go of that sweet promise. Not yet. The day is coming. I give him a piece of the truth. "Dead."

* * *

Declan doesn't say much for the rest of the day. Avoids me, actually, as much is possible for someone stuck inside. He responds with a grunt when I tell him I'm going out, and Ismael and Murat are with him when I return, burdened with jugs of water and some vegetables I managed to pilfer from an unguarded supply truck.

They've brought him a boot, a stiff walking cast in lieu of crutches. The smile on his face as he tries it out changes it.

Beneath the swelling and the angry colors on his skin I can finally tell he's a man you'd look at twice. Maybe not handsome, not in the traditional sense. Too rough, and not in the rough bad-boy way. Hardened by experience, incidents that can't be undone.

He catches me staring and the smile fades. I wish it hadn't. I wish it had stayed. I like it, and I want to see more of it. I want to know what I could do to put it back on his face.

The boot, however, means he's got more freedom. Freedom means he's got everything he needs to get around on his own, and can go back to his flat. Or someplace else. He doesn't need me. These few days have my fragile walls shuddering, so it's probably a good thing if he leaves before they come crashing down.

"Mila's home. She says to come by." Ismael flicks a dismissive glance in my direction. He resumes his conversation with Declan and Murat; something about soccer. Futbol, as they call it.

Putting away the vegetables, I slip back out of the flat without a goodbye from any of the men. I'd expect that of Ismael and possibly Declan, but Murat? We might not be close—my fault, I know—but he's always had a grin for me.

The street's empty and far too quiet. The crack of bullets in the distance is faint enough for me to assume the fighting must be in a different neighborhood today. I take my precautions anyway, the cold, damp air searing my lungs. My conversation with Cristian was cut short the other day, and I wouldn't put it past him to search me out again.

I take the long way around to Mila's, backtracking and looping. She doesn't live too far from me, only two blocks over, a walk that would take ten minutes, tops, if I was heading straight there. Instead I detour and check out the site of a supply off-load scheduled for two days from now. Confirmation of the offload would be nice, as well as what it is. The clinic's antibiotics need to be replaced, and Declan could probably do with a painkiller or two that's harder hitting than ibuprofen.

Mila yanks the door open like she'd been waiting impatiently on the other side since I'd left my flat. "There you are." She gives my hair a critical once over. "Too shaggy. You wait too long. Again. Come." She leads me into her kitchen, where the straight-back chair is set in the middle of the floor, the tools of her trade laid out within easy reach. After the salon she worked at was trashed, she elected not to stick around to help with clean up. The neighborhood it was in was one of the first to fall to the rebels, and it was too dangerous, she said, crossing the invisible boundary every time she had to go to work. Her clients come to her.

She runs her fingers through my hair. "Unless you have decided to grow it back out?" She hadn't wanted to cut off my hair when I came to her two years ago, but I refused to leave until she did. One more way to sever the ties to my old life.

"There is a club opening tomorrow night. You should come. Dance. Drink." Comb trapped between her teeth, she snips away at my bangs. Tiny hairs tickle my nose and I try not to wiggle it too much.

"A club opening? Really? Who's spinning?" My girlfriends in college would drag me out dancing and pour a couple of drinks into me to get me on the dance floor. It was the only way I didn't feel self-conscious.

"No one," she admitted. "It is not a true club, not like what we used to have." Most of the dance clubs and lounges had shut down in the past few months, the streets too dangerous to be on at night. When boundaries shift on a whim, you could be safe one hour and in the middle of a hot zone the next. "It is like a…what do you call it? A speakeasy, I think. But it is a place to go, relax, have some drinks with friends. You come. Dance."

"I don't have anything to wear." Going to a club, drinking, possibly dancing, isn't much of a commitment. I could handle it. I enjoy Mila's company on occasion, when I'm sick of living in my head and the one-sided conversations with Ismael start to grate. Working up the nerve to leave my flat in the dark might take some doing, though.

She comes around, frowning as her gaze rakes over me. "You are much smaller than me. Not much smaller than Zlata." Zlata is her younger sister. "She should have something you can borrow. You have shoes?"

I don't think she means sneakers or boots. "Probably not the kind you're thinking of." I had an impressive collection of heels I'd left behind in Pittsburgh, thinking I wouldn't have much use for them while we were here. Ryan was going to be busy with his thesis research, and money would be tight. Going out wasn't a priority. The two pairs I brought with me are in the back of the closet in the flat I left yesterday. I'm never going back. There's nothing left for me there.

Mila gives a final snip, swipes the comb through my hair, and unclasps the cape, dusts off the back of my neck. She gestures for me to follow, and we head for Zlata's bedroom.

Her sister's closet is full to bursting with clothes. Mila laughs as I stand there, mouth open in shock. "She likes clothes. She has been going nuts, trying to get the newest styles and not succeeding." Rifling through the tops, she plucks out a couple of slinky, skimpy, sleeveless creations and tosses them on the bed. "Her pants would be too big, I think."

"Is that a nice way of saying I've got a scrawny ass?" I say. I know I've lost weight since I got here, with the running and foot shortages.

"Yes. Too skinny. You have no hips." I like this bluntness.

"Yeah, well, you should have seen them before. I could have given JLo a run for her money." If JLo had gone on a starvation diet.

She picks up one of the tops and holds it up, a shimmery dark purple thing. Lips pursed, her eyes dart between me and the shirt, then she shakes her head and drops it, selecting another. This one is grey, almost matte. I like it. I pluck it from her fingers before she can discard it.

"Try it on," she demands. Turning around, I exchange my sweater for the top. Mila's face lights up as I face her again. "Yes. Good. Another." She hands me a cap-sleeved top in bright red.

"Cap sleeves? Seriously?"

"Cap sleeves. Seriously." I spin around, clutching the shirt to my chest. Zlata's leaning against the doorjamb. "Mila, what have I said about my closet?"

"I- I- I'm sorry." I hold out the red top. "I'll take it off."

"No. It looks better on you anyway. Keep it. But try on the red one, too. I do not think it is your color, but let me see."

Cheeks heating, I pull off one top and trade it for the other. "No. Just...no. Cap sleeves and me do not get along."

Zlata nods sagely. "They do make you look childish."

"I think you mean child-like." I strip aside the offending shirt and reach for a black scrap of fabric.

"I think my English is not as good as it could be and you should come around more. No, not black. Blue." Zlata brushes past me and pushes through the tops on the bed. "Mila, you have my blue tank top?"

Mila's got her head in the closet. "You mean this one?" She waves a cerulean number in triumph. The color reminds me of Declan's eyes, flat and full of depth at once, like a simple twist of movement or trick of light will take it from innocent to wicked.

Both sisters whistle as the fabric slides into place. Draping low in the back, the neckline higher than I'd expected, it flows over my skin, caressing it.

"Makes you look like you have tits," Zlata says approvingly. My mouth drops open to retort when she grins. "Shoes." She crawls into the closet and starts rummaging through the detritus on the floor.

"I'm a 36." It took me a while to get the European sizing down.

Her butt wriggles as she backs out of the closet on her knees. "These should fit. You have better pants?"

"I've got jeans without holes in them, if that's what you mean."

"It will do. We make it work. You come with us tomorrow night. Have Murat or Ismael bring you. Is not safe to walk at night. Especially not in those shoes."

Dusk is settling over the city as I run home an hour later, stomach tumbling from the time spent with Mila and her sister. I'm coming out of a stupor, a coma, the long-held anguish crumbling bit by bit. I can't go home, but maybe it's time I start thinking about this place, finding a way to live rather than survive. The war can't go on forever, and if I'm here, I'll be close to Ryan.

I suppose, in a way, I have Declan to thank for that. For insisting I hold his hand when all I wanted was to disappear into myself again.

He's slumped on the couch, a book in his hand. He doesn't glance up as I walk through the living room to the bedroom and put away the new clothes. For the best. Just because I'm reconsidering my misanthropic existence doesn't mean pursuing an attachment to the enigma currently taking up space in my flat. He'll leave eventually, and I don't want to waste my time on something already stamped with an expiration date.

Enough.

He continues to ignore me when I wander out into the living room. "So do you need help getting your stuff back to your flat?"

"Why would I need help?" He lowers the book.

I wave a hand at his walking cast. "You can get around on your own now. You don't need someone helping you."

"Doesn't mean I can go back. You saw what it looked like, didn't you? It's probably being watched."

The cushion makes a soft *whuff* as I flop down. "What happened in there, anyway?"

He shrugs. "Wish I knew. Came home and found they'd trashed the place."

They. "Which they?"

"Either side. I'm guessing government since it was their boots kicking my arse. One of them kept asking me where it was."

Cold surges under my skin. "Where what was?"

"Rebel headquarters."

"Why would they think that?"

Another shrug. "From the way they trashed my flat, they probably think I took a picture of it."

I sit up. Declan's just become more dangerous. "Do you? Do you know where it is?" *Please say no.* Please let it be the truth. Please don't be another weapon for Cristian to use against me.

He doesn't answer me right away, just takes in my rigid posture, the fingers twisting together in my lap. The nerves tightening my mouth and screaming under my skin. Every second that passes takes the likelihood he *does* know something higher. If he knows, he can't stay here. I can't have that in my house. I'm about ask him again when he answers.

"No."

CHAPTER EIGHT

"No?"

"No," he repeats. He sets the book on the coffee table with a sigh. "One of the soldiers must have seen me hanging around with my camera someplace, followed me home."

"So they trashed your apartment and jumped you when they found you on the street." It sounded pretty typical of them, using whatever means necessary to get what they want. Both sides are big fans of it. When we could still access the outside world with regularity, the international press called it one of the most brutal conflicts in modern history. "Why are you here, anyway? You said it's an assignment?"

"I asked for it. No one was getting recent footage, and the pay was three times what I'd normally get for a high risk assignment. Hard to pass up." He shifted on the couch. "You?"

I shouldn't have asked. I should have kept my mouth shut. Questions lead to conversations I don't want to have. "No lying, Nora," he adds, seeing my hesitation.

What difference does it make, who I tell? If it's Declan or Mila or someone else? "I…" The words stick in my throat. Swallowing doesn't help. I drop my gaze, drop my voice. "My fiancé was here, working on his thesis. I got stuck after they closed the city. Can't get out."

The embassy had been a pit of chaos when I'd gone for the

third time. I finally managed to get inside and in front of an official, who took my passport and went off to whisper with another official. Unfortunately for them, they weren't quiet enough, and I overheard snippets, fragments of their sentences. Things like "watch list," "terrorist," "Communist sympathizer," and "arrest". It was enough for my addled brain to kick into flight mode, and when they made the stupid mistake of leaving me alone in the room, I crept out the door and down the hall to an emergency exit.

I never went back. The few emails I managed to exchange with my parents after were full of anger and hate. They'd never approved of Ryan and his desire to finish his degree here, didn't approve of him putting their daughter in danger. We'd never expected that the instability in the neighboring countries and rising animosity toward Russia and its dictatorial overtures that smacked of Soviet Russia would brand us as traitors.

"You're an American citizen, right? Why didn't you get on one of the transports?" The incredulity in Declan's voice is tinged with exasperation. What, the pitiful little female wasn't smart enough to find her way out of the maze?

"Why did you ask me about Ryan? This morning," I continue at his questioning look. "You asked me who he was." *After you kissed me.*

"You were murmuring his name in your sleep. Women in my bed don't normally whisper another man's name." He smirked. Oh, you smug, smug man. If it hadn't been for the nastiness his face had already experienced, I would slap the look right off it.

"Why did you kiss me?"

"Same reason."

I froze. "You kissed me because I was saying Ryan's name?"

"I kissed you so if you started mumbling some man's name in your sleep again, it would be mine."

If I had any pleasurable thoughts left of those frantic minutes this morning, they disappeared with Declan's words. Guilt and pain tumble together in my chest. I'd kissed him,

I'd *enjoyed* kissing him, I'd wanted more. And he's sitting here telling me it was nothing. All I can think is my hand needs to connect with his face and possibly my knee with his groin.

"You don't have to worry about it happening again." My tone is flat, bearing nothing of the pain clawing at my insides. Kissing him back was a mistake, one I won't be repeating. "Tell me, does that usually work? Do women fall for that sort of arrogance?" I never had. Not until he'd blasted his way through and demanded I give in.

His response is cut off by a massive boom. My bones rattle as my back comes into contact with the floor, the weight of Declan's body a balm and a hindrance. Shouts from outside are muffled as he curves around me, covering me completely.

Even as battered as he is, he's immobile. A steel wall between me and the outside world. My hands curl into fists, clutching at his sweatshirt. A second boom, as loud as the first, rattles the windows. He drags me into a sitting position before making his way to the living room window. "Looks like smoke. A couple of bombs, probably. It's some distance away, so they must have been big ones."

Bombs. Not in this neighborhood. We're safe, at least for tonight. My brain says otherwise, and my teeth clack together, hard and fast little sounds accompanied by whimpers I can't control. The world becomes a sifting, changing grey.

"Nora." I stare blankly at Declan, kneeling in front of me. How'd he get there? Wasn't he by the window? "Jesus." He reaches for me, and I jerk to the side, scuttling out of range.

"Please don't." I don't need his comfort. I've made it through these alone before. I can do it again.

His gaze goes wary, one hand outstretched, and I weaken, curl my fingers around his. "We're all right, lass. Safe."

Safe. Another boom. A night of bombings. "Where did they get the bombs?" I whisper.

He scoots toward me. "Depends on which side it is. Could be Russia. Could be China. Could be some other European country with a vested interest in the outcome." A gentle brush of fingers, tipping my chin up. "How did you stay calm enough to get me out of the street?"

Huh?

"Focus, Nora. Talk to me. The street. You distracted them somehow, yet the last two firefights you've cowered."

"I—" Focus. He wants me to talk. A distraction from the increasing noise outside. "There weren't any guns. They weren't shooting. You were just...lying there. Taking it." Ryan, yelling at me to get away. Those screams that had to have ripped his throat raw. "I couldn't let them do it. Not again. Not like Ryan."

Declan goes still, his hand flinching as another boom sounds, farther away. "What did they do to him?"

Killed him.

"Did they beat him? Is that what happened?" God, yes. Stop talking, please stop talking. "They beat him to death. Were you there?"

"Yes." Barely even a sound, only a hint of it.

The quiet between us is punctuated with sirens. The bombs stop going off, but Declan maintains his position, thumb stroking the point of my chin. I like this version of him. I can almost forget the insulting and asinine comments he made moments ago. They burn at the back of my mind, embers ready to flame up when called. I don't need them now.

Declan, though, thinks our tender moment is over, now that the bombs have all exploded. He trails his fingers along my jaw and drops his hand, using it to push himself to his feet. He's probably tired.

Instead of heading for the bedroom, he limps toward the kitchen. Just as well. I need to change the sheets. As I stand, he reappears, holding two glasses of water. He holds one out to me and lowers himself to the couch. "You want to start or should I?"

Start what? I follow his gaze to the copy of *The Master and Margarita* sitting on the table. "Um. I can." I find the bookmark and begin reading. Margarita's about to take flight, her maid Natasha at her side. This is my favorite part of the book, almost nonsensical in nature.

The pounding on the door minutes later makes me drop the book. It continues as I pick it back up and place it carefully on the table, the sound echoing in my skull. "Nora!"

Ismael.

I hurry over and yank open the door. "What is it?"

"They blew up two of the hospitals. Or tried to. Parts are unusable. Doctor Gudelj needs you at the clinic."

Outside? I have to leave now? My skin will shred under the stress. I'm already shaking my head and stepping back when I run into a solid human wall behind me. "But it's already so low on supplies. There's practically nothing left. It won't be of any use." There hasn't been a medical supply truck in a couple of weeks, and my last grab-and-dash was aborted after I saw the number of guards on the truck.

Declan's hand is a solid, comforting weight on my shoulder, squeezing gently. "Ismael, start knocking on doors. People can spare a couple of towels." The other man gives him a narrow look, as though he's debating whether to take his orders, then turns and starts banging on doors.

Declan tugs me back inside and picks up my coat. "Ready?"

"I *can't*. Do you have any idea how hard it was, not being able to leave, that day I found you? You wouldn't let go of my fucking hand!"

"Would you have left?"

"Yes!" Yes, without a doubt, I would have left.

His expression turns to stone. "So why is the doctor requesting your presence now?"

"I steal the medical supplies for the clinic. From the transports. Not enough of the aid actually gets doled out, so I started stealing. I've helped out at the clinic before, when it's open regular hours. Sick people are one thing. Injured people, no. I can't. I can't." I'm babbling, backing into the corner, away from him.

They're almost icy, his eyes, the detached way he watches me cruel. "Sometimes seeing a pretty woman at your side makes the pain fade."

The statement makes no sense and has no bearing on our

current dilemma.

"The day they jumped me. You want to know why I wouldn't let go of your hand? That's why." He holds out a hand and I stare at it, wanting to recoil and unable to because there's a wall at my back. "The doctor must think you'll be of some use if he wants you there. We know the bombs are in another part of the city. We hear anything that sounds remotely close, we turn around and come back."

His gaze softens ever so slightly. I won't be alone. Someone will hear me if I scream this time. Panic bleeds out, leaving behind a strange calm. I can do this—walk through the dark streets, guns and shouts and bombs going off around me—for all the Ryans in this city, if it means I help one more person stay alive.

"Ismael will take me. Stay here. You can't keep walking on that leg. Doesn't it hurt?" I tug my coat from the hook on the wall.

He reaches over my head and grabs his coat, his weight balanced on his good leg. "I can handle the pain." He threads his good arm through the sleeve, and I reluctantly adjust the other side over his injured shoulder. I shouldn't find it sweet and a bit endearing that he won't leave me to face this alone. *Sweet* is not a word I associate with Declan. I crimp my lips to keep the smile from blooming.

"You lied," I say, shrugging on my coat. His hand engulfs mine. He doesn't hold it like it's breakable. His grip is sure and says I'm stronger than I think. It adds another layer of calm. I'll be fine. *We'll* be fine.

"I've been known to on occasion. Which time was this?" Ismael waits at the head of the stairs, and Declan nods to indicate we'll follow. He lets go of my hand to grasp the rail and hops down the steps.

"You said you weren't complicated." The street isn't as insane as I feared. A few people are hurrying toward the clinic, arms full of first aid supplies. I scan the street. I've yet to run into Cristian after dark, though that's more because *I'm* not likely to be out after dark. Seeing nothing out of the ordinary, I point to a narrow alley across the street. "Come on."

I wind an arm around his waist and we hobble across the street, Declan's weight pressing on me. I slip free to peer into the alley. It's as black as pitch from where we're standing, but I press forward.

"Shortcut?" Declan asks mildly.

"Something like that. Put your hand on my shoulder if you need to."

The blocks pass in relative quiet, sirens still screaming in the distance. The shouts are getting fainter as we approach the clinic. The roundabout route takes longer, hampered by his cast, but it's a good thing I'm being paranoid because as I creep around the corner of an alley, three blocks from our destination, I spot him.

Cristian's got a bag over his shoulder.

"Shit." I turn to Declan. "Can you get to the clinic on your own?"

He lifts a brow. "I think I remember where it is. Why?"

I shake my head. "Nothing you need to concern yourself with. Can you get to the clinic or not?"

His already inscrutable face is even more difficult to read in the dark, the inky black of the alley deepening the bruising and hollows of his face. "Three blocks more, right?"

Relief trickles through me. "Yeah. Well, four, really. Go back to the other end, turn right, then right at the corner. The clinic's on the left, but there'll probably be people around it."

He gives me one last piercing look and limps off into the gloom, one hand trailing along the brick for balance. Unable to see the other end of the alley, I count to a hundred before poking my head out onto the street. Cristian's under a streetlight, glancing this way and that, and I wait until he's looking the other way before I dash out into the middle of the street, curving toward him so it looks as though I came from the other side. Little things, misdirections, any trick I can think of to throw him off.

He sees me on his next scan but doesn't acknowledge me, moving out of the pool of light, head jerking to the side. I jog over. "Nora." I stifle my flinch as he kisses first one cheek, then the other, such a European thing to do. "You are going to the clinic?" Cristian's given me first aid supplies on occasion, knowing I bring them directly to the neighborhood clinic. He must approve, is all I can think. Good for him.

"Something about a bombing at one of the hospitals." *Be quick, you fucking bastard.*

He gives me a sober nod, in full soldier mode. No room for charm. "Two bombs at the university hospital and another at one of the bigger clinics. Two wings are destroyed, many dead. Your clinic is farther out and likely won't see many injured, but is best to be prepared." He hands me the small rucksack, and a quick check shows me bandages, wipes, and packets of things that must be pills. Antibiotics or painkillers. "You should go. Do not hang about." Another peck on the cheek and he disappears into the city, toward the sirens.

Well. For once, he didn't push the spy thing. Maybe we're turning over a new leaf. No more delays. Hefting the bag, I spin around and run smack into a wall of muscle.

"I couldn't find the clinic."

Declan.

CHAPTER NINE

I scowl up at him, heart racing. "It's not that hard to find."

He jerks his chin toward my bag. "What've you got?"

"Medical supplies." Hoping to stave off further questions, I open the bag and show him. "They're probably starting to wonder where I am."

The tactic works, although from his face I can see he wants to ask more questions. I stare him down until he lets it go and we cover the remaining blocks to the clinic in silence.

The clinic itself isn't the hive of activity I'd thought it would be. One door is propped open for easy access, lights flickering in the reception area. The clinic's two remaining nurses are scurrying about, cleaning up as best they can, and they barely manage a wave hello as we pass through to the rooms in the back.

Declan finds a tall stool and sits, mouth twisting in a grimace. I toss the bag on the floor and move the shelf unit away from the wall, cringing as it screeches along the floor. With Cristian's contribution, we should be okay on bandages and antiseptic wipes for a little while. I roll over a cart and hand him the bag. "Dump everything out and let's see what we've got."

Declan unzips the bag and upends it over the cart, the contents spilling into a small mound. A few pill packs land on the floor, and I scoop them up. "We've got bandages, a couple roles of medical tape, a new pack of needles, wipes, and..." I squint at the Cyrillic writing printed on one of the packs. "I have no idea what this is. Drugs of some kind." I sort out the packs, matching the writing, and end up with three different, tiny piles. "I'm going to find someone to translate these."

I pass Murat in the hall and tell him about the pills, and he goes off to translate while I track down Doctor Gudelj.

"Ah, Nora! I do not know if you are needed, but is always good to have extra hands, yes? Just in case." Despite the tension in the streets, he's in remarkably good spirits, his eyes twinkling with amusement.

"I brought more supplies. They're in the back room. What do you need me to do?"

He hands me a towel. "They must be sterilized. Just in case."

It's a familiar process—heating the water, praying the pipes have enough to fill the pot, waiting for the water to boil, the metallic clank as the tongs and scissors and scalpels hit the sides. I leave the needles out; with the new package they won't be necessary unless there are a lot of wounds to stitch closed.

Leaving the tools to cleanse themselves, I hurry into the back room. "What are they?"

Murat points at a pile. "Penicillin." Next pile. "Doxycycline." Last pile. "Some sort of painkiller. A...what would you call it? Common?"

"Generic? Non-name brand?" I guess.

"Yes, generic. Possibly. Generic of Vicodin. Or something. The doctor can tell you for sure, if you need to know."

"I do." If he has me handing out pills, I need to know what to give them. "I'll ask." As soon as Murat leaves, I swipe a packet from the tray, giving Declan a blank stare when he raises a brow. I close the door behind Murat.

Once it clicks shut, I hand it to him. "You'll want these later."

"The painkillers?"

"Yeah. Even if your leg doesn't hurt so much now, it probably will later, especially if you stay on your feet for very long. They'll help you sleep."

He tosses the packet from hand to hand, his gaze locked with mine. "We need to go by my flat tonight."

"Your flat? Why? Do you need more clothes?" His flat is even farther from the bomb sites, so there isn't likely to be much traffic. It's a smart idea, going when people are distracted. Whether he can make it is another question.

"My equipment."

I frown. "I didn't see anything when we were there, and Murat didn't mention anything." Though that means nothing; I doubt Murat would have noticed much of anything in the flat.

"That's why I need to go back. If they got the film and my laptop, as well as the cameras and lenses and shit, I'll have to replace it all when I get home, and I'd rather avoid that."

Frankly, I'd be more worried about staying alive. "Once the doctor cuts us loose we can go."

He slips the packet into his back pocket and hobbles to the door, his touch gentle on the small of my back as he follows me out into the hallway. We head to the reception area to wait.

And wait.

And wait.

And wait some more. Cristian was telling the truth. Only a few injured stagger through the doors, and they are in better shape than I anticipated. We are too far from the bomb site, it seems.

Close to midnight, the doctor gives us the okay to leave, since his nurses are crashing in one of the exam rooms. If anyone else needs care tonight, they'll get it.

"Are you sure you're up for this? It's kind of a long walk." About a half an hour's walk, give or take, between the clinic and Declan's trashed flat. My body already aches, and I'm not injured.

His smile is grim. "I wait much longer, they might find it. And if any of the pictures on my computer or the film are what they're looking for, I'm truly fucked."

Okay. To Dolac Malta we go.

It's slow, bordering on arduous. It's clear by the time we

reach his building he's in pain, sweat glinting at his temples, tiny lines radiating from his eyes, bracketing his mouth. Hoping he'll take it as the support it's meant as, I slip an arm around his waist. As small as I am, I can still bear some of his weight. He jolts, surprised, then leans into me, and hops up the stairs on one foot.

I risk flipping on a light. His flat is the same, a mess inside a disaster, and again I'm struck by the urge to put together the pieces of his photos to uncover the puzzle. Instead of searching the debris for his cameras, he limps into the bedroom and flops onto the bed with a groan, his good leg dangling over the side, foot braced on the floor. "Fuck," he mutters.

I wander in behind him. "Take one of the pills."

"Not yet. I'll take one when we get back."

Sadist. "Want me to look? Where do you store everything?"

His nod is more like a suggestion rather than a definitive movement, and when he speaks his voice is tight with pain. "Under the bed. There's a loose floorboard. Pry it up. There's a flashlight on the bedside table."

I locate the flashlight and hold it up in the dim glow of the street light filtering into the room. "Busted." The glass is cracked and the bulb is missing. "I can find it. Any spiders under there?"

"If there are, I'll kill them for you." He shuts his eyes, mouth tight with pain.

"Gee, thanks." My dry tone covers up the silly little flutter in my stomach at his offer. Such a male thing to do. Kill the spiders once the woman squeals. Which, of course, I would. I hate spiders.

Getting on my knees, I grope along the floor, feeling for cracks. "You know, this kind of reminds me of that scene in *The Saint*, the movie with Val Kilmer? Where Simon and whatshername are shackled in the van and she's on her knees, trying to get her heart pills?"

"And he says, 'While you're down there...'"

"'...mind getting the knife out of my boot?'" I smile at the quote. "So full of innuendo."

"Good movie, too. Aren't you a little young to have seen it?"

"They have these handy things called DVDs. I saw it in college." Movie nights were our alternative to going out and getting trashed every weekend. "God, I haven't seen a movie in years." I'd loaded a number of them onto my laptop before we left and brought a few along as well, but I haven't watched many. Not since Ryan died.

"The city isn't completely cut off from the outside world."

It might as well have been. Cell coverage is spotty, Internet connectivity worse, and they'd stopped delivering mail regularly months ago. On the rare occasion a mail truck makes it through the city's borders, people flock to the post office, hoping for news of the outside. Yes, we have electricity, running water, news coverage and satellites, if you know how to find it.

I just made the conscious decision to avoid contact with the world outside Sarajevo. To protect my family and friends, I told myself, give them plausible deniability.

"I know," I say quietly, "but it hasn't done me any good." Cold, flat words, tainted with anger from my parents. Confusion from my brother. Grief and disbelief from Ryan's family. Ignorance from my friends, unaware of how dangerous it's gotten over here. And once I left the embassy, going home stopped being an option.

There. There it is. A slight crack in the floorboards. The edge digs into my fingertips as I pry it up. "Is there a light or something on that table?"

He flicks on the bedside lamp. "Better?"

I snort in response and stretch out on my belly. Two large camera bags sit on top of a sleek laptop, cables jumbled and catching on the edges. "You'll have to check the camera bags yourself." Stacking the equipment on the floor, I scoot back and come up on my knees as Declan sits up, placing his feet on the floor. "Do you need to rest longer?"

He winces. "No. Not gonna make it hurt any less." He

unzips the first camera bag and pulls out a lens. "There's a bag in the closet for the laptop. Unless they trashed that, too."

It takes a minute to find it, buried under a small heap of blankets and sheets and towels, some ripped to pieces. I slide the laptop inside along with the cables and zip it closed. "Where did you find a dark room in this city?"

"Didn't. Why?"

I lift the strap over my head, settling it across my body before picking up one of the camera bags. "There's photo paper all over your living room."

He grabs the second camera bag and slings it over his good shoulder. "I've got a small printer. It's easier to see how a photo will turn out if you print it. Computer screens can distort things."

"Oh." We make our way out of the flat, pausing at the top of the stairs. He refuses my help, clutching the bannister as he clumps down the stairs. The street is eerily quiet—no more sirens, no more shouts. The sky's cleared enough for the moon to cast its fitful light over the broken buildings, and I stare up at them as we pass, for once not caring who finds me.

The tumbled bricks and splintered wood, glass shards glittering in between, hurt to look at. "This used to be such a beautiful city, and they keep destroying it. You have to wonder if they're going to give up someday and just let it rot." It's not the first time the city's been split apart by a violence so fierce it rubs out its history. We pass an abandoned church, the doors hanging from their hinges, the façade stripped of anything of value. Nothing's sacred here anymore. Not even God.

Declan huffs out a breath. "It's still a beautiful city. You need to look past the destruction."

I could. But it's safer, familiar, to sink down, let the gloom wrap itself around me like a warm cloak. Shaking it off, rebuilding the hope inside that I can make this new life work for me is a terrifying prospect. I don't want to face it without Ryan. That wasn't the plan.

"How long are you here for?" My brain's folding in on itself, dragging me to that place where I spend days in bed, unmoving.

"What day is it? I was probably supposed to contact the extraction team a day ago. Or more."

I smirk. "Extraction team? What is this, SEAL team six?"

His answering laugh blows away the shadows crowding my brain. "I don't know what they'd call it. That's what I call them. A highly skilled group of people who are supposed to get me out of a city no one can get into."

"How *did* you get into the city? All the checkpoints are under heavy guard, and I heard the countryside isn't much better than the city."

He's quiet for a moment, the thunk of his boot echoing off the buildings. "It's not as bad, but it's getting there. I was dropped a few miles from a checkpoint and walked in."

"But that must have taken hours!" I knew it was possible to sneak out of the city on foot; plenty of people had done so already. Every so often I'd start making plans of my own before I remembered I had no money, no passport, and no clue how to go about sneaking into another country and not get tossed out. It's easier to stay put, even as it chips away at my sanity.

"I needed the pictures."

He doesn't say anything after that, and we walk the rest of the way to my flat in silence. Once inside, it's clear the distance was more than he should have gone, his hair damp with sweat, lips flattened with pain. He fishes the pills out of his pocket, pops two free of the pack.

I stop him before he can swallow. "Go on. I'll get you some water." I point through the open bedroom door and follow him inside, scooping up wayward clothing and tossing it in the closet. After filling a glass in the kitchen, I bring it to him, waiting while he swallows the pills. I grab one of the pillows and take it out to the couch.

He's climbed into bed when I return for an extra blanket. Too different, too many faces, and I can't reconcile his earlier words with the man in front of me. "You didn't really mean that, did you? Earlier?"

"If you're going to be vague about it, yes, I meant it."

I open my mouth to continue, and some part of my mind scolds me. The horse is dead. It's time to stop beating it. This aching, beaten man is far more complex than he'll admit. That's all I need to know.

And I'll do well to remember he only kissed me so the next time I murmur a man's name in my sleep, it'd be his.

"Never mind," I mutter. "Good night." I shut the door behind me, strip off my clothes, and fall onto the couch, squirming to pull the blankets over me.

The dreams that come are fractured, fragments of Ryan and I, pieces of Declan, and always, always a city bent on grinding itself into the dust.

CHAPTER TEN

Obviously, the "club" doesn't open the next night.

Murat comes by with detailed descriptions of the carnage, and my anger rises with each word. Pointless, completely and utterly pointless. Innocent people dying because not so innocent people think it's a good tactic to keep others in line.

Declan just gives me a mild look as I sit fuming, hands clenched into fists. "Going out?" he asks once Murat leaves.

"No," I mutter. I'm not stupid enough to go tearing through the streets to find Cristian and demand an explanation for the government's actions. This isn't my war, anyway. Who wins isn't my concern. I can't bring myself to stop stringing him along, not yet. The information he unwittingly passed on is why there were Molotov cocktails at the ready the day Declan was beaten.

And I can't quite give up the hope that he might be able to help clear my name so I can go home.

Morning slides into afternoon, into evening, into night, and we wake and do it all over again. Days pass. We spend hours sitting in the quiet of my flat, sometimes reading, sometimes having actual conversations where those little tidbits you glean about one another are exchanged. He's the oldest of five and older than me. Our mutual love of *The Master and Margarita* leads to the discovery of other favorite books and movies, though his taste in music is atrocious. I tell him about the time I convinced my brother I was Santa's special helper and could get him anything he wanted for Christmas as long as he was my slave. He told me how he'd dislocated his shoulder twice before, once playing rugby, once reaching for a shot on location in Kabul.

"You've been to Afghanistan? By choice?" Another level of hell. A hot, swirling dust storm of hell.

He shrugs, then rotates his injured shoulder. He can do it now without the fine lines of strain running over his face. "The money was good."

"I'm beginning to sense a pattern here," I say dryly. "You just love being tossed into volatile situations, don't you?"

His grin is bright and quick. The bruising on his face has mostly shaded to yellow, the swelling negligible. The expression shouldn't be charming. It is, and it disturbs me on a level that's still insulted by the cocky bastard who pops up at random moments.

It's cozy, disconcertingly so, and I'm frustrated by the fact that he doesn't touch me and goes to bed each night in *my* bed while I'm left with the couch.

We have more company. Ismael, bearing alcohol. Doctor Gudelj to check his shoulder. Zlata comes over and flirts outrageously with Declan, and he's borderline rude. It doesn't deter her in the slightest. In fact, I think she gets off on it. Strange, having people over, after month upon month of keeping my location a secret.

"You have a sweetheart waiting for you? A lover? She must be anxious." Zlata's fingers run down his forearm, and I can see the skin twitching from here.

He leans forward and picks up the glass of water on the table. "I just take them as they come along. We fuck, I leave, I come back, she's no longer in the picture. It's a good system." That grin again. Yes, definitely disturbing.

Zlata's hands are wandering again. "I like the way you think." Her smile is slow and sly.

Subtle, Zlata. Real subtle.

Mila takes one look at him and immediately pulls me into the kitchen. Her words tumble over themselves and she loses her English in her excitement, but based on her sister's reaction I think she's telling me how hot Declan is. Which is weird, because he's not.

She blushes and fumbles her way through a stilted conversation with him, or stilted on her part, since all she seems to be capable of is staring.

By the time she leaves there's a black cloud hanging over my head. I haven't left the flat since the night of the bombs, and I can't handle being trapped in here with him.

Except up until the sisters showed up, I hadn't felt trapped.

"I'm going to see if there are any vacant flats around." I slip on my sneakers and grab my coat. My legs are begging for a run.

"Why?" He's fiddling with something on his laptop and keeps his eyes on the screen.

"Because I'd like my bed back."

He glances up, one side of his mouth lifting in a smirk as he studies me. "You got something against sharing?"

The proposition combined with his expression, so smug, so arrogant, should not have heat gathering between my thighs. "Why would I want to share a bed with a man I know is just going to shunt me aside sooner rather than later?"

"Because it would be fun." Lacing his hands behind his head, he leans back, eyes glinting with amusement.

"Not my idea of a good time." I shrug my coat on. "You're getting a new flat. I'll be back in a while."

His smirk drops away, a blank mask sliding into place. "Good luck with that, lass."

It rained earlier, the wet chasing away the stench of smoke. I've let too much time lapse. I swing through one of my usual routes, the end point one of the supply drop offs. I need to find new ones. Can't become predictable. The old storefront is boarded over and empty, the back loading dock a perfect place for food supplies to be unloaded, away from the prying eyes of the neighborhood.

Edging through the broken door hidden behind a stack of crates, I let my eyes adjust to the gloom of the interior before tiptoeing forward, listening for voices. I switch on the tiny flashlight stuffed in my pocket. They've been here recently, and I snag a few cans of food and a loaf of sandwich bread, then break the seal on a refrigerated crate. Eggs! Oh my god, actual eggs. And butter. Saliva pools in my mouth. Drooling would be a bad idea.

My cache of burlap sacks hasn't been moved, and I grab one and fill it with the food I'm swiping. Stashing it near the exit so I can sneak in and carry it home later, I head for the next alley, the next drop. Medical supplies. The clinic's okay for a while, supply-wise, which is a good thing because I missed the truck and the crates have been moved to their final destination.

Winding through the neighborhood, venturing further out in search of more information, I almost miss Cristian as he stalks down the opposite side of the street. The fury I'd felt when I learned of the waste laid to the hospital rises, and I struggle to bank it. Anger won't do me any good here.

I suck in a breath and step out onto the street, hurrying across to catch up to him. "Cristian!" I hiss.

He whirls around. The heavy scowl on his face transforms into a bright smile, one that's not entirely faked. "Nora." He reaches out and pulls me to him, kissing my cheek as usual. Then he crowds us into a doorway. Always so concerned we'll be caught. I'm grateful for his paranoia, though. In a neighborhood where the residents have consciously chosen to remain neutral, being seen fraternizing with either side brings up questions you can't answer.

"Did you do it? Did the government blow up the hospital?" Crap, there goes my anger.

He freezes, then nods slowly. "It was necessary."

"Really?" I say bitterly. "It was necessary to blow up people who were unable to defend themselves?"

Ice hangs from his words. "It was necessary to stop the rebels from regaining strength and advancing. Many of those who died were their soldiers or sympathizers. The few that weren't were unfortunate collateral damage."

Collateral damage. I am collateral damage.

"I'm sorry it upset you." Is he? His sincerity meter appears to be running low. "I know you want this to end so you may leave, but if you help us, it would be over much faster. You are small and quick. You like to play in the shadows. We will train you to. Help us win, and I will get you home."

Home. His promise is familiar, but for the first time, it's completely hollow. That tiny flare of hope has drowned in its own wax, left to flicker too long without someone to tend it. "My answer hasn't changed," I murmur, unable to give him an outright no. It's a false hope now, but better than none. "I just want to stay out of the way. This has to be over soon, right?"

He sighs. "I wish I could tell you that. We are getting close, but war doesn't stick to a schedule." He tips my chin up, and my skin shrieks in protest at the touch. "I'll win you over." His grin isn't anywhere near as charming as Declan's. "I couldn't get any more nectarines. This will have to do." He reaches into his pocket and pulls out a small box.

Prying open the lid, I squint at the contents. "Chocolates?"

"Of course. Sweets are hard to come by."

I hold them out. "Cristian, I can't keep taking food from you."

"What is the expression…Humor me? Humor me, Nora. Life is hard right now. Let me make it a little easier." He kisses my cheek again, squeezing my hand for good measure before ducking out onto the sidewalk again. I give him thirty seconds, stuffing the box into my coat pocket, then begin following him.

He doesn't disappoint, the stupid man, confident as he is that no one would think to follow him. He leads me to one of the few bars still open for business. The back door is propped open, and I sneak inside, careful to stay out of view. Murat, bless him, gave me a minirecorder several months ago when I started relaying some of the more relevant information I got from Cristian. Murat never questioned where I got it, and he's translated more than one conversation from the recorder. He wants to know as badly as me how much longer we'll be out of the line of fire.

I managed to snag some batteries on a recent supply run, replenishing our depleted stock. There's plenty of life in the device to find out what the plans are for our neighborhood.

The stench of cigarettes and stale beer waft around me. Gag. Ugh. It's a dirty, filthy smell. I don't know how anyone can stand it.

Sometimes when I track Cristian, I get lucky and he's in a place I can keep an eye on him, get close enough to record the conversation. Other times I have to be patient and wait for him to leave, so I can follow his compatriots. Again, useful information. I have a stockpile of it. If I had a rebel contact, I could sell it for a hefty sum.

All I need to know is when and where the next supply drop will be, but when I peek into the main room of the bar, Cristian is sitting in the far corner. There's no convenient spot for me to sidle into. I could wait. It might be hours, and I need to get the food back to my flat, but I could wait. Avoid the man ensconced on my couch, dinking around on a laptop.

Frustrated, I creep out through the back and wind my way through the streets to a small cemetery. The orderly rows of headstones, dotted here and there with grand monuments, carry a false sense of calm. I know better. I know many of the new headstones, the even newer unmarked graves, are soaked in fury and violence.

Ryan Terrance Standford. Such an upstanding, proper name. The pale grey stone was the best I could do, once I was forced to put him in the ground here. Old anger and grief murmur soothing, mindless words.

The scent of fresh dirt drifts under my nose and the damp ground soaks through my jeans as I kneel in front of his headstone, tracing his name and blinking back tears. It will never stop hurting. Never. This rip inside me will continue to bleed.

"It's getting worse," I whisper. "You wouldn't recognize

the city anymore. It's broken and crumbling." Like us. "I'm trying to get on with it, you know. Not be the grieving widow who can't let go. But it's pointless. I can't go home. I can't stay here. Every time I try to think of a solution, I remember you're here and I can't do anything."

It hurts, Ryan's ashes in the ground below me, a tiny piece of him in a box in the bottom of the closet. Knowing that if I leave I'll be giving up more than just what's left of him. I'll be acknowledging that my stasis is over.

It's already over. It was over when Declan grabbed my hand and wouldn't let go.

"I miss you so much, baby. I love you." Bringing my fingertips to my mouth, I press the kiss into the stone. More fraud. I need something real. Solid. Ungiving.

Some*one*.

Bad idea. A truly terrible idea. I'm tired, emotional, and irritated. I can entertain bad ideas, but executing them? No. Once I do, I can never unexecute them.

It starts to rain as I jog through the streets, circling and detouring to pick up my bag of food. Rivulets snake under my coat collar, my hair plastering itself to my head. My jeans get in on the action as well, sticking to my legs. I drip all over the floor as I climb the stairs to my flat. Hopefully the bread stayed dry. Well, dry-ish.

Declan hasn't moved from his spot on the couch, his eyes glued to the monitor of his laptop. He grunts in response to my hello, and I leave the food in the kitchen. I squish past him to the bedroom, wincing at the trail of wet behind me.

Peeling off my clothes is a lot of fun, the fabrics heavy and adhering to my skin in places. I drop them on the bathroom floor and retrieve a towel. My teeth are starting to chatter as I pull on a clean pair of panties. "Hey, Declan? Could you put on the tea kettle?"

His answer is unintelligible. I toss the towel through the open bathroom door and dig through the clothes I piled into the closet in an attempt to straighten up the tiny room. I have a pair of fleece pants. I swear I do.

Thunk. Thunk. Thunk. I shut the door, didn't I? Dammit, where are those pants?

"What did you say? I didn't hear—" I whirl around, sweatshirt clutched to my chest. "Oops. Sorry." The wide, sly smile doesn't make him look the least bit sorry.

"Out. I asked you to put the kettle on. I'm freezing, and I want tea. Out." Turning my back, I tug the sweatshirt over my head and resume hunting for the pants. A strangled noise behind me must be my imagination. As is the flash of heat in Declan's eyes when I glance over my shoulder. "What?"

No one should be able to move that fast with a walking boot on. I'm braced against the wall with my legs wrapped around his waist before I can blink, desire shadowing his face. "Want me to warm you up?" he murmurs.

"No." Dammit, I was going for strong. Not breathy with need.

"Too bad." He takes my mouth and a searing heat zips through me like a wildfire. *Yes.* I need this. Need him, need his hands clamped on my hips, need his lips and tongue and oh god his *tongue.* When he drags his mouth away, I moan and tip my head back to give him better access to my neck, biting my lip when his tongue completes a particularly wicked maneuver at the fragile spot under my ear.

Lacing my fingers through his hair, I plunder his mouth as he does mine, wanting him to be as crazy with this need as I am. It swirls between us, a whirlpool threatening to drag us down, and his hand slips under my sweatshirt and finds my breast.

I want to know what his skin feels like against my mouth. I want to taste every inch of him, and then go back and do it again. I want him under me, over me, inside me, making me forget, making me live.

The heat of his hand and his mouth is gone as quickly as it came on. I stare at him, confused, dazed with lust. He stopped. Why did he stop? Especially when I can tell how ready he is?

He slides his hands down my thighs and unwinds me from his waist, dropping me on my feet. "Warm enough now?"

And he limps out of the room, cast thunking with every step.

CHAPTER ELEVEN

That's it. Twice now he's kissed me, wound me up, then dropped me like I'm diseased. He's not getting away with it this time. I storm into the living room. He's lowering himself to the couch, booted foot hovering in the air over the coffee table. "Where the fuck do you get off? You think you can be that callous and expect me to just...let you do it whenever you want?" I fist my hands on my hips and glare at him.

"You know, your mouth says one thing, but your legs..." He stares pointedly at my bare legs.

My ragged emotions coalesce and settle on one singular feeling: anger. Red edges my vision. The world narrows to the space around his head, lighting it up with bright gold fury. "You. You *fucking* bastard. Is that how you treat women? Like tissues? Use once and toss them away?" Even as anger catches the embers of desire he'd stirred, I realize I've got a choice: I can follow through on my thoughts from the cemetery, or I can back off.

My body overrules my brain and says *go*, propelling me forward. I stalk over to the couch and straddle him, determined to leave him wanting this time. *I'll* do the touching. *I'll* rule this kiss, these fleeting caresses. Fisting my hands in his sweatshirt, my eyes meet his and my heart sputters to a halt. The intensity on his face is frightening, air sticking in my lungs. He pushes his face close to mine. "*Yes*, that's how I treat them. Most of the time, because I'm not around and that's the only way I can get it through their fluffy heads. But you—Do you have any have any idea how badly I want you? You're not ready. I'll break you. Tiny little pieces of Nora."

His hissed words hammer at the fog cloaking my brain. "What the fuck are you talking about?"

"Don't play stupid now." Cupping a hand around the nape of my neck, he kisses me. Hot. Possessive. There's a claiming in this kiss that wasn't there before. I am *his*, his toy, his to use, his to discard, for as long as he'll have me. He'll smash my defenses so there's no use putting them up again. His tongue finds every tiny crevice in my mouth. Stroking, enticing, cajoling my response from me.

The first tremor works its way up my spine. Another harsh kiss, taking me deeper. Another tremor. He breaks the kiss, his forehead propped against mine. "Tell me you were ready for that. Make me believe you, and I'll take you to bed right now." He strokes a hand down the back of my neck and eases away, his gaze searching and sober. "What do you want, lass?"

The potent, liquid darkness of his mouth…soon. Maybe. I'm afraid if I wait I'll talk myself out of it. I'm afraid this is the wrong choice, that my heart and my brain and my body won't accept him.

Only one way to find out.

I scrape my teeth over his lower lip and thrust my tongue into his mouth, hoping he won't notice how badly I'm trembling, that he'll think I'm shaky with unquenched wants. I have to know the difference, the way his skin feels under my hands, how his broad shoulders and long, tall body fit with mine. "Let me touch you," I beg.

He groans. "Christ." He jerks me forward, hands streaking under the hem of my sweatshirt as his mouth covers mine in a bruising punishment of a kiss. The fierce possession I'd felt earlier is magnified a hundred thousand times, and the doubts slip away like water down the drain. Hands roaming along my waist and up to span my ribs, he palms my breasts and I gasp into his mouth, his touch searing through me.

"Take it *off*." Pulling at his sweatshirt, unable to get it over his head, I wish my hands were strong enough to rip it apart. He lets go of me long enough to drag it off, and I'm rewarded with the sight of his lean, muscled chest, the bruises faint splotches on his skin. Warm, almost hot to the touch.

My brain shuts down. Just completely stops processing higher thought, and all I can think is *want*. I am laden in it, drowning dying gasping with *want*. And what I want more than anything right now is to feel his skin against mine.

Whipping off my sweatshirt, I press myself to him, clad only in my underwear. I'm no longer cold. The shakes are still there, growing more and more violent. Control's slipping beyond my grasp and instead of making one last desperate lunge for it, I fling it away and attack his mouth, his jaw, his neck, fingernails scoring a trail over his abdomen.

I am tiny in his arms and strong as titanium, ready for the next assault. He launches it, two-pronged with little finesse. An arm around my waist, bowing me up, presenting my nipples for his eager mouth. His free hand shoves into my panties and finds my clit, rubbing in steady, smooth circles.

"That's it," he mumbles against my breast. He bites down on the sensitive tip and tugs, drawing a sharp cry from me. "Responsive, aren't we? Let's try this." Without warning, he plunges a finger into me, and I arch back, lost to him, my hips mindlessly jerking before following the slow pump of his hand. "Fuck, you're tight."

The words are a bare whisper, hard to hear over the roaring in my head. He strokes his fingers in and out, in and out, faster, dragging me closer, higher, that bright, shiny orgasm within reach. *Don't stop don't stop oh please oh please dear god don't stop don't stop don'tdon'tdon't.*

He stops.

He doesn't stop for long. Cursing, shaking, he yanks me up with one hand as he pushes at his sweats with the other, freeing his cock. Oh. *Mine. That* is mine. I scoot back on his lap and grip him at the base, stroking upward. The head is slick, and I spread the moisture around, leaning forward to kiss him.

Fabric rips as he shoves his hand back into my panties. His hips twitch and lift, and I match my rhythm to his, the edge of release right in front of me and still beyond my reach. I give him a final stroke and let him go, hitching my thumbs into the waistband of my underwear and pushing them down. They get caught around my knees. I get them to my ankles. Good enough. Crazed with need, body straining for release, I glide my hand along his length, squeeze once, and shift my hips over him.

"Nora, condoms—"

I drop down. He splits me in two, it's been so long. There's a stitch of pain deep inside. I've gone too fast, but I don't care. Circling my hips, I lean forward and cover his mouth with mine, sucking on his tongue as our bodies find a rhythm that suits us, suits the frenzy screaming to get out.

Grinding on him tears a whimper from me as the first waves of pleasure roll in. Rocking forward and back, forward and back, his thumb in my mouth, trailing over my breasts, heading south. I groan at the touch. *"More."* I pick up the pace, place my hand over his, show him how I want it. Fast. Almost painful. "Pinch me," I beg. "Harder." Things are getting slipperier. Hotter. Tighter. I trail the tip of my tongue up the side of his neck and suckle a kiss below his ear, smashing his hand between our bodies. "Again." Lacing my fingers through his hair, I place kiss after kiss along his jaw, his throat, raining them along the line of his shoulder. The sensations are pulling me under—the harsh sound of our breathing, the salt of his skin under my tongue, the sultry press of his lips at my throat, his clever fingers manipulating me and egging me on. Everything is white and getting brighter, shining silver as we move against each other.

"Nora."

"Don't stop," I whisper. His eyes have darkened and gone mad. "Don't stop. Too close. Too close to stop." I cradle his head in my hands and kiss him, his lips on mine completing the circuit.

"Nora. Lass," he whispers against my mouth. "I'm not going to—"

I splinter, crash into a thousand tiny pieces, the soundless scream locked in my throat as everything implodes. Through the flood of release I'm aware of Declan's hands on my hips, clamping down as he thrusts upward. A shout. One last smashing wave of orgasm, and I'm limp and sated.

He gathers me close, tucking my head into the crook of his neck. Our ragged breathing is thunderous in the aftermath, competing with the heavy, speeding thump of my heart. He presses a kiss to my temple. "Good thing I didn't try that earlier. Might not have lived." He strokes a hand down my back.

I chuckle. "I'd have revived you."

Nap. After stupendous sex, one needs a nap. I yawn and snuggle closer. The hand stroking over my back pauses. "If you'd waited two seconds longer, I could have told you there are condoms in my camera bag."

His words penetrate at the same time I become aware of the wet warmth seeping across my thighs. Scrambling off his lap, I glance down in horror. This is what happens when I think of bad ideas. I act on them, and make monumentally stupid decisions.

Unable to look at the horrible mistake on my couch, I stumble away and into the bedroom, then the bathroom, shutting the door behind me. The damning evidence of our frantic fucking trickles farther down my legs. Flipping on the shower, I duck under the water and arch away from the stinging cold drops. I deserve the cold. A fair punishment for not taking the time to think.

Though just because I'm punishing myself doesn't mean I can't be quick about it.

I lather up and rinse off, the soap sluicing away the scent of sex and Declan. And I immediately wish I hadn't. I wish I'd taken my time, explored him, experimented. Used a condom.

Ryan and I hadn't used one for the last two years we were together, the only barrier between us and an unexpected and mostly unwanted pregnancy the IUD I'd had inserted. We'd wait each month for my period to come, anxious and trying to hide it. It took a few months, but we finally accepted there wouldn't be kids until we were ready, and the sex had gotten even better after that. The hindrance of having to carry a condom around when we dared a quick fuck in the park or in the shower or in an elevator was gone.

I shut off the water, chilled enough my blood is like ice under my skin. There's no point in regretting what happened. Not just that we'd had mostly unprotected sex, but that we'd had it at all. I couldn't, really, not when it felt so good. Not when I want to do it again. And again. And again. Not when I want to let him drag me off to bed and never get up, let him pin me to the mattress, tangle in the sheets.

The tiny voice telling me sex is supposed to mean something isn't as easy to ignore. Especially since, with Declan, there isn't much hope it ever will mean anything. I don't doubt he was telling the truth when he told Zlata about the women in his life. His crass and hurtful words lent too much credence to it. And I'd left my days of one night stands and fuck buddies behind when I met Ryan.

A temporary lapse, then. Now that we'd gotten it out of our systems, we could control ourselves. I'd help Declan out until he'd healed enough to go back to his flat, and everything would be fine.

Declan is still on the couch when I come out, though he's pulled up his sweats. "Bathroom's yours, if you want to take a shower." He gives me a stiff nod and gets to his feet, avoiding my gaze as he walks to the bedroom.

He returns as I'm making some tea. His hair is damp, and he's clad in jeans and a sweater. "Couple things." I shoot him a questioning glance. He holds up a finger. "One: I've never gone without a condom before. I might not be one for a relationship, but I'm always careful. You?"

"I had an IUD put in a few years ago. An intrauterine device," I explain. "It's a form of birth control. I haven't been with anyone like that other than Ryan." I don't bother telling him I haven't had sex since Ryan died. That's pretty much a given.

He studies me for another moment before holding up another finger. "Two: if you think that was a mistake, you tell me now, because I'm going to take advantage of you any chance I get.

"Three: you don't belong here. You're coming with me when I'm leaving. Four," he continues, ignoring my shaking head, "no more sleeping on the couch. You sleep in the bed, next to me, regardless of whether we keep fucking." He turns toward the living room. "Ismael said something about a football match. Surprised anyone still has TV reception these days. I'll be back later."

Space. However he phrases it, it's distance, and it hurts and it doesn't. I struggle to match his nonchalance, throat aching with the effort. I manage to push one side of my lips up in a smirk. "Don't try to hobble home drunk."

His teeth flash in a grin. "Worrying about me? How sweet." He disappears from view, his next words preceded by the front door opening. "I'll see you later."

Will I? Despite his words, I've never felt more uncertain in my life. Wobbly. We'd be better off not repeating the incident on the couch. The harshness of war hasn't changed my outlook on romance; I want the hearts and flowers, the rainbows to go with my thunderstorms. Ryan gave me all of those and more. I never thought I'd want them again. I *don't* want them again. I'll never get them from Declan.

His promise to take me with him? How's he going to manage that, when he can barely take care of himself?

I putter around, making myself scrambled eggs and toast for dinner because I can. I'm restless and tired and unable to concentrate. We finished *The Master and Margarita* and, after some heated arguing, agreed on another book to read, George Eliot's *Middlemarch*. I'd wanted to read it ever since I'd seen the BBC miniseries eons ago, and had the fun idea of reading a section, then watching it. It was one of the DVDs I'd brought with me. Declan declared it boring and only gave in when I threatened bodily harm. We hadn't started reading yet.

I could read it anyway. It's not like we *have* to read together. I've got plenty of other reading material for him to choose from.

The flat feels empty without him.

I settle for rewatching a silly romantic comedy on my laptop and drowning my confusion in vodka, swiped from Ismael's stash, the shots interspersed with the chocolates from Cristian. Over a week has passed since Declan took up a spot in my life, jerking me out of my grief-induced slumber. I want to rewind, want to find the strength to walk away instead of letting him clutch my hand like it's the only thing tethering him to this world.

Angry, I shut off the laptop, put the vodka back in the freezer, and make my way into the bedroom. I change the sheets and hunt up a pair of Ryan's boxers to pair with my sleep shirt and climb under the covers.

Cold. I am so cold. Cold and alone and lost.

It's sometime later that I'm woken by the mattress shifting. He's here, in my bed, close enough to touch. Close enough to hold me and wrap me in his strength and tell me I'm not the only one who isn't sure what's supposed to happen next in this scary new life.

I tense, waiting for him to move. Willing him to.

He doesn't.

So I huddle on my corner of the mattress and pray for sleep.

CHAPTER TWELVE

"Explain to me again why you're going there? What, the information in Carnegie Library isn't good enough for you?"

Ryan's laugh was a full-bodied thing, his body vibrating around me as he held me in his arms. "It's not that, babe. It's the resources plus the environment. The country's stable enough, but some of their neighbors … And Russia … Damn. Firsthand experience."

In Ryan-logic it made perfect sense. In other people logic … crap. It still made sense. "You'll be gone for a year?"

The flickering lights glowed around us as candle flames danced, blanketing the room in shadows and warmth. His arms tightened. "We'll be gone for a year. You can't let me go by myself. Who's going to make sure I eat? And shower?"

I managed a laugh around the lump in my throat. "Are you sure it'll work? I mean, quitting my job isn't a big deal, but how are you so certain the funding will come through for two people?" His assurances his housing allowance would cover both of us battled with my doubt that it wouldn't because we weren't married.

He kissed the curve of my neck and rolled away. His bedside table drawer scraped open and shut, and then he was back, surrounding me once more. He handed me a piece of paper. "Written confirmation, as my lady requested."

The letter did, indeed, state his housing allowance was for the two of us, and my stomach calmed, my heart squishing with joy and love that he'd go that extra distance for me. How had I gotten so damn lucky?

"And if anyone has any doubts, this should set them straight." He reached around me again and held out his hand. It was shaking so badly I grabbed his wrist to steady it, and the candlelight caught and flickered on what he was holding up between two fingers.

A ring.

A shiny, lovely ring.

"You're mine, lass. For as long as I want you in my bed."

What the—I squirmed around until I was facing him. Instead of the smirk I'd expected, Declan's face was intense and possessive. Frightening, that intensity. His hands more so. He skimmed one over my hip and cupped my ass, shifting me closer. His words were a soft caress on my lips as his mouth brushed over mine. "You don't belong here."

God, that hurts.

That dream, that memory of Ryan's proposal, perverted by the intrusion of Declan and his arrogance. It's all the more insulting for the ghost of the heavy warmth of Ryan cradling me in his arms.

This ghost is far more substantial than it should be. Slowly unwinding myself from the fetal position I'd curled into, I slide my legs down the bed, stopping when my foot runs into the stiff, hard plastic of his boot. What the hell is Declan doing? He'd been on the other side of the bed last night. Now I'm completely dwarfed by him. My head rests on one arm, his other binding me to him, ass to his groin. This can't be good for his ribs. Not to mention his shoulder. Does this man have no care whatsoever for his own well-being?

"Mmph." The arm around my waist relaxes slightly as his hand sneaks under the hem of my t-shirt. His mouth teases the curve of my neck, a ticklish sensation that never fails to heat me up. "Too many clothes," he mumbles. He suckles a kiss at my nape.

Caught between a bittersweet memory and Declan's temptation, I lie still. Do I get up? Do I get rid of the boxers? How badly do I want his hands to wander farther than they have?

Then he sighs and pulls me impossibly closer, his hand

molding my breast.

He doesn't move after that. For all intents and purposes, he's fallen back asleep. The heat of him soaks into my back. It hurts almost as much as the dream. Being held, protected.

And that's the difference. Declan's hold is as possessive as it is protective. He'll stand between me and the bad guys, every time. From the shape of his body to the strength in the sleek coils of muscle, he fits around me in a way Ryan didn't. It shouldn't feel right. It does.

Ryan never held me like he could scare all the monsters away with a single growl.

Tears gather in my throat. *Go away*. I press my face into his arm and will sleep to come.

Sleep is more like a fitful doze, the light in the room shifting as the minutes pass. Dammit. I don't want to get up now. I don't want to leave this circle. But I can't just lie here.

Giving a little wriggle, I try to pry the arm pinning me to him away. He only tightens it with a grunt. Wriggle, push, squirm. My pajamas are twisted and I'm still not free. I'm going to have to wake him up.

"Don't stop, lass. I was enjoying it." He presses a kiss to the top of my head.

"I'm sorry. I didn't mean to wake you."

"Too late. What are you going to do with me?" The question is punctuated with a roll of his hips. It's pretty obvious he's got a plan in mind.

He answers for me by tugging at my shorts, and I lift my hips and kick them off. I'm not conceding anything. I'd have to take them off to put on my sweats once I get out of bed anyway.

"Now the shirt," he murmurs. More wiggling and squirming, and I'm finally free of the confining fabric, his morning erection a hard lump against my butt. He groans softly. "Feels good."

That's a snort worthy comment if I ever heard one. "I'm short and skinny. You actually enjoy having bones poking you?"

He skims a hand over my hip. "Slim. Not skinny. Always liked small women." His warm breath caresses the back of my neck.

"Weirdo," I breathe. Teeth close over my nape.

"Not weird. They're much stronger than people think." Kisses form a burning line over my neck to my shoulder, winding around and up to my ear. "Sexy." He palms a breast, rolling the nipple.

That shuts me up, and I focus on his touch and how my body reacts, surging toward each new caress. He torments me from behind. Doesn't move me around so I can touch him. Manipulates me for my pleasure, or his, or both. Hands and mouth bringing me to a fever pitch, so when he snaps the sides of my panties and pulls them off, when he rolls away and I hear the familiar crinkle of a condom wrapper, when he lifts my leg and holds it in place, braced on his hip, all I can do is moan as he thrusts forward.

"Feels better. Christ, Nora, fantastic." He moves his hand from my leg long enough to guide my hand to my clit, pressing my fingers in small, fast circles, the slickness of my arousal growing with every plunge of his cock. "*Yes*. Like that."

It's sweaty and sticky and a step above the basest form of fucking, the bed squeaking with the effort. Tiny flutters ripple through me. "Close." My voice is hoarse with lust.

His strokes pick up speed, his fingers joining mine in their efforts to send us tumbling into the abyss. I strain toward it, forgoing breathing because I need this orgasm more than I need oxygen. Almost. There. I'm throbbing with it, the keening noises leaving my mouth embarrassing. Almost...

"Oh, *god*," I gasp. The climax races outward, squeezing me hard, the force of it setting off Declan. He sinks his teeth into the curve of my neck, and if I wasn't panting for air I'd have laughed at the vampire trick.

Soaked in more ways than one, my heart struggles to slow down. I'm not sure I can move any time soon. Declan gently lowers my leg, rubbing my hip. "Perfect start to the morning."

"Right." I snuggle into him, heedless of the sweat clinging

to our bodies. "Dammit, I just changed the sheets last night."

"I guess we'll have to make sure they get very dirty, then. Wouldn't want to waste a load of laundry." He strips off the condom, tying it off before he maneuvers me until I'm on my back. Huge. He's huge above me. One hand smooths along my side, over my hip, down my thigh. He hitches my leg around his waist. "Again," he growls.

His kiss brooks no argument. I'm in bed, so is he, and we'll fuck until we can't move any longer and the sheets are thoroughly used. His injuries don't hold him back. It's a slow, total devastation. I lose myself in the chaos, coming back to myself only to arch toward him, going taut as a bow.

I'm wrecked.

Sheets tangled around my legs, Declan's weight pressing me into the bed, my brain sputters into gear and reminds me I'm capable of coherent thought. The sex temporarily short-circuited it, but now that it's reset itself, the doubts creep in.

Those doubts remind me I picked the worst possible person to jump into the intimacy pool with.

"Hungry?" I think my legs might work. I push at him and sit up, sucking in a breath as the room spins. "It's past time for breakfast."

"Sure," he yawns. He sits up as well and glances at the walking boot around his lower leg. "This didn't bother you, did it?" His grin is sheepish and a little heart melting and I remind myself he may not be around long enough for me to see him lose the cast.

"Nah." My legs wobble slightly as I hurry into the shower. Sore at the hips and between my legs, I brace myself against the shower wall for a minute, searching for balance and not finding it. Shit. Mistake. A horrible, horrible mistake, and I'm making it over and over again.

Somehow I manage to get myself clean and out of the shower, resisting the urge to cover myself. He's already seen everything. Either the view unobscured by lust will put an end to things, or he was telling the truth earlier and he likes small women.

The appreciative grin is confirmation enough, though the smacking kiss he gives me solidifies it. Then he grabs the plastic bag sitting beside the bed and hobbles into the bathroom. A few curses later the shower turns on, followed by more cursing. Oops. I must have used up the hot water. I toss on Declan's sweatshirt and some sweats and hightail it out of the bedroom.

Eggs. I should ration them out, but I can't. Delicious, delicious eggs. Unsure how he likes them, I scramble five and pour them into a skillet. He clomps out as I'm divvying up the spoils, pleased that the toast turned out unburnt, despite having to use the broiler.

"Thanks for—are those eggs?"

"Yup. Came in on the latest supply truck." I hand him a plate and carry my own to the couch.

"How did you get these? From what I've heard, most people haven't seen an egg in months." Most of the meat and other protein—the good stuff, anyway—is snatched up by the government and the rebels. The rest of us get what's left over.

"Magic." I shovel a forkful of egg into my mouth, burning my tongue in the process.

He eats in silence for a few minutes, watching me the entire time. It's disconcerting. Gone is the domineering, coaxing lover. He's been replaced by the detached, aloof version of Declan. He's nicer than douchebag Declan, but still not my favorite. The way he shuts down after any physical display irks me. Is that what he does with his other women? Shut them out so they'll catch the drift and walk away without being told?

"How'd you get the eggs, Nora?" he asks quietly, setting his plate aside.

Before I can answer, a sharp *ratatattat* cracks the air. It's followed by shouts and more gunfire, and I drop my plate on the floor, my hands shaking so hard the strength's left them. Declan sets his plate on the coffee table and scoots over on the couch. I shake my head. He ignores me, yanking me across the remaining distance, and the instant I'm plastered against his chest my hands still. I hate this. I hate how utterly *weak* I am. I hate that I can't get over it.

We wait, long, drawn out minutes, to see if there's more. There isn't.

"Give me another few weeks. Most of the shots didn't turn out. Then I'll contact the extraction team. They can handle both of us." The circles he rubs over my back are anything but soothing.

I push at his chest, breaking free of his hold. "No," I croak. "No, don't bother. I'll be all right."

One brow rises. "You'll be all right? What's going to happen when I leave? You'll go back to hiding under the bed?"

I jerk up my chin. "I said I'll be fine. I *will* be fine. Stop worrying."

Hands on my shoulders, he holds me in place. "I doubt it. You've looked shell-shocked after every firefight so far."

I don't tell him he's right, that it's gotten worse as the fights have gotten closer. "Leave it, okay?"

"I'm getting you out of here," he says grimly. "Fight it as much as you want, you won't win."

I get to my feet. "There's no point, okay? I'm stuck here. Even if I could get out, I have nowhere to go." I throw out a hand and point to the bookshelf. "All those? Those, this country, Ryan's thesis—they all landed me on a terrorist watch list. I can't get into the US. I don't have a passport any more. I haven't the faintest idea how to go about clearing my name, and I don't know where I could go that I wouldn't be immediately deported to Guantanamo." Snatching up my plate, I stalk out of the living room.

It's out. One more secret is out, and I can't take it back. It's a relief, in a way, not having to dodge any longer. He'll leave, and I'll stay here, and ne'er the twain shall meet. Meet again, anyway. Unwilling to dump the eggs that stayed on the plate when I dropped it, I stick it in the fridge and start tidying up the kitchen.

"I'm still getting you out." Declan, standing in the doorway, a scowl drawing his brows down, darkening his face. "You'll break before much longer, Nora, and giving into madness in a place like this will only end in death."

"Really? Then yippee, bring it on," I say sourly.

The plate clatters on the counter. "Shut up. Just bloody well shut up. I'll find a way to get you out of here. Don't argue," he adds when I open my mouth to protest. He limps to the sink and slaps on the tap. "Give me a few days."

He can take all the time in the world. It won't work.

Doesn't he realize he can't make promises like these? Ones that he has no hope of keeping? Hope is the worst four letter word in the English language. Hope is a dangerous thing to have in this slice of hell.

He shuts off the water and turns around, dragging me to him. Hands in my hair, he sucks the breath right out of me as his mouth covers mine. My arms wind around his neck, hanging on for dear life. I want to soak this up, store it away for when he's gone. His tongue teases and flicks, drawing a moan from me, and he eases away. "A few days," he repeats. "I'll figure something out."

A few days. A few days until I learn how this man plans to save me.

CHAPTER THIRTEEN

"You know, when you asked me to come with you, I didn't agree to be your sherpa." A heavy camera bag bangs against each hip with every step.

Click.

I'd thought tagging along with Declan while he shot some photos might be interesting. A tenuous peace seems to have fallen over the city, pierced here and there by a gunshot or two, or a scrabbling, scrapping fight, but nothing major. Nothing on the scale of blowing up the hospital or an actual battle on the street outside your flat.

Color. He wants color. The combat photos he lusts after are too far out of reach, something he can't get as long as his leg is in a cast, so he's making do with what he's already shot. And grumbling about it. The man is growing ever more displeased with his injuries.

He spins around, a move surprisingly fast for someone in a fat, heavy boot, and snaps a picture of me before I realize what he's doing. "I'll make it up to you." That charming grin, the one that transforms his face and does funny things to my stomach. I know exactly what he means. The last couple of days have been spent in a sweaty, twisted heap.

He never lets me touch him for long. Turns the tables and makes me so weak and dizzy with want it doesn't occur to me until later that I'm allowed nothing but the most cursory of touches.

It's taken me a few times to recognize it for what it is: a ploy to avoid true intimacy. I shouldn't be upset about it. After all, I don't have much to give anyone. Nothing but a dead lump of tissue and a cracked and battered soul that requires repairs on the most fundamental level. I'd be better off torching the whole thing than trying to rehabilitate it.

I've started avoiding snuggling after sex. I wonder if he's noticed.

He raises the camera again. *Click. Click. Click.* "Would you stop that?" I flap a hand at him, irritated.

"No." *Click.* "New series. How women survive war. Could be a big seller." I flip him the bird. *Click.* He laughs. "Play nice."

"I'm sorry, I don't know the meaning of the word. What is this 'nice' you speak of?' I smile prettily at him, lips spreading wider as he laughs again. I love that sound. Rough, almost harsh, a strange combination of darkness and light.

Click. He lowers the offending device finally and fits the lens cap back on. "Let's go."

Wandering through the streets of my neighborhood, I'm shocked to see how little has been destroyed. Pockets throughout the city are full of buildings reduced to dust, the bricks and stones being carted off bit by bit to shore up other structures. But here the buildings still stand, more or less untouched. Lights flicker in storefronts, the displays aiming for cheerful and falling short of the mark.

We pass a small grocery, one I'd gone to on occasion in the beginning, when I still had money to spend. I cringe at the sight of Mrs. Vucik, pasting on a smile and returning her wave of hello. I haven't been able to tell her I blew up her car. Part of me is sure she won't mind, not once she knows the story, but that means working up the balls to *tell* her I blew it up in the first place. She loved that car. Her enthusiastic gestures, combined with Murat's murmured translations of how she enjoyed having the independence to get out to the country to see her son, make guilt a heavy mantle on my shoulders.

"Need anything?" Declan jerks his head toward the shop.

I do. Feeding two people means I'm running low on most things, and my stock has never been huge to begin with. I'm fine with stealing from the supply trucks. I'm not fine with stealing what's left on store shelves. I imagine if the war goes on much longer I won't have to worry about it. The last convoy of goods bound for the various stores around the city was over six months ago. Fresh food, unless it's been smuggled in somehow, isn't found in those stores any longer. People line up at the makeshift warehouses for most of their supplies these days, paying exorbitant prices. Sometimes I join them. Most of the time I've already snuck in and stolen what I needed.

"I'm good." We've got enough to get through another day, two possibly. Enough time for me to poke around in places I shouldn't be and see what I can find out.

Apparently he doesn't agree. He grabs my hand and drags me into the store, shoving a basket into my hands. He stalks through the aisles, ignoring my whispers as he tosses cans and packages into the basket. I trail after him as he walks up to the cash register, prying the basket from my hands.

"Declan! I can't afford this!" He brushes aside my hissed words and pulls out a handful of bills, exchanging them for the bags of food.

"I've been eating your food. Think of it as paying a debt." His mouth thins as I squint up at him. "I've seen your cupboards. You might be able to stretch it out, but that's not enough for two people. This'll last a few days. Maybe. And it's only going to get worse."

It wouldn't surprise me if another food shortage hit. It has in the past. Sometimes it lasts for months, others only a week or so. There's no way to predict them. Laying in supplies would be smart, except it's impossible to do, given how expensive everything is.

"It's not your job to take care of me, Declan. Besides, you don't like doing it anyway."

He stares at me. Doesn't he remember his own words,

thrown at me in the first days of our acquaintance? "Right," he says shortly. His eyes freeze over and he shuts down, aloof Declan firmly in place. "Hate to say it, but me leg's starting to ache."

We start the trek to my flat. "Did you know you slip into stereotypical Irish talk sometimes?"

He snorts. "I do?"

"Yeah. 'Me' instead of 'my' is the common one. You don't do it very often. And 'lass.' Still not convinced that's Irish."

"The Irish have had lasses for centuries. You'd rather I used the even more common *mavourneen* or *a grha*?"

"No, thanks." I've read enough romance novels to have a passing knowledge of terms of endearment in a number of different languages. He wouldn't mean either one. I adjust one of the straps of the bags across my chest. "Why'd you bring both cameras when you've only used one?" He'd had it slung around his neck the whole time we'd been out.

"Never know when it'll be needed." He gestures to a doorway. "If I put it away and take out the other one, will it make you feel better?" I stick out my tongue. "Ah, now, are you prepared to use that?"

"Well, I *would* except you won't let me," I retort without thinking.

Heat sparks in his eyes, and he drops his bags to cup my face, his mouth over mine a whisper of sensation. "Have you been holding back on your talents? For shame," he murmurs.

My response is lost to his mouth, claiming mine and reminding me who's in charge. Him. Burdened as we are by bags, I can't get as close as I'd like, which is skin on skin. At one point, adventurous me would have thrilled at this, knowing I was getting off feet away from total strangers, any of whom could walk by at any moment. But that part of me died along with Ryan.

At least, that's what I tell myself, to reason away why I can't sink into Declan's embrace, lose myself in the battle of lips and tongues we're engaged in. Because the truth is closer to impossible.

I can't trust this man enough to let go like that.

"Clever mouth. Clever tongue," he whispers, the sound hoarse with desire. "Should go home and find a use for them."

Somehow I think it'll end as it always does, me writhing helpless beneath him, as pliable as a cooked noodle, begging for more. Anything to lose myself in that morass of feelings.

I wish I could tie him up. Take my time and learn him the way he's learning me.

Wait. Why do I care if I'm a selfish lover or not? I get off, multiple times, every time. As long as he continues to do so, why would I want to change that? This distance he's keeping between us is there for a reason, I suspect, and I don't want to speculate on it.

One last kiss and we step out onto the sidewalk again, Declan's other camera looped around his neck, bags of food in hand. "You going over to Murat and Ismael's this evening?" I ask. Television broadcasting is more reliable of late, and he'd been over there several times for football matches. Me, I haven't set foot in their flat since I'd roused them the day Declan was attacked.

"Likely. They said something about whiskey. Though I'd kill for a Guinness." We round a corner and wait for a flock of teenage girls to stumble out of our way, chattering and taking up the entire sidewalk. They're all skinny legs and ponytails, and when they see Declan they giggle and elbow each other in the ribs, heads bent toward one another to murmur about how hot he is. Normal. I'd almost forgotten there were families around, mothers and fathers and sons and daughters, ranging in age from toddling to doddering. "And yes, I promise not to stagger home drunk and take advantage of you." He snickers. "I'll make sure I'm sober for that."

"Har." The street looks familiar. They all are, really, though this one sticks out. Especially the twisted hunk of burned out metal.

Mrs. Vucik's car.

The vise on my lungs comes out of nowhere. Multi-colored spots and tendrils flash and zip through my vision, obscuring the street. Declan, curled up, groaning. The shouts and sickening thunks and cracks as fists and steel-toed boots meet flesh. Smoke and debris and blood. Dirt. Damp. Gasping about hell. We're in one of its circles, unable to die and unable to escape.

Someone's calling my name. Declan. Or Ryan. I'm not sure which, they've amalgamated into the same person. Broken and left to die. One gave up. The other didn't. I manage a lungful of air and it makes me dizzy.

I can't see anything.

Large, warm hands, cradling my head, turning it this way and that. A fist pounding into my back, rubbing in between my breasts. Meaningless, soothing words. Grey encroaching and retreating. Something pinches my cheeks. The sidewalk stares up at me, my head between my knees, and the blood rushes to my head where it belongs.

"Christ." Heedless of the camera bags hanging off me, food bags scattered on the ground Declan crushes me to him. "Scared me," he mutters.

Scared *him*?

"Don't make a habit of it." He eases back, peering into my face. "You started gasping and wheezing. Looked like you were having trouble seeing."

I nod, swallowing to wet my throat. "Panic attack. Or something. Recognize this place?"

He glances around and frowns. "Should I?"

"You were jumped right over there." I point to the middle of the street, roughly where he'd been lying. "I blew up the car with a Molotov cocktail."

"Huh." He studies the car, then removes the lens cap from his camera and starts clicking. "Where's the alley? You made me crawl to an alley." He limps out into the street. "Never mind. I think I've found it."

How can he switch off like that? Just ... act like nothing happened? Like this isn't the site where everything changed and I was jolted awake after sleeping my way through the last two years of my life? The blood's been washed away by the rain, but the stain is forever imbedded in my memory, merging with another that had a different outcome.

A crack. A rip. A fault line tripped.

"Declan." Shaky. I'm shaky. My voice is shaky. "I'll see you at home." *Come with me. Make sure I'm okay. Keep me safe.* He grunts and continues shooting.

The next few blocks pass in a fog. It would have happened eventually. The neighborhood is bigger than most, so it would have been possible to avoid the block all together, but not practical. And Declan's reaction wasn't completely out of character. The initial spurt of concern, quickly overtaken by disinterest.

It stings.

Fine. It fucking hurts.

Good thing he's going out tonight. Good thing I am as well. The delayed opening of Mila's club is happening tonight. A night of dancing and drinking with women who could very well be friends. A night free of the sinuous bonds of desire chaining us together.

"Nora."

I stumble, Cristian catching me before I can faceplant onto the sidewalk. "Cristian. What are you doing here?" I've never seen him this close to my flat before. Another block, and he would have found out where I've been hiding.

"I have been looking for you. I did not have a chance, the last time we met, to ask you for your answer. We can't wait any longer."

Oh. That. I sigh. Putting it off won't do me any favors, and it's past time for me to stop leading him on. "I'm sorry, Cristian. I can't do it. I don't speak the language, for one. And I don't know where you got the idea that I'm good at sneaking around."

He smiles. "You are better than you think if I am not able to find you at whim. The language barrier we can get around. You will learn. You must know some of it. You have been here years already."

Actually, I'm terrible with languages. The rudimentary

French I took in high school has long fled the scene, the basic verb tenses and conjugations finding no purchase. "My answer is no, and it's not going to change."

His eyes widen in disbelief. "You do not want to go home? You want to stay here? Die here?"

"Cristian, your offer sucks. Once the war is over, I'd be able to get out." If I had somewhere to go. "It would only make a difference if you could get me out *now*. You can't. You'd need information all the way up until the bitter end." I shift Declan's camera bags against my hips. "Your side wins, you'll have the clout and pull to offer favors. Now? You've got nothing." Oh, this is going to anger him. I can tell. I stifle a flinch and the instinct to apologize, to promise to think about it a while longer.

Sure enough, his jaw tightens. "I have done you favors already. Medical supplies. Food. You will see none of these. You have friends here? Loved ones? They will be forced to choose a side." Many people were choosing to *not* choose, staying firmly in the middle. It irked both sides equally, to the point some were being forced to pick a side or face death. Way to score new recruits.

"I have no loved ones here. You already took him from me." Tired of holding it back, tired of patching the walls of my well, the pressure builds. Cracks appear. The walls bow outward. "Your soldiers beat him while I watched. For what reason? What was he to you, that you had to break his spine? Were you scared of what he might do? Were you afraid people would take his research to heart, that it would ramp up the protests to steer Sarajevo back to communism?" I push a finger into his chest, riding the wave of fury. "Did you enjoy listening to him scream for mercy? Beg for it to end? Did you not hear *me*? No one did. Not then. I was as invisible as he was. Congratulations. You took us both." God, I want to kill him. Rip him apart with my hands. Feel his blood slick on my fingers. "Get out of my face," I growl.

A standoff, and only one of us has a gun. He breaks the contact first. "They will have to choose," he repeats and stalks off.

CHAPTER FOURTEEN

"Nora. Your roommate. You should have brought him." Zlata's dark eyes glitter in the spotlights dotting the club.

"What for? He's got a busted leg. Can't dance. Plus, he's white. White men can't dance." The cocktail is better than I'd expected. The whole place is better than I'd expected. The industrial feel suits the environment. An actual DJ would have been nice, but the sound system is several steps above decent. It's been a mix of club hits I recognize and those I haven't, plus some truly old school R&B. TLC's "Creep" was playing a moment ago.

"You are thinking of American men. Yes, they cannot dance. But the Italians, the Spanish…" Mila licks her lips and smiles.

I snort. "Declan's Irish. I doubt he's got any more rhythm than your typical American frat boy." Ryan had had two left feet. He'd been happy enough to let me go off with girlfriends for the night instead of embarrassing both of us by trying to dance.

"Who cares about the dancing or his leg? I just want my hands on him. I can do that at the table." Zlata's laugh is a husky, sensuous thing, but there's a steely determination to it. She wants him, all right, and she's going to go after him.

I guess the question is whether I should step aside or tell

her to back off.

After the run-in with Cristian, I'd gone home and opened a book, staring at the pages as though they would give me the answers to the questions flooding my brain. When the door to the flat opened and Declan greeted me, I didn't answer. The last thing I needed was to talk to him, because all it would do is add to the confusion.

He'd pulled out his laptop and started loading pictures, and after a while, I'd actually managed to focus on the story in my hands. The silence had become companionable, and I'd almost forgot our circumstances. Just a couple enjoying each other's company, doing their own thing. I'd made dinner, and he'd left to go watch a football match while I'd showered. I'd made it to Mila's without freaking out, and I was pretty damn proud of myself I hadn't fallen to pieces today.

The panic attack on the street didn't count. Besides, I didn't cry, didn't try to hide, didn't sleep away the afternoon like I would have in the past. As little as three weeks ago, I would have huddled under the covers until I managed to fall asleep.

I'm fairly certain that if I hadn't stumbled upon Declan in the street, I wouldn't be here tonight. I wouldn't have made the conscious choice to socialize. Violence has a way of provoking meaningful actions. But something's holding me back. Something's preventing me from putting Ryan in a little box labeled the past. Some*one*. Someone with a lovely accent and the ability to make me think I can start over. Someone who holds me in the middle of the night and tosses off thoughtless comments during the day.

Declan's kind of an asshole. Why I'd want to stick with him is beyond me. I'd be better off with a nice guy. Declan is not a nice guy.

"You're welcome to him, babe." I down the rest of my drink.

"You do not want him for yourself? If I am taking such a man from you, I should replace him." Zlata waggles her eyebrows. "What kind do you like?"

"I think you mean type," I say dryly. "I'm not interested."

She frowns. "How can you not be interested in men? Many varieties to choose from. I know I want to sample as many as possible."

I used to own my sexuality as much as she does. I miss that version of me. I push my glass into the center of the table. "Dancing. I'm dancing. Either of you coming?"

Mila shakes her head. "I need more alcohol first." Zlata's eyeing the bar and a few of the men ranged around the end of it and doesn't answer. With a shrug, I slide off my stool and make my way onto the dance floor.

It's not so crowded I have to worry about getting elbowed in the chest, which is sometimes a problem, being as short as I am. My joints are creaky and stiff; I could have used another drink or two myself. Normally I'd have a good buzz on before I'd venture out like this, but the track switches to an old David Guetta song, one I loved back home, and I forget about needing alcohol and Declan and betraying Ryan and the war outside. Nothing matters but the beat pulsing its way up from the floor. Lights flash, the volume rises, and the bodies around me undulate in synchronicity.

Hands appear at my hips. Caressing them. Molding them. They're unfamiliar, pulling me backward so I'm flush against a hard, lean chest. Also unfamiliar. Someone's aggressive. Glancing over my shoulder, I'm met with a sly grin and dark eyes. Pretty. Since his hands haven't wandered from my hips to my ass, I let him stay.

A few more beats, and he spins me around, catching me in a smooth, obviously practiced move. He grins again, then leans in, lips brushing my ear as he shouts into it. Shaking my head, I lean back. "American!"

Understanding crosses his face, and he bends forward again. "My English not so good. I am Danilo."

"Nora." I see no reason not to enjoy this man's attentions. It doesn't happen often. I was used to my girlfriends being picked off one by one when we'd gone dancing in college. Going home with a guy I'd met in a bar was never appealing to me anyway. Getting the chance to flirt was good enough.

We dance a while longer, and he's good. Surprisingly good. He knows where to put his feet and if his hands drift every once in a while, he moves them fast enough to territory that won't get them cut off. So when he points to the bar, I take his hand and follow him.

What Cristian never could understand was I'd never needed to learn the language. Enough people spoke English, or a bastardized version of it, for Ryan and I to get around without issue. Though standing at the bar with Danilo makes for some awkward moments. His English really is as terrible as he claimed.

Mila catches my eye and gives me a thumbs up, and I grin. She can believe whatever she wants. And Danilo is good-looking. Almost sinfully so. Sipping my drink, I try to keep the conversation going, and it sputters a few more times before it goes out. I give up and we head back to the dance floor.

There are more people, crushing us together. The alcohol is a pleasant, warm burn in my belly, but it doesn't make me brave enough to throw all caution aside and grind against Danilo the way some couples are doing. My exhibitionist streak never went quite that far.

Beats rise and fall, the bass line throbbing through my body. Sweat trickles down my neck, along my spine. I needed this. This night, this carefree night. A night away from my brain. As long as my feet keep moving I don't have to think.

A few songs later, I stretch up on my toes and yell into Danilo's ear, letting him know I need a glass of water. He grins in response, kissing my cheek for good measure, before squeezing my hand and moving away. My cheeks heat with pleasure. I'd forgotten how fun harmless flirting could be. Maybe I'll try to find him later and do some more of it.

I make my way off the dance floor, skin tightening with awareness. I swear I'm being watched. Scanning the bar, I spot Declan on a stool, his booted foot propped up on the lower rung of a neighboring one. I head toward him. "Didn't expect to see you here," I call out over the noise.

"What the fuck was that, Nora?" He jerks his head toward

the dance floor. A muscle jumps in his jaw.

Why does Zlata find him so attractive? The scowl on his lips drags his whole face down, dark brows lowered over blue eyes like shards of ice. The last of the bruises have faded, leaving behind a slight yellow tinge. His jaw is scruffy since he hasn't bothered to shave in several days.

Not attractive. Not in any traditional sense. But he makes you look twice, and then he catches you looking and you're stuck.

I sigh. "Dancing. I was dancing. And before you go all caveman on me, he kept his hands to himself."

Declan grabs my hips and jerks me forward. "I saw where his hands were," he grumbles. He strokes down and cups my ass. "They didn't belong there."

I lift a brow. "And yours do?" I close my hands around his wrists. "It's sex. Don't pretend it's anything else."

He flexes his fingers, making me yelp. "Isn't it?" Dangerous. When he softens his voice, that lilt becomes dangerous. I'll believe anything he says.

"It's not," I murmur, distracted. His mouth is *right there*. All I have to do is lean forward an inch. "Let go of my ass." His hold softens, but he doesn't relinquish it completely. "Declan—"

"I didn't like it. Watching him put his hands all over you. I know I can't dance, not with my leg in a cast. That's no reason for another man to paw at you."

That's enough for me. I dig my fingers into his arms, smugly satisfied when he hisses as I poke at his injured wrist. I yank his hands away and take a step back. "Do you think we can have a conversation without you manhandling me?"

He glowers, and I step in so we don't have to shout so much. "We have sex. Spectacular, amazing sex. It's what you wanted. Spectacular, amazing sex does not entitle you to act like a jealous boyfriend."

The sneaky bastard palms my ass again, bringing me to him. "I never said it was just sex, lass. I said I don't do relationships. I don't go in for flowers and love notes. That doesn't mean it's nothing more than getting naked. Call it spending time together, if you like."

I scowl at him. "How about I call bullshit? That's what it sounds like. We 'spend time together' because we live together."

"I call it exactly that. Do you think I don't enjoy spending time with you, Nora?" Feathery, teasing kisses burn on my skin as his mouth works its way over my jaw, drawing me closer. I dig my fingers into his thighs as his tongue flicks over my earlobe. "Are you certain it's not more than sex?" he whispers.

I'm certain he's a manipulative, selfish man. His words find their mark, though, as his mouth continues to taunt. He doesn't have to spend all that time in the flat, talking to me. He's already proven he can get around on his own, regardless of whether his leg is paining him. A moan escapes as he kisses the delicate skin below my jaw. I scramble to hold on to my frustration. "Stop it."

He lifts his head, lips an inch from my ear. "If that's what you want."

It is. My feet are stuck. They won't move. I have to move away from him, free myself before he changes my mind for me.

"Nora?"

Decadent. That's what my name sounds like, coming from his mouth. Is it such a bad thing to take from him like this, when he so clearly wants to give? It's the best kind of distraction, the most beautiful reminder that life goes on, even in the midst of destruction. Is it so bad to take comfort from that?

I turn my head toward his and kiss him, sinking into it. Sometimes I think this must be what dying feels like, the air in my lungs burning to be released, unable to escape because my mouth is otherwise occupied. Then his teeth nip into my lip or his tongue curls around mine, and I figure if I'm dying at least I'm going to enjoy it.

It happens so fast I'm not sure it's real.

Thunder rumbles, a fast, fierce roll. Someone screams. The

shrillness of it pierces the thrum of noise in the club, drawing murmurs. Another scream, accompanied by yelling. Constant yelling. I whip my head around, trying to break free of Declan's arms as I search for the source.

Everything slows. A flash, a crack, a rumble, and he picks me up, shifting his hands to lift me onto the bar. A wince of discomfort crosses his face as he boosts himself up. His mouth moves. There's smoke. He pushes me over the bar, and I land in unfamiliar arms. The bartender. He shoves me below the bar and Declan's on his knees in front of me, dragging me toward him. I shove at his chest. I can't see. I need to see. I have to know what's happening. But Declan's strength gives him an advantage and he won't let go.

Let me go.

Then it's dark and sound rushes back. Another crack, more smoke. His arms tightening, pressing my face into his chest. Screaming. So much screaming. My mind blanks. He pushes me to the floor, stretching out over me. A protective shield. Bad. Something bad must be happening.

Flashes of light. Smoke. A bomb? One side is trying to blow up the club? While I'm in it. While Zlata and Mila and my new buddy Danilo are in it.

Who knows how long we lie there behind the bar. Another explosion, more smoke, a hell of a lot more yelling, and my face getting smushed against Declan's shirt. One hand around the nape of my neck, the other arm braced at my lower back. He's going to absorb whatever comes. It isn't fair. He shouldn't have to. He shouldn't be here. None of us should. All we're doing is having fun, and they—whichever side it is— have decided we can't anymore.

The screaming hasn't stopped and it's getting smokier. The place is burning around us. The bartender tugs at Declan's sleeve and points toward the end closest to the entrance. Leave. He's telling us to get out now before it collapses around us.

We could be stumbling into an ambush.

"Follow the bartender!" Declan's shouting in my ear. He

pushes me after him, and I shake my head frantically.

"There has to be another exit! They could be waiting outside!"

"No choice!" He points to the back of the room. Flames are licking the far wall, where the back exit would likely be, eating into the walls with glee. "Come on!"

Crawling to the end of the bar, I peek to my right, to the rest of the club, and all I see is chaos. A fiery, whirling mass of it, flames and smoke and creaking furniture. Bodies. God, the *bodies*. Eyes smarting from the smoke and tears, throat stinging, I crawl along the floor to the entrance. Fire's starting to work its way forward, judging by the increased screams.

Someone steps on my fingers. A woman falls in front of me, then scrambles to her hands and knees and staggers on. Everyone's forgotten that smoke and hot air rises. Everyone's forgotten you drop to the floor in a burning building, not stand around like a herd of sheep, rolling your eyes in fear and confusion, waiting for the border collie to come along and make everything all right.

My knees are crying along with the rest of me, the unforgiving floor bruising. Palms slipping and skittering on something I'm best not questioning, it's an agonizing crawl to the entrance, navigating through fallen tables and chairs, around people milling about, pushing each other in their attempts to find the way out.

The short hallway leading into the main part of the club is clearer. An enterprising soul propped the door open. My legs aren't working. My brain isn't working. Other club goers are rushing past us, squishing us into the wall. Mila and Zlata aren't among them. I can't back up to go search for them. No room to turn around.

I pull Declan to his feet and we stagger out, into the bracing cold.

The nightmare isn't over.

CHAPTER FIFTEEN

I've stumbled from one level of hell straight into another.

The street outside the club is crowded with soldiers and club goers drifting around, their shouts and whimpers a blanket of noise. Smoke and dust choke the air. It's hard to breathe. I'm cold. I'm *freezing*. I left my coat in the club. Goosebumps pop up, and I shiver, wrapping my arms around myself to hold in the warmth. I should go back and get my coat.

Declan catches me around the waist before I can dart for the entrance.

"Let go!"

"No." I'm trapped by steel girders, his chest a wall at my back. "The building's on fire. Or didn't you notice that?"

I try to elbow him in the gut. He simply grunts and limps backward, dragging me with him. "What are you going to do, Nora? Get yourself hurt?"

Hurt. So much hurt. Pain. There are bleeding people everywhere. Shambling past. Crying on the sidewalk. Lying stretched out on the dirty, dirty street, inviting infection.

There are *bodies* inside that building.

Danilo might be inside.

Mila and Zlata might be inside.

Sirens rise in a wail, drowned momentarily by a thunderous *crack*. Dust and smoke billow outward. My throat closes off, and I double over, Declan curving over my back, our bodies wracked with throat-ripping coughs.

I blink the tears from my eyes and straighten, scanning the street for Mila and Zlata. Danilo staggers out of the gloom, and I fight Declan's hold until he releases me. Blood drips from Danilo's nose and forehead. He tries to smile as his eyes light with recognition, the expression twisting in a grimace. There's a cut at his hairline, the source of the blood on his forehead. The warm red coats my fingers as I run them over his face.

"Are you hurt anywhere else?" His grasp of English has to be good enough to answer this question. It has to.

Before he can answer, he's waved over by a black-clad soldier, and my hands fist at my sides. The street's crawling with them, their boots stomping through the clumps of people, weapons at the ready. I step back, watching Danilo's shambling progress through the street toward the soldier. Experience has taught me that where there's government soldiers, there's Cristian, and I don't have the strength or patience to deal with him.

The dark and the smoke and the dust are blinding. I squint against the gritty air, heart in my throat, nerves screaming and poised to jump at first sign of the soldier who won't leave me alone.

A hand clamps on my arm and I swing around, my fist bouncing off a solid bicep. "Jesus. Watch where you plant that fist." My eyes have finally given up the ghost, and tears stream unchecked down my cheeks, the grit stinging and burning. Declan's hand is huge and strangely gentle as he wipes the damp from my face. "Can I take you home now?"

Take me home. Take me far away from this chaos. "Where's Mila and Zlata?" My throat is raw, smoke and dirt crawling into the tiny crevices each cough tears open. Every word hurts. Every *breath* hurts. I'm rasping like an asthmatic after a sprint. But I won't leave without knowing the sisters are all right.

He tugs me farther away, the noise and the swirling, writhing mass of humanity behind us growing bigger as troops begin pulling people out of the building. At first they're lumps. Bricks? Rubble? I wish I were that lucky. It's not the wreckage of the club. It's the bodies, the limp, broken shells I knew were in there and hoped I wouldn't see.

I can't stop watching. More. More and more, soldier after soldier, carrying people out. Too many. It goes on forever. They blur together, and the only thing holding me up is the band at my hips and the wall at my back. Some part of me is aware it's not a wall and a band but Declan, though why he hasn't pulled me away from the horror show in front of me I don't know.

He does seconds later, our progress awkward because he won't let me go and his cast hampers his stride. A familiar figure stumbles through the smoke and dust. "Mila!" Declan calls.

Oh, god. Mila. Mila's alive. She cradles her left arm like a child, and there's a gash along the side of her face, blood seeping from the wound. She doesn't register Declan calling her name, just stares at us blankly.

"Mila?" I ask. Nothing. Eyes wide and unseeing, she sways on her feet, and Declan shoots out a hand to steady her, keeping his other arm around me. He can let go. I'm okay. Mila's not. Mila is definitely not. Her lack of response is disturbingly familiar. Shock.

Careful not to move too quickly, I reach up and cradle her face, turning it toward me. The cut on her face isn't deep, the blood dripping from it almost congealed. I swallow bile. "Do you know what's wrong with her arm?" Though he's right next to me, I have to shout to be heard.

Declan shakes his head. "Broken? Dislocated shoulder? I can figure that out pretty easy." He presses his fingers along the socket. Mila starts and moans, jerking away. "Dislocated shoulder. Hold her hand." I take her right hand in both of mine as he steadies her, grasps her injured arm, and shoves it back into place.

She jumps, stumbles, and doubles over, retching. When she's done, she wipes her mouth on the back of her hand and straightens. "Nora? *Nora.*" She lunges forward and catches me in a hug, hissing with pain and dropping her arms almost immediately.

"Where is Zlata?"

She blinks and peers into the gloom. "She found Ismael before the explosion. He was bored, as usual. She was scowling. As usual." She takes a tiny step toward the club, then another.

Declan stops her. "If she was with Ismael, he probably got her out. Best thing you can do is go home and wait for her."

She starts to protest and winces. "Yes. Home."

The way is slow and painful, each step a victory as we get farther from the wreckage. Mila's sunny cheer is buried under worry for her sister and doesn't put in an appearance. We leave her in her apartment after she insists we leave. She doesn't have to do much to convince me. I want the relative safety of my stolen flat.

We cover the remaining blocks, dragging ourselves up the stairs and into the apartment. We collapse on the couch on opposite ends, Declan groaning softly. There was a bomb. In the club. The walls collapsed. There was fire, and smoke, and dead people. So many bodies.

Nausea surges, and I lurch to my feet, racing for the bathroom, barely making it in time to empty my heaving stomach into the toilet. Hollowed out and weak, it'd be comforting to succumb to unconsciousness right about now, but the stink of smoke reminds me of the charred remains of the club goers. I need a shower first. Then I'll sleep.

Stripping aside my ruined clothing, I turn on the tap. Please have water. Please have *hot* water. I'm rewarded with a spurt of hot water, hot enough to peel the flesh from my bones, the pressure better than it's been in weeks.

"Nora?" Declan opens the door as I'm about to step into the shower. His gaze cuts past me to the stall. "Good idea." He ducks out and returns with his trusty plastic bag. Making quick work of his clothing, he gives me a crooked grin as he sits on the toilet lid to adjust the bag over his cast. "Might want to get under there and start soaping."

Right. Showering. Standing stupefied isn't on the agenda.

The shower's crowded with the two of us. His cast doesn't make it any better, either. We move slowly, and he nudges me around, substituting soap for shampoo, his strong, deft fingers working it into a lather and soothing my scalp.

I'm exhausted. A few cursory swipes of the towel and I pronounce myself dry. I don't even have the energy to pull on my sleep shirt or underwear. Squirming under the covers is the most I can do.

He slides in beside me and pulls me to him, and his skin rubbing over mine ignites me. I need to erase tonight, with its death and shock and terror. Replace it with life. With sweat and gasps and endorphins. My lips search his out, and I whimper as I tangle my fingers in his hair. Alive. Vibrating with it. So warm. Warm, firm, assured and in control. He's all these things and exactly what I need.

It's not enough. I need to be surrounded. I hook a leg over his hip and roll onto my back, pathetically grateful this man knows his way around the bedroom and takes my hint with ease.

Then he stops, stares, forearms bracketing my head. "Don't stop," I plead. "Why'd you stop?"

He dips his head and runs his tongue along the curve of my neck, nipping into my ear. "You're looking for a distraction, lass?"

Yes yes *yes* please fuck me now. I rock against him, grinding my clit into his hardening cock. He hisses out a breath and shuts his eyes, tendons in his neck standing out in stark relief. I do it again.

His eyes snap open. "You'll pay for that."

He plunders. There's no other word for what he does to my mouth, forces it open and strokes inside, drawing my tongue into a duel with his. My hips jerk as he sucks my tongue into his mouth, releasing it to nibble on my lower lip.

I pull back and flick my tongue along the shell of his ear, planting kisses along the way as I work back toward his mouth.

His talented, incredible mouth. Sometimes I think he'll make me forget my own name just from kissing me. And if there's any time to find out if he can, it's now.

God, I want him to. I want him to wipe away the nightmare of tonight with strong, firm strokes, replace those awful memories with ones of lust and need.

He works his way along my jaw, down my throat, pausing to nuzzle my breasts, pinching and tugging at my nipples as I squirm under him. The farther down he goes, the less friction I have, and I'm soaked and desperate by the time he deigns to move on over my belly. Soft, soft kisses around my belly button, hands clamped on my hips to hold me in place.

It's too hot in here. I buck my hips up. "Declan. *Please.*"

When he finally runs his tongue over my clit, I want to cry. Cry, beg for more, grab his head and hold him there until the world ends. The heat ratchets up, and everything narrows to his wicked, wicked mouth, teasing and sucking and stroking and oh *fuck* he's using his fingers and I'm blind and deaf and—

I bow up, scream dying in my throat, stretched taut and he's relentless, driving me on, the pleasure so keen it's a blade, slicing clean through and leaving me bleeding. I don't care. If it means I'm consumed by this white-hot pleasure-pain, he can drain me.

And he keeps going.

And going.

His fingers twist along with his tongue, and he hurtles me headlong into another orgasm, the sensations racing through like fire on oil, melting my bones, turning my blood to lava. I will die. If he doesn't stop, I'll die.

But he does, and because he does, my clit throbs with anticipation while he fumbles for a condom. He bats my hand aside to roll it on, plunging into me, straight through swollen tissues still shuddering with aftershocks. It bends me in two, my back arching so far off the bed something cracks.

"Wait. Wait wait wait. Don't move," I whimper. There's no air. He's used it all.

"Like this?" He rocks forward, nudging my oversensitive

clit. A high-pitched mewl escapes. "Or this?" A circular movement, tiny bolts of pleasure zipping through me. "Maybe you mean like this?"

He rears back until he's almost on his knees, palming my ass and lifting me to meet his deep, lazy thrusts. My hands fist in the sheets, every cell on alert and ready to burst.

His eyes bring me back as he fucks me at his leisure, the blue glinting in the shadowed room, hooded and inscrutable.

With a sudden fury he flips us over and slams my hips down as he thrusts up, setting off more tremors. *This*. A thousand times this. This room, this bed, this moment, this single breath of air, tension mounting and ready to break, taking us to pieces on a night that could have crushed us both.

"Touch yourself," he growls.

Of course. We're not done yet. He'll wring every last drop from me. I asked; he's delivering. In spades. Rolling my hips, my hand snakes down to where our bodies join, stroking gently.

"Harder." He sits up, trapping my hand between us, threading his fingers through my hair and yanking my head to the side to ravage my neck. The closeness presses in, presses my hand into me, harder, faster, sweat making us sticky.

I have nothing left. He's already taken it all. I can't give up. The horizon opens up, and it's there, bright and vicious, stars bursting as I shake from the impact of release, dimly aware Declan's grinding into me, his shouts ringing in my ears.

I'm a void. I'm ready to be filled. Strait-jacketed in Declan's arms, he lowers us to the bed and shifts us to our sides, my face flush with the crook of his neck, legs twined together.

He doesn't let go.

CHAPTER SIXTEEN

Click.

"Would you put that damn thing away?" Declan's pointing his camera at me. Again. He's done that a lot lately.

"Can't. New series, remember?" *Click.*

"Women in war or something, right? Don't you need more than one subject?" I turn away from the window and glare at him. His grin only makes me scowl harder.

Gunfire erupts, and from the sounds of it, it's farther away than yesterday. Small comfort. Since the bombing at the club almost a week ago, I haven't had the courage to step outside the flat. We have enough food and water to last another day or so, but running this close to the bottom has me on edge. Well, more than I was already.

"Hold that." *Click.* He lowers the camera. "Jesus. Bloody good shot there." Thumbs jumping all over the place, he mutters to himself, then starts rooting around in the camera bag at his feet. He holds up a cable on a triumphant shout and plugs the smaller end into the camera.

He's done this a few times, gotten lost in his pictures, talking to himself and fiddling with his laptop. I've learned not to interrupt him; he gets snarly. The firefight picks up again. The crack of bullets echoes along the streets. I press my nose to the glass and crane my neck as much as possible—right, then left—trying to determine where the fighting is. The closest drop point for supplies is about five blocks away. If the guns are in the opposite direction, I can run over. Getting out of the flat will do me good, though if I think too long about venturing out when guns are actively blazing, I talk myself out of it. Dying of starvation is more appealing than dying of a gunshot wound.

"Nora?" He gestures to the cushion beside him. "I want to show you something."

Probably one of the many, many pictures he's taken over the last few days. I wander over to the couch and flop down, squeaking in surprise when he wraps an arm around me and hauls me to his side. A shudder rolls through me as something rumbles in the distance, and his hold tightens. It sort of amazes me how quickly I've gotten used to having someone hold me when the battles pick up.

On the screen is a picture of me. There are slight shadows along my cheeks, and my eyes are huge. And sad and scared. It doesn't take an art genius to see the emotions on the screen.

"This is what I want," he murmurs. "You're perfect. Your face shows every facet of this war." He flips through the pictures, and I'm there—smiling, scowling, staring at some unseen thing. "Everything people associate with violence, you've got written on your face. I don't need any other subjects. Just you."

I have no words. What am I supposed to say, anyway, to a statement like that? I don't want to be wanted for what I've gone through. Those scars will never go away, and he wants to make them public. For people to fuss over and offer sympathy when they have no business doing so.

"You need my permission, don't you?" I hate that my voice is shaking. "To sell them, to display them?"

"Technically, yes." He strokes his hand up and down my arm. *Relax*, he says, maneuvering me closer to his warmth. "Vulnerability isn't a sin." He scrolls until he comes to another picture. Just how many does he have of me? If he were anyone else, I might think it's sweet. This is Declan, though, and the next time he goes to Murat and Ismael's, I'm going to go through and delete every single one of them. "Not when its opposite is determination." Fierce. Fierce and weary, faint lines between my brows, mouth thinned. I'm standing as tall as I can. I remember this shot. I'd managed to talk myself into leaving the flat two days ago. I'd gotten as far as lacing up my sneakers and exchanging my sweater for a more serviceable sweatshirt.

Then gunfire erupted on the street below and I went scurrying into the bedroom.

Declan reported it wasn't actually on the street below, that he couldn't see it all. It hadn't been enough to convince me to leave the bedroom. I'd stayed huddled in the corner, refusing to let him touch me. I had to get through this one on my own. I had to prove I could. He was making me weak. He left me in the corner and retrieved our newest book, stretching out on the bed to read. We were making solid progress with *Middlemarch*, and he read until I was calm enough to crawl onto the bed beside him and take a nap.

"If you use that picture to demonstrate determination, I'll punch you and destroy the photo *and* the file. You know what happened after you took it." I can't stop staring at it. For a brief, brief moment, I'd had courage, something I'd lacked over the last few days. Longer, possibly. A hard commodity to come by, and I could use some now.

He kisses my forehead. The tender gesture stings every time he does it. "Doesn't matter what happened afterward. It's what happened during that counts." He taps the screen. "Think about it," he says, capturing my chin in his hand. "I look at these, and I see a vibrant, determined woman scared of her own shadow at times, yet unwilling to give up. I see that, and I see something beautiful. I want to show the rest of the world that beauty."

I stare at him. Every time I convince myself he's a selfish bastard, he says or does something to make me reconsider. He closes the photo program and I'm stunned to see *another* picture of me. I'm his desktop background. "Can't get enough of you." He grins and captures my mouth in a fierce kiss. "Think the internet gods are with us today?" He's been trying to access his email for days without luck. When I'd moved in I'd jerry-rigged a modem to the existing landline, giving me slower than slow internet access. It's spotty at best.

He lets out a whoop as the connection goes through, and he wastes no time accessing his webmail. New mail. He clicks it open, gives it a quick scan, and sends a one word reply before I have a chance to really read it over his shoulder: *No.*

"No what?" He's saving the email to his desktop. Smart move, considering the connection could break at any moment.

"Didn't your mother teach you it's rude to read over people's shoulders?" He gives me a look and angles the computer away, the screen no longer in my line of sight.

"Yeah. Your point is?"

He snorts and continues reading. He skims it again, then calmly, deliberately, lowers the lid of the laptop and puts it aside. "I asked them to come up with a plan to get you out. They have. I don't agree with it."

Disappointment uncoils in my stomach. "Declan—"

He continues like I haven't said a word. "I knew they were good, but fuck, they're *good*. We're supposed to meet the team near the southeast roadblock in a week. It's the most difficult one to patrol for either side, so our chances are good. We'll need to secure your passport from the embassy, unless they've taken it with them."

Breaking and entering. One more thing to add to my repertoire.

"You'll have to stay with me for a while, once we get to Galway," he adds

"That's all fine and dandy, but I can't go. I can't take the risk I'll get taken into custody and sent to prison once I set foot in another country. Particularly one that's friendly with the US. My name will be on the, what do they call it—manifest? Passenger load? Nora Eddington, suspected terrorist. Ding ding ding! Alarms go off, guards rush in, and I'm shipped off to a tiny cinderblock room while I wait for an attorney who'd rather be anywhere else to cut through all the red tape."

"There's a different name on the passenger list." Something in his tone makes me go still. Growly. He doesn't like what he's about to say.

"What name?" I'm not going to like this. I know it.

He continues like he didn't hear me. "The team says the easiest and quickest way to get around this is to get married. Buys us a little time. Shit idea's what I think. There's got to be another way."

Married. Married to Declan. *"What name?"* What name will I have that I'm not going to like, besides his?

"Nora Moran. Maiden name Standford."

My mind goes blank. Everything is white and fuzzy, and I can't hear the fighting any more. He's staring at me, braced for impact, and it claws its way to the surface. *Standford.*

"How—" Grief chokes me. "How could you?" How could he be so *cruel?* He blurs and solidifies. Tears drip and hit my cheeks with a searing, stinging heat.

"I don't like it either. That's why I said no. Where the hell are we going to find a priest, anyway?

The room is too small. There's no air.

"They'll think of something else. It's what they do," he says soothingly. Like I'm a fretting child.

Whatever progress I've made in the last few weeks is washed away with a few careless words. I'm right where I started, in a hole, doing my best to bury myself.

I stare at him, forcing my brain to work. To process. He promised he'd get me out. This is how we do it. This lie we make the truth. But right now, I can't be in the same room as him.

Sucking in a breath, I scrub the wet from my cheeks and get to my feet. "Are you sure they'll be able to find another way?"

"They will. If they can't, fuck it. We'll just get a divorce or some such shit later." He sounds distracted; I bet if I look down he's got his laptop open again. I swallow a sob.

A divorce. The perfect bookend to an unwanted marriage. I move to the bedroom. Once inside, I locate my sneakers and put them on, then exchange my sweater for a sweatshirt.

I'm right, he's got his laptop open. He doesn't glance up when I walk by, heading for the door. "Declan?"

"Hmm?" Distracted. Definitely distracted.

"Why Standford?"

This gets me a look, a quizzical one. "It was your fiancé's last name, yeah? I figured it'd be easy for you to remember. Why?"

How can he be so...*oblivious* to everything? I shake my head. "We need more food."

He frowns. "We've got enough for another few days. We'll be fine."

We'll be fine. Fine. Fine. I don't know the meaning of the word anymore. I am *not* fine. "We need more food," I repeat and slip out the door before he can say anything more.

It's raining. The smattering, miserable kind, the kind that soaks in and chills you deep into your marrow, and you'll never get warm again. Raindrops ripple into one another in the puddles, and I keep my head down, keeping close to the walls. I don't hear any more gunshots. Hopefully they got tired of killing each other for the day.

The rain does a good job of clearing my head, though. It can't clear away the pain. If it could, I'd stand in every storm to roll through the city until my soul was pink and shining, rather than the dull red it is.

Two years. Two long, miserable years alone in a city where I haven't put much, or any, effort into getting to know my neighbors, into getting my ass out, into clearing my name. I allowed myself to be crippled.

Allowed. There wasn't any allowing about it. Watching Ryan die will stay with me for the rest of my life. I don't have the skills to process it, to consolidate it and shove it into a tiny box where I can take it out and examine it when I feel like it. It's a ghost I can't shake loose. I don't want to.

But I can learn to live with it. To do that, I have to leave, not stay, like I thought I could. I have to start over, create a life for myself without Ryan. Declan's wrong. This idea, this horrible, horrible idea, has a shot. It could work. The simple, low-key plans are always the ones that work.

Someone tried to rip up the cemetery fence. They ought to be ashamed, ripping off a cemetery. Cemeteries never hurt anyone. This silent garden of dreams and hopes, both realized and unfulfilled, should be the one place anyone can go to find peace.

There's mud on his headstone. I wipe it off, tracing over his name. "Hey, baby. Guess what? I'm getting married." The laugh that escapes sounds bitter and spooky, echoing around me. "I'm getting out of here," I whisper. "I don't want to leave you. Not here, all alone. Though I guess we're all alone, aren't we?"

Rain streaks down my face like tears, and I sit there until my legs fall asleep and I'm starting to shiver with cold. "I'll get you out. I'll come back, and I'll take you home, where you belong. Your family deserves a part of you."

"*Pile moje.*"

Bending over, I press my lips to the headstone, heedless of the mud and other nasty things that are likely on the granite. I rise and rub my hands together to bring the feeling back as I turn to Cristian. "What do you want?"

He steps forward, hands at his sides. "A loved one?" He gestures toward Ryan's headstone.

"Only one I have in this city."

"I am sorry. I can help you. You want to send the remains back to America, yes?" He holds out a hand to me. "I can do that for you."

This time, my laugh is harsh to go along with the bitter. "What, like you helped before? Your government is the reason he's buried here, instead of there, where he belongs. Your side refused to allow the remains beyond the barricades. You know what? We could probably lay this whole mess at your feet. Causing a situation where the rebel faction felt they had to take up arms. Refusing to listen and using violence to prove your point. It takes two sides to create a war. You don't want to help me. You want *me* to help *you*, and I've said no. I'll keep saying it until I'm dead or out of the city."

His eyes narrow. "You have to choose a side. You cannot hope to survive if you do not choose, and you should choose wisely. We will prevail."

"Good for you." I brush past him, whirling when his hand closes around my wrist. "Don't, Cristian. A smart soldier knows when to take a strategic loss," I say softly. "I'm an American. I don't belong here. Mine is not the heart or mind you need to win."

His gaze turns calculating, and finally he releases me. "Go. You are right. I have no use for you. But neither do I have any reason to ensure your safety anymore."

I have a distinct feeling I just skirted a shaky line. Cristian is a wild card, and falling on his bad side could have made my life the past few years a lot worse than it was. I don't take any chances as I leave the cemetery behind. The route I take to the food warehouse is long and circuitous, my body warming gradually with each loping stride.

I'm soaked and exhausted by the time I get back to the flat, and Declan yanks open the door, ready to pounce. "Don't. Don't touch me right now." He backs away, and I shove my bag of food at him. "I need dry clothes."

He's staring at the food like he's never seen it before when I come out. "It goes in the cupboards. I've seen you rummage through them often enough I know you know where everything goes."

Metal clinks against the countertop as he sets the bag down. Then he reaches for me again.

"I said don't touch me. Please." He frowns. "We should do it."

"Do what?"

I twist my hands together. "What they said. Get married. It'll divert suspicion for a while, right? I give the priest a different maiden name, and we enter Ireland as husband and wife. They'll be looking for a Nora Eddington. Not Nora Moran. This way leaves a paper trail and looks legit on the surface. I can ask for asylum or whatever, give me even more time." I lift my chin. "You don't need to worry that it means anything. You're getting me out, and I appreciate it. It's nothing more than that and good sex."

Say something. Say anything. Tell me you're not going to take back your promise. Tell me I'm getting out while my sanity is still somewhat intact.

He limps around me without a word, and I shut my eyes. He's not going to do it. He's not going to give me that chance.

"Nora."

I open my eyes and glance over my shoulder. "Yeah?"

His mouth opens, shuts, opens again. "I'll see if Murat knows someone." He moves out of the doorway, and seconds later the front door opens and shuts.

CHAPTER SEVENTEEN

The only thing about this day that resembles what I'd imagined my wedding would be like is the church. Old stone, old stained glass windows, dark in the flickering candlelight, words echoing through the sanctuary to lose themselves in the shadows.

No attendants. No Ryan waiting for me at the altar. No wedding dress. Instead I get a depressingly empty building straight out of a Gothic novel, an old guy in a pointy hat, and a man who, if he glowered any harder, he'd be one of the gargoyles guarding the place.

I can't understand a single word the priest is saying. Mila and Murat tried to translate the words, but the best I can do is focus on the phonetics and say my part at the appropriate time.

Declan hasn't said a thing since we arrived.

The calmness that had settled over me once I'd made my decision cracks under the strain of his silence. A piece of the duct tape holding me together rips. It peels away with an agonizing slowness, making room for the sharp lance at his growled, "I do."

To love and to cherish. 'Til death do us part.

'Til divorce do us part.

The kiss is a cursory peck on the lips. His hand is warm around mine as we walk down the aisle to the narthex. It's done. I am Mrs. Declan Moran. A name he didn't want to give me. A name that gives me hope.

The six of us crowd into my flat. Mila insists on toasting us, and Zlata agrees. Toasting involves alcohol, which makes it okay. They break out the vodka and the glasses, and the sisters both insist on saying some bullshit on our future happiness.

Right.

Several shots later, I'm loose and warm. The Cyrillic letters of our marriage certificate squiggle on the page. It's a piece of paper. A means to an end. Nothing worth making a huge fuss over. And despite his assertions to the contrary, Declan's taken such delicate care with me.

Maybe he cares. Just a little bit.

The aching void fills as I study Declan, his scowl as he talks with Ismael, his tight smile as Zlata tries to flirt with him. I have a place. A place to rest a while, to figure out my next steps. I'm not naive enough to think this ceremony will bind us for the rest of our lives. I can have him now. Now is good enough for me.

"Mmm. That is a good look." Zlata sidles up to me and pushes a tumbler of vodka into my hand.

I squint at her. "What's a good look?"

"Yours. It says there's a man over there you want in your bed. You should go for it. He is yours."

"It's not a real marriage, Zlata."

"There were vows. It is real."

"Temporary," I allow, blinking to clear my blurred vision.

She smirks. "That should not stop you from having a wedding night. He is yours," she repeats. "Claim him."

I don't want to claim him. But he may have other uses.

Sex with Declan makes me feel more alive than I have in months. My attempts to move forward, to make friends, to try and find some stable ground to build on here, haven't taken hold. I frown, struggling to think through the vodka clouding my brain. Maybe I'm going about it wrong. Maybe instead of cleansing myself in fire or water, I could use sex as a tool for renewal.

135

Am I stupid enough to think it might actually work? It could. Even if it doesn't, at least I'll enjoy trying.

"You're right." I swallow half the liquid in the glass, wincing as it burns down my throat.

"Of course I am right." She bats her lashes. "He is good, yes?"

"Good?" She pops my buzz with an elbow to my ribs.

She leans in, her eyes trained on the men on the other side of the room. "I think he would just...what is the word? Take over?"

"Dominate," I murmur. He certainly takes control, but he doesn't give me any orders. Or any choices, for that matter. What he wants in bed is what he gets because he takes it. And I let him because it's such a trivial matter, really, when his attentions always leave me babbling incoherently.

"Yes. Dominate. Such a delicious word." Her eyebrows waggle and I snort out a laugh. Her sly grin fades. "You will let him take care of you, yes?"

I don't like having to take care of someone else.

"I'll let him take me to bed. I can take care of myself." Means to an end, I remind myself.

She gives me a look. It says I'm lying through my teeth, but she lets it go and catches her sister's eye, her chin jutting imperceptibly. Mila understands the almost invisible signal apparently because she announces it's time to go and Murat and Ismael need to make sure they get home safely.

You wouldn't think four people leaving would be chaotic, but somehow it is. In the confines of my flat, the goodbyes and well-wishes tumble over each other, layer upon layer of sound. The alcohol doesn't help matters. The two bottles are mostly empty, sitting on my scarred coffee table surrounded by glasses.

After the noise of company, the silence rings in my ears like tiny bells. Declan hasn't touched me since we left the church. Time to change that.

His gaze is harsh and cold as I straddle his lap. My fingers curl into his shirt, anchoring myself. We've done this before.

Tonight is no different. The vodka gives me the courage to ask for what I want.

"Fuck me," I whisper. "Now."

If he's going to take what Ryan never got, there's no point in doing it halfway. Who cares if the vows mean nothing? Who cares if everyone knows it's a charade? I need to finish this out, strip myself bare, and drain the last bitter, blackened part away. I'll either be emptied, never to fill again, or reborn.

Fury turns his eyes blue blue hard blue, a frozen lake. Spurred by the alcohol warming my belly, flooding my veins, I crush my mouth to his, hoping for a response.

I get one.

It explodes out of him and overwhelms me. His mouth commands mine, dictating my reaction. Wet, sinful, with a hint of mean. His tongue flicks, strokes, curls around mine, his teeth nipping a fraction too hard. The pain is a welcome distraction. Firm lips burn kisses along my neck, his tongue darting out to taste the crazy-sensitive spot below my ear. His mouth curves as he does it again, biting softly. His fingers dig into my hips. I'm not going anywhere unless he wants me to. I don't *want* to. Declan's possessive displays show me those caring parts he refuses to admit are there, and I need them tonight.

He grips the hem of my sweater, tearing his mouth away long enough to drag it over my head. My bra strap snaps against my arm as he tugs at it, his mouth swallowing my hiss at the sharp sting. Fingers pluck and pinch my nipples. Teasing. Tormenting. Sending electric jolts straight to my core, erasing everything else. *Yes.* I'm purging. I'm breaking. And when his mouth closes over a nipple, his tongue swirling around the sensitive flesh, my head falls back in abandon.

He rips the button off my jeans and shoves a hand into my panties, drawing a high-pitched whine from my throat as his fingers thrust into me. Hard, brutal, pleasure barreling through swollen flesh, whipping me up and snapping me back. I grind on his hand, not caring how insanely wanton I must look.

The climax leaves me limp in his arms, half-dressed and

breathing hard. "Get up," he growls. "Bedroom. Strip."

I slide off his lap, my legs weak and trembling with the effort to hold myself up. The bedroom's too far away. I'll never get there before my legs give out. My hands don't want to work, fumbling with the bra hanging off my arms. He comes up behind me as I enter the bedroom, pushing my jeans and underwear over my hips and down my legs.

The buttons on his shirt fight me as I struggle to pop them free, stubbornly holding the fabric together. Tearing his shirt becomes my only option, and the heat of his chest singes my hands. He's real. He's solid. He's here. His belt buckle scrapes over a knuckle as I will my hands to work faster.

Oh, praise the little baby Jesus, he went commando.

We fall on the bed, mouths clinging to one another, hands reaching for each and any part we can get at. He rolls us so he's on his back, and before I realize what's happening, he scoots down, pulling my hips up at the same time.

The first lick is firm, hot, and I almost fall over and smother him. Bracing myself on my forearms, I try to steel myself for the assault.

Foolish of me to even try.

I wanted him to destroy me. He's leveling me, digging down and demanding more than I thought I had. His tongue, his fingers, his teeth—he uses everything, walking that fine line of pain and ecstasy. He scrapes and bites and torments, bringing me to the edge and never letting me fall over. Once. Twice. Three times. Up and up and up and up.

Finally he stops, leaving me throbbing and clawing at the sheets. I glance down, trying to see his face. It's grim. "On your back."

On my back. Yes, yes please. I scramble to comply. I'm no longer capable of thoughts longer than a single word. *Want fuck now hard yes.* A crinkle, a rip, and it's *time.* He looms over me, expression distorted and twisted in the darkened bedroom. He yanks up my hips and hunches over, his mouth millimeters from mine. "Who am I?"

What?

"Say it," he hisses. "Say my name. Tell me you know who's in your bed. Tell me you know who's fucking you."

He is. He's under my skin, inside my head, surrounding me. Taking me. There's no Ryan here. There's just us. Him. Only him. What Declan's done to me leaves every other sexual experience I've had in the dust. He's reset my programs. He's exactly what I needed. What I *need*. I need him to finish this out.

"You," I breathe. "Declan." I kiss him hard. "Fuck me." No please. He doesn't get a please.

For one long, agonizing second, he doesn't move. His anger slips, revealing something so inexplicably tender, I swear I'm imagining it because it's gone in a blink.

His hips slam into mine with little finesse. I arch up on a gasp, then dig my heels into the mattress, determined to match his pace. It's a torturous bid for pleasure, oblivion within reach. Without being asked, I work a hand in between our bodies and rub the taut bundle of nerves there, spearing my fingers down in a V to slide around the root of his cock with every stroke.

Sweat beads and slips. The room fills with the sounds of flesh smacking flesh, his grunts, my whimpers. His mouth is everywhere. My lips. Jaw. Ears. Neck. Marking me. Branding me. Shattering me to glue me back together. I suck his tongue into my mouth, dark satisfaction surging as he groans.

Not much longer.

I clamp down on him as the pressure builds. Fingers moving in tight frantic circles, the first wave comes in a rush. Rising. Towering. He's growing harder. Harder. I pinch my clit, the sting of pain flinging me over the edge.

It's his name I scream, just like he wants me to.

"Fuck!" He goes rigid above me. His hands will leave bruises. Right now I'm too dazed to care. He collapses, and we become a damp, sticky heap, his weight pressing me into the bed. I probably ought to protest. He feels good. Solid. Real.

He moves before it gets too hard to breathe, rolling to his side with a soft groan, sitting up to deal with the condom.

When he lowers himself back down, he drags me to his side, possessive to the last. His hands move in soft lazy circles over my back. They lessen as his breathing deepens and slows.

* * *

Morning comes, grey shifting light harsh on my gritty, burning eyes. I couldn't sleep wrapped in Declan's arms. Not after last night. Not after we wrecked each other so completely. How could I have been so stupid?

The smart thing would have been to avoid him. Sleep on the couch. Instead I chose to extend this mockery of a marriage and consummate it. Knowing Declan only did it out of a twisted sense of obligation makes it worse.

There's no caring here. Certainly no love.

He stirs against me, his hold shifting into a sleepy caress. Despite the sensations wrung from my body last night, his touch has me aching for more, yearning for it to mean something. That yearning is the final nail in the coffin as he slips inside, half-asleep and dreaming of uncomplicated women who want nothing more than a quick screw and a pat on the ass as he shows them the door.

I squeeze my eyes shut and match his lazy rhythm. It's the gentle push/pull of the ocean, to and fro, advance and retreat. This is not us, this soft, sweet lovemaking. But here, in the early morning quiet, I can pretend we're like any other newlywed couple, sated from the night before, eager to start our new lives together. His mouth finds mine with a sweetness I didn't know he was capable of, and the last piece of the old Nora shudders and dies.

He whispers my name as we fall, plunging into the unknown.

I've never been more afraid of what comes next.

CHAPTER EIGHTEEN

They came out of nowhere. One minute we were walking home from the university, the next we'd been pried apart and several large men in uniforms had surrounded Ryan, knocking him to the ground. The kick to the stomach ensured he'd stay down.

Slap. Thunk. Crunch. Hands, fists, someone had what looked like a billy club. I struggled against the hold on my wrists, twisting my arms around in their sockets trying to free myself.

The shouts and taunts sounded like gibberish, punctuated with groans and wet smacking sounds. My throat was raw from screaming. It didn't do any good. They continued to beat the life out of Ryan.

After one last shrill scream and a crunch of bone, they spat on him and left, the man holding me back releasing me to follow his comrades. I ran to Ryan's side, scared to touch him, needing to know he was okay.

"Someone will come. Someone will help us." It seemed safe to hold his hand, so I did. His grasp was weak in mine.

"Don't leave," he rasped. His eyes were glazed over, and it looked like he was having difficulty focusing.

Wind swirled around us, sneaking tricky fingers under my coat. Why hadn't anyone come? He was getting weaker. His already loose grasp was faltering. "I need to go get someone. I'll come right back. I promise."

"Too late." A shudder worked its way through his body. "Cold." His lips were turning blue, his skin paling.

"Here." I shrugged out of my coat and draped it over him. "Is that

better?"

The corners of his mouth tipped up in a smile. "I love you. So much it hurts sometimes." He drew in a ragged breath, coughing once as he exhaled.

"I love you too, you dork. And you're going to be fine." I bent forward to kiss him, panic and dread spooling out through my limbs. His eyes were so dull now. Flat. "Let me go find someone. Call an ambulance."

He shook his head, face twisting with pain. "Too late," he repeated. "Just stay."

I'm shaking.

Someone's shaking me. My throat aches. My pillow's damp. Opening my eyes, I'm met with a glinting blue stare. Declan. Swallowing soothes some of the tightness, and a few deep breaths does the rest.

I haven't had many nightmares since Ryan died. I'm grateful to whatever's suppressing them. Nightmares on top of the waking one I'm in would have put me out of commission a long, long time ago.

"You're okay?" Concern shadows his eyes.

I nudge his hands away and sit up. "I will be." Honesty. I owe him that much. We are friends, of a sort, despite being bound to each other in a way neither of us wants. "He didn't die right away," I say. Maybe it would have been easier if he had. He'd passed out, though it had taken hours for him to stop breathing. The bruises on my knees had imprinted themselves on my brain; I couldn't leave him. He'd asked me to stay, and it was the last thing I could do for him.

And never, in those agonizing minutes, did anyone come out to help. Too afraid, or too indifferent, to show simple kindness to a pair of strangers. The locals must have had some inkling of what was stirring before Ryan was attacked. It's the only explanation I can think of that keeps me from hating each and every single person I come into contact with.

"I never did find out why they'd singled him out. Was it wrong place, wrong time? Or did they know who he was? His thesis was controversial. His advisor had backed him, though, so we thought the only danger he'd be in was once he went to defend, and they'd attack him with words, not fists."

Rubbing my hands over my face, I push back the blankets. Tea. Tea will take away the last of it. I won't get any more sleep tonight.

I pad out to the kitchen and feel my way around, faint light from the street lights outside making fuzzy shapes of the living room. I put the kettle on and root through the cupboard searching for a clean mug and the last of my herbal tea. It's good stuff, my one luxury I've had consistently while I've lived here. They regulate everything from bread to meat to fresh vegetables, but I've never had any problems getting my hands on tea.

"Is there any vodka left?" Declan limps into the kitchen. I find the bottle in the freezer and hand it to him. He unscrews it, takes a swig, and makes his way to the living room.

Once the tea is brewed, I join him on the couch, curling up with my mug and a blanket. "I tried to have his body transported home. Bosnian officials wouldn't let it beyond the borders." The only kindness those officials had shown was to have the body cremated. "Are you ready to get out of here?" I ask, changing the subject. Steam floats off the surface of the liquid, sinuous tendrils wafting under my nose.

"No." He chuckles at my surprised noise. "I didn't get what I came here for. I've missed a good deal of the actual fighting because the war is more unpredictable than expected, and that's saying a lot because war is never predictable. I got the shite kicked out of me because they thought I saw something I didn't. I've got half a story. I didn't earn my fee, which means I'll have to return some of it or come back in when I've healed enough to do so. Or they could choose to send me elsewhere. Won't know until I get home."

It occurs to me I don't know exactly what he does, other than go into places he's likely to get killed and take pictures. If we're both going to be up, we might as well talk. "So you, what, have an agency or something that sends you on shoots like these?" He squints at me in the dark. "Just asking. I don't really know that much about you." Though if I think too much about it, it feels pointless, like we're going backward. He's already seen me naked, already seen me at my most vulnerable. Not to mention our impending divorce. Do I really need to know anything about him?

Vodka sloshes in the bottle as he tips it up for a drink. "It's an agency, I guess. Media outlets need photos of all kinds, so they send people out like me to get them. We're not their regular staff so they don't have to pay out insurance policies if we're killed on the job."

"Where else have you been?" I sip my tea, wincing as I burn my tongue, and settle into a more comfortable position.

He's been all over. He was in Japan after the tsunami and Lebanon during a spate of fighting with Israel. He spent time in Libya when they knocked Qadafi out of power and sold a series of photos from Baghdad for a hefty sum.

"Hurricane Katrina was one of my first assignments. Getting there was too easy." Another swig of vodka. He doesn't follow up the statement with anything else. Based on the coverage that was sanitized enough to show on the local news, he doesn't need to.

Gunfire erupts in the distance. The familiar, manic *tatatatatat* prickles my skin with each bullet launched from the barrel. Not nearby. My shoulders tense.

Declan sets the bottle on the table, picks up *Middlemarch*, and flips it open. His arm comes up. I stare at it. He shouldn't have done that. Does he think I'm going to fall apart when the firefight's obviously nowhere near here? I shake my head and take another sip of tea. He glares at me until I put my mug on the table and crawl across the couch to his side, tension draining from my body when he pulls me closer.

I hate how soothing his voice is.

* * *

"It is good you are leaving." Mila gives me an authoritative nod, then passes me a mug of tea. "This is not your fight."

"It's not yours, either." The heat seeps through the ceramic and singes my fingertips. I set the mug on the floor. "That's one of the many downsides of war. It's almost always someone else's fight."

Mila and Zlata are ridiculously well adjusted for what's going on around them. Or maybe they're desensitized to it. Violence is funny that way; it can keep you on edge or lull you into submission. It seemed it had the latter effect on the sisters.

"True," she agrees. "Enough war. Tell me about Declan. Mysterious man who does not flirt with my sister? I never thought that would happen. *Everyone* flirts with Zlata."

"Not everyone." Zlata wanders out of her room and throws herself down on the couch. "She gets tea and I do not?" She pouts. When Zlata pouts, she does it in that annoyingly cute and sexy way that you admire and despise at the same time. "But I know why he does not flirt back. You saw them in the club together? Before the bombs blew everything to hell?"

The three of us shudder, remembering the horrible night.

"She is right. I saw you. There is a story there, and you do not leave until you tell it." Mila waggles her eyebrows at me, and the sisters give me their full attention, expectant grins on their faces.

I groan. "There isn't anything to tell. We have chemistry. The marriage is for...what, diplomatic purposes only? He's doing me a favor because I can't get transport out of the country. I lost my passport somewhere." Untrue—breaking into the embassy had proven to be futile. The fighting had been particularly heavy in that area since Declan had relayed the plan of attack. With him unable to run or otherwise be of much use, that left me, and the fighting was too intense for me to be able to get near it without chickening out. Even an accusation from Declan that I was a coward and wanted to be miserable for the rest of my life didn't work. "We're friends. Sort of."

They give me skeptical looks, and Zlata opens her mouth to say something when someone knocks on the door. Grumbling, she slides off the couch and goes to open it, and Mila takes the opportunity to lean toward me.

"You are not friends with him." She shoots a quick glance at the door. "Or he is not friends with you."

I follow her gaze. Declan had gone over to Murat and Ismael's before the three of them trooped over here for a movie night, and he stands near the door, blue eyes fixed on me. It's intense, his stare, full of things I can't begin to understand and don't particularly want to. It'll make leaving him that much harder to do.

"Whatever," I mutter and pick up my tea. Then there's conversation overlapping conversation, giggles, Zlata insulting Ismael and scowling at his impassive face. I'm surrounded by noise. A low hum of humanity, these people I've known for months now and what I actually know about them you could fit on the head of a thumbtack. My stomach sours with the knowledge I don't have time to rectify my mistake. We leave tomorrow, and I can't cram months of missed conversations and laughter and advice into a few hours.

"That man." Zlata thumps down on the couch next to me, ignoring my curse as the tea slops dangerously close to the rim. "You want someone who does not flirt back? Ismael. He is not even worth the effort. Too—" She waves a hand around.

"Stubborn? Hard-headed?"

"No. I am those. He is…oh! Complicated!" Her smile lights up her face.

I snicker. "Men like to pretend they aren't complicated. You should have seen the look Ismael was giving you a moment ago."

She turns so she's facing me fully, her back to the rest of the room. "And what look is this?"

"Like he wants to bend you over a table and spank you, then fuck you senseless."

Her mouth drops open, eyes going wide with shock, and just as quickly she recovers, a sly grin tugging at her mouth. "Oh. Yes. I can use this." She plucks the mug from my hands and sips. "Mila always makes better tea than I do. Anyway. Declan looks at you like that."

I roll my eyes. "I told you. Chemistry."

She continues like I didn't even speak. "He also looks at you like he doesn't know what he's supposed to do with you."

Well, that doesn't make me feel any better.

Handing the tea back, she rises and wanders toward the kitchen, pausing to smile up at Declan and rub herself against him. A classic move. Aim for jealousy. Too bad for her, Ismael isn't paying attention. He's focusing the brunt of it on what Mila's saying and he's actually smiling. The sight is so surprising I can't help smiling myself.

"You must do that more often." Murat sits beside me on the couch. "Makes the sadness go away."

"Haven't had much to smile about," I murmur and take a sip of tea. "Are you ready for tomorrow?" Murat and Ismael are our escorts. They're coming along to help carry our crap and try and keep us from getting shot at.

"Of course." He sounds offended.

"You know you don't actually need to do this, right? We can get there okay." The southeast border is one I've only heard about, never seen, but I'm confident I can find it, even with Declan in a cast.

"We said we would escort you. We will."

I open my mouth to protest some more and think better of it. "Want to tell me why Ismael's so studiously ignoring Zlata?"

Murat chuckles. "She drives him crazy. He wants simple. She is not simple. Too wild. She is not good for him."

I think of the way she eyed those men at the bar, and I'm inclined to agree. Zlata's not ready to latch onto one man for an extended length of time. We chat for a while longer, and I tease him about the neighbor woman he's been avoiding for weeks.

"You might as well give in, hon. It's a war zone. I think it gives you license to screw whomever you want."

He has the grace to look disgusted. "Why would I want any woman who just lies on her back and spreads her legs? No. She must participate. Ludmila already looks like a dead fish. I do not need to sleep with her to confirm it."

Laughter sputters out before I can stop it. "God, Murat, tell me how you really feel."

Mila holds up a DVD. "Sit."

147

Everyone finds seats, and Murat moves over to allow Declan to sit next to me.

Our dynamic shifted on our wedding night. Not forward or backward. More like sideways. He's quicker to offer comfort when the sounds of war pick up, slower to show affection any other time. Since that night, we haven't had sex. We talk less. We're drifting further apart and coming closer together.

It's the drifting I hate. It's the drifting I'm grateful for. The security he offers is easy to mistake for feelings. I thought maybe he cared. Just a little. Now I'm not sure. But I *am* sure I'm not ready to have feelings for him.

I wish I were whole again. It would be easier to hold off, to stay away, to not want to give in to the need to curl up against him and have his arms wrap around me, fighting off my demons for me instead of letting me battle them myself.

As the opening credits roll, the windows rattle with the impact of an explosion nearby. Mila combats the rising sounds of the firefight by turning up the volume on the TV. Zlata inches closer to her sister, the two of them clutching hands. Someone shuts off the lights and Declan looks over at me. It's a look that says it's okay to lean on him, to be scared shitless that maybe we won't make it out in one piece tomorrow. I pull my knees up and wrap my arms around my legs, resting my chin on top of my knees. I'm not leaning on him tonight. Not when I might have to do it to get through tomorrow.

Maybe he doesn't know what to do with me. I don't blame him. I'm not sure what to do with me, either.

CHAPTER NINETEEN

I'm jostled awake sometime before dawn. Eyes gritty and burning from lack of sleep, I snuggle deeper into the warmth surrounding me.

"Sorry, lass." I crack open an eye. My brain wakes up. I'm on the couch. Or *a* couch. The cushions aren't quite as lumpy as mine. Declan's spooning me. If the others can see us, we're probably giving them the wrong idea, especially after my assertions it's little more than chemistry and an obligation. Who cares? I'm too damn tired and he's nice and cuddly.

Last night swims to the surface. The movie hadn't ended late, but the fighting had picked up and neither sister wanted anyone to leave. Too dangerous. After much grumbling, Ismael and Murat agreed to stay, sprawling out on the floor. Declan had simply pulled me down on the couch and curled around me, as much as was possible for a man as tall as he is, and told me to go to sleep. So I did.

Hard to believe it was only a few weeks ago that I'd badgered him into crawling into an alley with me. Hard to believe that numb and entirely broken woman was me.

Now he's trying to unwind himself. "Where you going?" I mumble, clutching at the arm wrapped around my waist.

He tugs it free and scoots around until he can get his feet on the floor. "I'll see you at your flat." My lids drift shut as he

149

rouses Ismael and Murat from their spots on the floor. There's a vague sense I ought to be more concerned with what they're doing so early in the morning, but sleep beckons and I'd much rather do that than worry about what mischief they're up to.

* * *

The nightmares are a tumbling mass of images and sounds. Indistinct. Blurry. Yet frightening all the same.

I jerk myself awake several hours later, lungs primed to scream. I swallow it instead. It's full morning now, based on the light streaming through the windows.

"Nora?" Zlata's standing wide-eyed in the entrance to the kitchen, a mug cupped in her hands. "You are okay?"

"*Are* you okay," I correct, "and yeah, I'm fine." Good thing she's not close enough to hear my heart slamming against my ribs, doing its best to break free of its cage. I point at the mug. "What's that, and is there more?"

"Greedy." Mila pokes her head out of the kitchen. "It is for you. Zlata was coming to wake you. It is almost time to go, yes?"

Unexpected tears prick my eyes, my throat tightening. "Yeah. I think so." I'm going to miss them. I'll miss what I could have had if I'd only tried. But grief does funny things to people. It took two years of my life, and regretting it now won't do any good. All I can do is get out and hope they survive, so we can meet again.

Somewhere else. Because I there is no way in hell I'll return to this city.

Zlata crosses the room and hands me the mug, a sad sort of knowing in her eyes. "You will be fine. We will be fine. Everyone will be fine." Then her familiar sly smile blooms. "Next time we meet, Declan will not resist me. He gets a...what do you call it? A free pass."

I snort and bobble the mug. "So how many free passes has Ismael gotten then?"

She scowls. "I have a new plan where he is concerned. Ignore him. He will come around."

"Good luck with that." I've ignored Ismael on more than

150

one occasion. It never bothers him. In fact, I swear he prefers it. I gulp down a mouthful of tea. "Ow. Fuck." Setting the mug on the floor, I push to my feet. "Thanks for the tea, Mila, but if it's as late as you say it is, I need to get going. I have a few things left to pack." The small portion of Ryan's ashes. The photo I rescued from our old flat. A couple of books.

She pulls me into a hug, the embrace tight and strong and fierce. "We will see you soon. Email when you reach Ireland. Tell us about Declan's home. And Declan." She gives me a wicked grin.

Zlata looks worried. "This is not smart. Letting you leave alone. We should go with you, yes?"

"No, it's fine. The fighting's died down, hear?" There's nothing but the normal noises coming from the street. No shouts, no guns. "It's not far." Neither sister looks convinced. They let me go after a few more goodbyes, and I check the street before I exit the building.

I've gone three blocks when I run into Cristian.

"Nora." His charm is gone. It's been replaced by a coolness. Some rifle-looking thing is strapped to his back, and he's wearing black combat boots laced over heavy black cargos. "You should not be on the streets. Especially if you do not wish to pick a side."

"I don't." In a fit of inspiration, I grab his hand. "I can't choose. I just need to get inside. Will you take me home?" A soldier with a gun will keep the errant bullets away, right?

His gaze travels down, then up, then over my shoulder. "Come. But keep up." He takes off at a brisk jog, boots beating a heavy tattoo on the pavement. I scramble to catch up.

We jog at a fast clip past the shops and flats that have been my home for the last two years, the grey and brown stones unwelcoming, yet comforting. There's been little destruction so far in this part. You'd think it was almost normal.

Almost. The soldier running next to me is not part of the normal.

I point out my flat on the opposite side of the street and he gives a stiff nod, checking the street as we cross. Panting a little, I pull open the door to the building. "Thank you."

His expression is solemn, the cold soldier's mask gone. "I would keep you safe. You are too…" He lifts a hand, trailing his fingers along my jaw. "…fragile. Too breakable to be in this war. You are deceptive, and that is why I knew people would tell you anything you wanted to know. You would be a good spy, Nora."

He's right about the fragile and breakable part. One flick and I'll fracture; another flick will widen the cracks and send me shattered to the ground.

He kisses my forehead. That's Declan's spot. So what if he hasn't marked it in a while. I suppress a shudder as I ease away, backing into the building and pulling the door shut.

"Declan?" The living room is empty when I come in. He'd better be here. I don't think his team will take me and not him, regardless of our marital status.

Crap. Where did I put our marriage certificate?

"Declan?" I poke my head into the bedroom. A dirty metal box sits in the middle of the bed, equally grubby clothing piled around it. What the hell is it, and why is it on my bed? Grumbling, I scoop up the filthy clothes and dump them on the floor, then reach for the box.

"Careful with that." He chuckles as I spin around. Black hair damp, water dripping onto his shoulders, he hobbles the short distance to the bed, one hand on the towel at his waist. "Didn't think you'd want to leave without it."

Want to leave without—

I suck in a breath. "What did you do?" My gaze drifts back to the metal box. It's similar to the one holding Ryan's ashes, only larger.

Larger.

"Don't tell me you're going to start screaming about desecrating a grave," he mutters. He hands me the towel he's wearing. "Here. Wrap it in that and pack it. We don't have much time."

Ryan's ashes. He dug up Ryan's ashes. I don't know

whether to yell or cry.

So I kiss him.

He stiffens, probably from surprise, before he takes over the kiss, tongue darting out and demanding entry. Sinful, filthy, and all kinds of wrong, not the soft thank you I was going for. I no longer care. I want to climb all over him. Lick the drops of water from his shoulders, his chest, work my way down…

Shit. He's naked.

He groans into my mouth and angles my head, deepening the kiss. A nip, a slide of his tongue, and I forget we're supposed to be getting ready to leave and press closer. His hands slip under my sweater and inch it up up up.

The pounding on the door halts his progress.

Panting and half-dazed with desire, it takes a few moments for my brain to restart. Once it does, though, it doesn't take nearly as long for me to jerk away and smooth my sweater into place. I hurry from the room, closing the door behind me and yank open the door to the flat just as Murat's about to beat on it again.

"Ready?"

"Almost." I head to the kitchen and pull the photo from the drawer, stuff it in the bag sitting on the couch, and slip into the bedroom to change my clothes. I don't have time for a shower, which sucks.

Declan's wrapped the box and left it on the bed, and he's stuffing clothes into his duffle. "They're here?"

"Murat is. Don't know where Ismael is." Stripping off my clothes, I dash into the bathroom and throw some water on my face, scrubbing down with a washcloth as best I can. Dammit, I wish Zlata had woken me earlier.

I turn to go back to the bed and run into Declan. "Nora." He tips my chin up. "We're not done."

That kiss. Too much heat to let it just…go. Images of the two of us twined around each other dance through my mind. No, we're not done.

Having any sort of conversation about the state of our sexual relationship while I'm naked, he's clothed, and we're about to run through a city under siege shouldn't be anywhere near my thoughts. The human brain prioritizes as it wants, though, and it's decided that this conversation needs to happen. It'll just have to wait.

I push at his shoulders. "I need to get dressed." He lets me by, but only barely, my body rubbing against his, his hands roaming over my naked flesh in an insanely proprietary manner. I pretend my skin doesn't tingle all over and pull on my clothes, folding the ones I'd worn yesterday to toss in my bag. Gathering up the clothes and the towel-wrapped box, I march out into the living room and stuff everything inside, zipping the bag shut.

Declan limps out with his duffle, and I sling one of his camera bags over my shoulder before picking up my own bag. The three of us troop down the stairs and out onto the street.

A dark blue two-door stands at the curb.

I'd been wondering how we were going to get to the pick-up spot. People still drive their cars, Mrs. Vucik's aside. It's just more and more of them are ending up like hers—a heap of smoking, twisted metal.

Ruminating over the car and where it came from involves time we don't have. Murat takes our bags and starts fitting them into the miniscule trunk, and Declan stares at the car, then at his cast. Three tall men, one short woman, and a car not built for people over midget size. Grumbling, Declan climbs into the backseat and stretches his injured leg out as much as he can. The boot knocks up against the back of the passenger seat. "Nora, can you shove that forward?"

I slide the seat forward and tip the back into place. With Declan's leg, there's room for three.

"Not enough room." Murat appears at my elbow and offers me a grin. "Ismael will drive you as close as he can get."

I'd thought I'd have a few more minutes with Murat. I'm not ready to say goodbye to the man who shared his home and his booze with me. His grin goes a little crooked, and I throw my arms around his neck and squeeze tight. "Thank you."

"You made life interesting. No thank you necessary." But

he hugs me back, and when he eases away his smile is a little sad. "We will see you again. You buy the vodka."

Choking out a laugh, I hug him one last time and climb into the passenger seat. He shuts the door and thumps the roof, which Ismael takes as his cue to start the car and drive off. The streets slip past, the sun shining on beaten-down buildings, civilians hurrying along the sidewalks. Over the dull roar of the engine I hear the familiar sounds of a firefight starting up, guns cracking, people shouting. A siren going off.

Out in the open. A moving car, a moving target. There was fighting nearby, last night, bad enough and close enough we didn't decamp for my flat. Where is it today? Is it sleeping, a dragon waiting to be woken with a fiery screech? I slump in the seat and twist my fingers together, trying to quell the rising shakes. I have no idea how close we are.

Ismael whips the car around a corner. People are running through the intersection up ahead, and he rolls down his window as he slows to a stop. Shots fired, loud and clear. Smoke wafts through the window, and he curses.

"The fighting must be up ahead. We will have to go around." Throwing the car into reverse, he executes a tight three point turn that has me scrabbling for the door handle. He speeds toward the street we'd turned off of.

This happens more and more often the farther we go, the streets Ismael turns onto blocked off halfway down or leading us farther into the fighting. Dread pools in my stomach and forms a hard, heavy lump. The fighting's getting worse. Ismael's grip on the steering wheel is tight enough to snap it off, his curses becoming louder and longer.

Another turn, another blocked street, and Ismael curses one last time before jerking the car into an alley. "Get out. This is as close as we can get. It should not be much farther."

My ass becomes cement. I can hear the screams from here, the small explosions and crack after crack of gun fire. Walk through that? Through hell? With violent projectiles flying in every direction? "No. Keep driving."

He grunts, opens his door, and hauls himself out of the car.

Terror blooms as he stalks around the hood of the car and jerks open the passenger door. He unbuckles my seatbelt and yanks me out. "Walk. You want to get out. You walk. We can avoid more fighting this way than in a vehicle that is too big for certain spots."

He has a plan? A route? A safe route? I can't stop trembling as I try to melt into the brick wall at my back, watching as Ismael helps Declan maneuver his way out of the back seat. Something blows up, a siren goes off, and the shouting gets louder.

Someone shoves a bag into my hands. Declan. He cradles my head and forces me to meet his gaze. "We'll be all right. Okay?"

It's not okay. It's never okay. Looping the camera bag he hands me over my head, I grip my bag tight enough to cut off the circulation in my fingers and fall in behind Ismael.

CHAPTER TWENTY

This is a place worse than hell.

The fighting is near enough I can make out individual words. They must be commands for the rebels or the soldiers to follow. Flank out. Man down. Go. Go. Go. It doesn't matter that I'm unable to understand what they're saying. War is a universal language, and you don't need a translator to know what's being said. Kill or be killed, you idiot.

Ismael inches out of the alley to check the street, and I edge back, thinking if I can get back to the car I can drive back to my flat. Declan wraps an arm around my waist from behind, and I stiffen.

"We'll be fine." His lips whisper over my ear. "He knows what he's doing."

Right.

He nudges me forward at a wave from Ismael. We creep across the street to the next alley, just as dark and narrow as the last. The sounds of the fight lessen as we hurry along, and I allow myself to relax slightly. Declan's right. We'll be fine.

And we are fine. We're fine as we walk as fast as Declan's cast will allow, a straight shot through alleys. We're fine as Ismael decides to take a chance and cut over a block, bringing us closer to our final destination. We're fine right up until someone blows up a car fifty feet from us and the shrapnel and flames send us to the dirty sidewalk.

Declan crawls over and covers my body with his, and I'm too limp from shock to protest his smothering weight. A second explosion rockets through the air. More shrapnel. More shouting. The air's clogged and laden with smoke and burning fuel and rubber.

My brain jumpstarts at the blood trickling from his temple. "You're bleeding."

He smears it with his fingertips and curses. "We've got to move." He rolls off me and struggles to his feet, stretching out a hand to help me to mine. "Ismael?"

Bleeding from several small wounds, his jeans dirty and torn at the knee, Ismael staggers to his feet and turns to glare at the fireball of a car. "Move. That way." He points at a tiny crack between buildings, and we hobble over to it. It's another alley, barely wide enough for a person to fit through. Shifting the bags so they're in front and behind us, we stumble through the alley to the other side.

It's clear and strangely quiet, like the battle being waged a few blocks away is happening in another city in another country. I dump my bags on the sidewalk and reach for Declan, scared by the blood still sliding down his face. He makes a face but puts up with my questing hands.

There's a rip in his sweater and another cut on the back of his neck, a few scrapes on his palms, but he's otherwise okay. He flashes that charming grin, and I scowl as I turn to Ismael.

He's not nearly as patient with me as I check him over. I'm about to pronounce myself satisfied when I see the spreading blotch low on his abdomen. Panic threatens as I yank up his sweater and see the dripping, seeping wound. "You should have said something." I rip off my sweatshirt and ball it up, applying pressure to the wound.

"Said what? It is not serious. We do not have much time left, and farther yet to go." But his face is pale and damp with sweat. He hisses when I press harder.

"We need you get you some help." Glancing around at the empty street full of empty storefronts, my stomach sinks with every passing second. It's like Ryan's beating all over again. No one will help. "Declan, can you start knocking on doors?"

Ismael shoves my hands away, taking care to clutch the sweatshirt and hold it to his stomach. "We will keep going. Zlata will not be pleased if you do not get out of here like you were promised."

Despite myself, I raise a brow at his mention of Zlata. "Oh?"

He nods, teeth clenched, and jerks his head in the direction he wants us to go. "So we go."

Not convinced he shouldn't get medical help immediately, I hesitate. Declan hands me one of his camera bags. "He's right. Likely missed vital organs. He'll be all right for a while yet. And this close to the fighting, no one's going to open the doors. He comes with us, they'll patch him up and drop him someplace he can be thoroughly examined."

Stubborn. Stubborn and foolish. But two stubborn men against me isn't a fight I can win, not when one of those stubborn men is Ismael, who can outstare a cat. Hefting my bag, I stalk off in the direction Ismael pointed.

A few minutes later we're moving at little faster than a stroll, thanks to Declan's cast and Ismael's gut wound. A battered SUV sits on the next block, a couple of men grouped around it. Declan raises a hand and catches the attention of one of them.

"Declan Moran! What the bloody fuck happened to you?" A small man in black combat gear hurries toward us, a scowl on his ruddy face. He stops short when he sees me and flushes a deep red. "Beg pardon, missus."

"Knock it the fuck off, Sean. Nora's mouth is as filthy as yours." Declan limps up beside me and lowers his duffle to the ground. "Got more important things to worry about. Man needs some help, and then we need to drop him somewhere safe."

Sean grumbles and snatches the bag from my hands, leaving Declan's sitting on the ground. "Cheerful sort, isn't he?" Declan puts his hand on my lower back and pushes me after him.

All told there are three men. They're dressed similarly in black, boots scarred from use. The other two men are brawnier than Sean, and the red-haired one, Aidan, is downright happy. He takes the rest of the bags and slings them into the car.

Rob, the third man, has Ismael stretch out on the back seat while he looks at the hole in his gut. "Not too deep." His accent is thicker than the others, and he seems to take great joy in poking Ismael in the stomach.

Declan and Sean are out of earshot, arguing from the looks of it, leaving me to listen to Ismael's grunts or try and make conversation with Aidan and Rob. I climb into the front seat of the car instead and crouch between the seats.

Ismael's eyes give him away, even as his jaw tightens. "I'll be sure to tell Zlata how stoic you were," I say dryly. He cracks a grin, one quickly wiped away at another poke from Rob. "Can't you be a little more gentle?"

Rob doesn't look up at my snarly tone. "Needs stitches." He rummages around in the kit he's placed in the footwell, coming up with a needle and thread. Threading the needle, he wipes the edges of the wound one last time with an antiseptic wipe and lowers his hand, needle pointed at flesh.

"Wait! Aren't you going to use anesthesia?" He's not just going to pull Ismael's skin back together, is he?

Rob finally looks up, annoyed. "You see any around here?" he snaps.

"S'all right." Ismael's words are slurred with pain. "Do not need it."

"Hmph." I clamber out of the front seat and jerk open the rear passenger door. Cold air drifts through the car, and goose-bumps pop out. I'm going to be freezing once the adrenaline fades. "Lift your head." He's done more for me in the last two years, however grudgingly it might have been. The least I can do is offer him some comfort. I settle his head on my lap and grip his hand, trying not to think of the blood smearing across my palm.

Ismael rolls his eyes, but his hand tightens with the first

plunge of the needle and every one thereafter. Rob pronounces him good twelve stiches later and ties off the thread. A streak of antibacterial cream and a soft cotton bandage and Ismael's ready to let go of my hand and get his head off my lap.

Rob helps him sit up, and he tugs his shirt back into place. He refuses to look at me. Typical Ismael. But he picks up my hand and rubs it between his own, soothing out the cramps from where he gripped it so hard.

Declan climbs in beside me. "About two hours' drive from here." He lowers his voice as he slips an arm around my shoulders. "We need to talk. Later." He punctuates the cryptic statement with a nip to my earlobe.

Sean shoves his way into the back seat, drawing a hiss from Ismael and a muttered curse from Declan. "Move!" he barks. The car rolls forward, and I can't help but duck my head as we speed through one intersection after another.

We pass lots where buildings were leveled, shops and homes with no glass in the windows. A smattering of people are on the streets. No one lingers. They keep their heads down while they hurry to the next safe place. A beautiful, proud city, reduced to this. Again. Those years of hard won peace, gone. I'm surprised the stones aren't crying from all the pain they've absorbed. Sarajevo is determined to tear herself apart.

Several turns later we stop in front of a neighborhood clinic, and Rob and Ismael get out of the car. Ignoring Aidan's orders I stay in the car, I scramble out after them.

"Ismael! Wait!" I don't know what it is about me he doesn't like, but I owe him. He looked out for me when he didn't have to, and he helped when I asked. Careful of his injury, I hug him, and to my surprise, he hugs me back. "Don't get yourself killed," I whisper. "Zlata would never forgive you for it."

He eases back and smiles, an actual smile, one as sweet and wicked and charming as Declan's. "I will worry about Zlata. Next time, you buy the vodka."

"Murat said the same thing," I mutter. "Go. Stay whole."

Declan lifts his arm when I slide in, exhausted and cold as the survival rush drains in a blink. It could have all been over then. Blown to bits. Bile rises, and I force it down, drawing in a breath, blowing it out. In, out. Repeat.

He holds me tighter as we drive up to a barricade. Aidan treats it like it's no big deal guns are being shoved in his face and offers his papers to the soldier, who squints at them, then into the car, then back at the paper, like squinting at it will clarify things. It's when he goes off to consult with another soldier I start getting even more nervous, and Declan rubs my arm, up and down, stroke after soft, soothing stroke.

Finally the soldier returns with the papers and waves us through, and I bury my face in Declan's neck until we're clear. The men stay tense and alert, constantly scanning the road, Sean twisting around to watch behind us.

"What are they doing?" I murmur.

"It's not all that safe out here, either," he murmurs back.

Fires in the fields, soldiers and rebels tramping along the roads, guns strapped to their backs, blockades and tumbled-down villages are sights I didn't expect to see as the countryside zips past. The war has spilled beyond the city's borders, and it's getting harder to keep my stomach in place.

The explosions in the distance don't help matters.

I'm sick and weak by the time we pull onto the small airstrip. The plane is larger than I'd expected, but after the sights on the drive over, I'm scared to get out of the car. It's only after another barked command from Sean that I reluctantly slide out, jolting when Declan's hand lands on my lower back.

From the size, I thought it would be some sort of executive jet, luxuriously appointed in leather, possibly with a bed in the back. There's no bed. There are several seating arrangements, the seats wider than your standard commercial jet. He guides me toward the rear of the plane, pulling me down as I hover uncertainly.

The rest of his team is finding their seats, and he shoves the arm up between our seats and laces our fingers together. It's odd, how well they fit, his hand swallowing mine. Like they're built to automatically adjust. His fingers are longer, wider, rougher, yet they're comfortable against mine.

"We'll be in Galway in a few hours." His thumb rubs over the back of my hand. "Sean's found an attorney to help with your terrorism case, but he's warned against filing for divorce too quickly. It would draw more attention than we need. I'm sorry, lass, but you're stuck being married until you can start proceedings in the US. Given how long it takes in Ireland, you'll have better luck once you're home."

"What do you mean, how long it takes?"

His mouth thins, and he shoots a glare at the back of Sean's head. "This is why I said it wouldn't work."

"Stop stalling."

He blows out a breath. "Divorce in Ireland is a tricky business. The couple must be separated for four consecutive years before it will be granted. According to Sean, though, if you file in the States, and remain there, Ireland will recognize it at the time it's finalized."

Stuck. I've left the ninth circle of Hell for…this. This bullshit on top of crap. If it had been anyone else, he might have had the decency to wait for the plane to take off, for the fear to drain away. This is Declan, though. There's no mistaking the frustration in his voice. If I'd had my doubts, the annoyance glinting in his eyes would have sealed it. Stupid. Stupid of me to forget this man wants no attachments of any kind. I let out a shaky breath, trying to squash the hurt, allow the anger to rise to the top.

"You really know how to make a girl feel special, don't you?" Slowly, deliberately, I free my hand from his and place it in my lap. When he reaches for it again, I link my fingers together to keep from punching him in the face and stare straight ahead.

Once the captain gives the all clear, I unlatch my seatbelt and stand up. "Nora?"

"Every time you open your mouth you just make things worse. So why don't you shut up?" Anger a slow burn in my belly, I walk to the front of the plane and take one of the empty seats near the door.

If I'd known there'd be more pain waiting for me beyond the gates of Sarajevo, I would have insisted on staying. At least there I knew what the pain was. I don't have a name for this. Betrayal, I guess. Selfishness. Tactless.

Something hollow and aching. Something that will never be filled. Not by Declan.

CHAPTER TWENTY ONE

He slides into the seat next to mine. I ignore him.

He doesn't get it. Of course he doesn't get it. He's male. Those burdened with the Y chromosome never understand when they're making asses of themselves until we point it out to them.

"Not talking isn't going to fix the problem." I have to give him credit. At least he's astute enough to realize there is a problem.

I turn away from the window. "Go back to your seat, Declan. Yes, there's a problem. It's a private problem, and we're not going to talk about it here."

"Tell me what I've done to piss you off this time."

"You haven't done anything wrong." The moment the words leave my mouth, I realize they're true. He's been nothing but honest and up-front about everything. I didn't go in blind. "I'm angry, yes. I'm just pissed at myself mostly. Nothing you need to concern yourself with."

He glares at me, and after I give him a bland look in return, one that costs me far more than he'll ever know, he heaves himself out of the chair and clomps down the aisle to his seat.

I don't think I'll be able to sleep, but I do, and the nightmares close over my head, Ryan's begging mixing with Declan's hoarse pleas for me to leave him. Hands and feet flying. Curses. Smoke and dirty, sooty air, blurring my vision, rolls of thunder as buildings crash to the ground.

The soothing words and soft caress along my cheek are completely out of place. I blink awake to find Declan kneeling in front of me, the concern in his eyes softening his face. "All right?"

No. Not all right. How can this man show so much caring and be so thoughtless and carelessly cruel? Essentially telling me I'm unwanted one moment and tending my nightmares the next? There's no point in lying, though. "Go back to your seat," I say quietly. I pull the blanket up over my shoulders, shutting my eyes again.

He leaves me alone for the rest of the flight.

As the plane begins its descent, I shift my attention to the ground below, the rolling green, the bay dotted with shipping vessels, the mountains in the distance. Sunlight glints off the water and spears my vision, and when it clears, we're close enough I can see sheep.

I'm in a land of sheep. Fluffy white sheep. Sheep on brilliant green pastures right next to the runway. A giddy smile spreads across my face, and I press my nose to the window, hoping to see more. I get smacked on the nose for my troubles as the plane bumps down.

It's not as windy as I'd expected, this close to the coast, though it's chilly. I tug my coat closed and wait for the others to deplane. Declan hobbles down the steps and jerks his head toward a waiting car. The others peel off and make their way to a nearby hangar.

The ride is strained and quiet. What little pleasure I'd derived from the sheep has dissipated, and Galway City's charm is lost on me as the car speeds through the streets.

Some of it returns when we pull up to a small grey house, well-kept but spare, on the outskirts of the city. There's no fence to mark off where his property ends and his neighbor's begins, and the grass could use cutting. The shadows of the mountains looming behind the house are lost to the darkening sky, and when I turn around to look down the street, the driver's unloaded our bags from the trunk. The faint hum of traffic from a nearby road isn't peppered with shouts and gunshots.

The inside is as bland and blank as the outside. It's obviously old, and again, clean and well-kept, but it's boring to look at. Or, at least, the living room is. The windows facing the street are covered in dark brown curtains. The furniture looks comfortable, but there's no rugs, no knickknacks, no *color*. A few photos hang on the walls, but no paintings, no posters. Just blank, white walls. If the rest of the house is like this, I'll sleep outside, thank you. At least outside has personality.

"You don't spend a lot of time here, do you?"

"I spend plenty of time here, lass. Why?"

Insulting his lack of decorating skills probably isn't a wise idea. I keep my mouth shut and set my bag on the floor.

And now I don't know what to say. We're supposed to have a conversation that I don't want to have because there are questions I don't want to ask, things I don't want him to know.

He asked. I'll have to answer. I just don't know how to start.

He solves the problem for me and cages me against the wall. "We're alone now," he growls.

"How very observant of you," I snap. "Move."

"Not until you tell me what the problem is."

I scowl at him. "Why didn't you tell me about Ireland's divorce law sooner?"

A baffled expression clouds his face. "It wasn't important. Marriage was the quickest way to get you out of Bosnia. Ireland's laws wouldn't have changed that." He narrows his eyes. "You're seriously pissed about that?"

The fight drains out of me, and I slump down. "Yes. No." He must hear the defeat in my voice because he lets me go, even helps me over to the couch. "Declan, you are one of the cruelest, most thoughtless people I've ever met." I hesitate, rubbing my hands over my face. "You know I was engaged. You've seen how Ryan's death affected me. So I think it's pretty obvious that marriage means a great deal to me. Yet you

167

treat it like it's a plague to be avoided at all costs. And that's fine. What's not fine is how you treat *me* because of it. You don't want to be married. You don't want to be tied down. You don't want some little woman worrying about you back home while you're out putting your life in danger. But we're married, and we're stuck together until we can find a way out of it."

I suck in a breath, aware Declan's yet to move a muscle since I started speaking. "You want me in your bed, but you don't want me in your life. And it hurts every time you treat me like you *care*. Like I matter. You hold me and tell me it's going to be all right when the fighting rages outside, or when I wake from yet another nightmare. I can't reconcile the two Declans." I can't look at him. What I want from him and what's best for me are two different things. He'll choose what's best for me. What's best for me will split me in two. "Who am I to you?"

Silence. I glance up. His face is hard as granite, eyes flat and cool. The silence stretches on so long there's no reason for him to answer any longer. The odd fluttering in my chest calms as it's replaced by ice. Maybe someday he'll tell me what's going on in his head. Maybe I won't be around anymore to hear it.

"Well." I rub my hands over my jeans. "I'd like to take a shower. Where's the bathroom?"

The question startles him out of his stillness. "First door on the left. Towels are in the closet at the end of the hall."

I find the towels and the bathroom. Stripping while I wait for the water to heat, I take a second to snoop through his bathroom cupboard before getting under the spray. Sweet. He's got a spare razor and shaving cream. I snag them and climb into the tub.

Hot water. Glorious hot water, pounding on my shoulders, streaming down my body. The pressure feels amazing after so long with piddly little streams of lukewarm water. His soap smells faintly of pine and reminds me of icy forests. It sluices away the dirt of war, and after using the razor I almost feel...feminine. Girly. Give me a dress and a pair of heels and point me to a club.

The yawn makes my eyes water. Sleep would be a better idea. The lack of it the night before and the gut-tightening tension of getting out of the country has fatigue rolling in. A nap provides the added bonus of avoiding further conversation with Declan.

Clean and dry, I wrap the towel around me because I was stupid and forgot to bring a clean set of clothing into the bathroom. I wander out to the living room, ignoring Declan sprawled on the couch. My bag's not there. "Did I leave my bag outside?"

"It's in the bedroom. Second door on the right." Distant. He sounds distant, like he's not in the living room but someplace I can't reach. The split breaks open a little wider, and I pad down the short hall to the bedroom, gently shutting the door behind me.

I can't do this. I need today to be *over*. I need this whole mess to be over. I want to be home, with my family, with Ryan, where I'm wanted and none of this ever happened and I am not a shell of a human trying desperately to remain upright and sane.

I want to sleep. Sleep until it doesn't hurt anymore.

That sounds like an excellent idea. Setting the bag on the floor, I drop the towel and slide between the sheets, the mattress like heaven and the worn cotton sheets warming quickly as I burrow under the covers.

But it doesn't come. Sleep, the bastard, doesn't want to join me in this cozy bed, where he'd be welcome. Sleep wants to dance around the edges of my mind and taunt me as tears gather, surrounded by the scent of whatever Declan uses on his laundry. It smells like him. Icy clean. The pillow under my cheek grows damp as I cry, stuffing one corner of the sheet into my mouth to muffle the sobs. The last thing I want is for him to come in here and placate me.

I'm safe. Finally safe for the first time in years. I won't be woken by sirens or the screams of my neighbors. I won't worry that the next time I step outside is the time a bullet rips through my head. *Safe* should equal *relieved*, and that's the last thing I feel. *Hurt* sits on my chest like a sandbag, growing heavier as the minutes drag past.

Tears can't flow forever. They stop, and, exhausted, I drop over the edge into oblivion.

* * *

I blink awake, the last wisps of the dream curling around me, Declan's sly, charming grin imprinted on my brain. Fucking hell. I couldn't get away from him even in my sleep. Getting Declan out of my mind and heart is going to be harder than I'd thought.

I stare at the ceiling until the call of nature drives me from the bed. It's full dark and the other side of the bed is empty; I can only assume Declan's in the house somewhere and unconcerned with what I've done with myself. I pull on a t-shirt and underwear and creep out into the hallway.

After my trip to the bathroom, I pad down the hall toward the living room, drawn by the dim light. He has his back to me, head bent over something on his lap. One of the floorboards creaks underfoot, and he lifts his head, glancing over his shoulder.

His laptop's open, the screen too far away for me to make out what's on it. But it's the look on his face that prevents me from moving closer. Closed off and out of reach, exactly like he was this afternoon. "I was just—" I wave a hand toward the kitchen. "Getting some water."

"Glasses are in the cupboard to the left of the sink." He turns his attention back to his screen, and cold washes through me.

It's a strange sensation. It's not born of fear or anger. As I fill my glass, a heavy feeling settles in my chest. Maybe if I go back to bed it'll go away.

Declan doesn't look up as I walk out of the kitchen, and once in the bedroom, I set the glass on the bedside table without taking a sip. The blankets wrap around me like old friends, drawing me in, telling me to take a load off and stay awhile.

Right now, there's no place else I want to be. I curl up, adjust the pillow, and slide into the black.

CHAPTER TWENTY TWO

Galway is quiet. There's no gunfire, no random explosions, no sirens or screams or rumbling trucks carrying soldiers. Whenever I wake, the noise of my dreams echoes, remaining like afterimages burned onto a screen. It doesn't bother me anymore. Strange. It scared the fuck out of me for two years.

The days blur together in a mess of shadows and warmth and soft cotton, the occasional clunk of Declan's cast on hardwood, strong arms like iron bands and familiar heat. Words flit through my ears, the difference between waking and sleeping a line so thin it doesn't exist most of the time.

Freezing air hits my bare legs, and I grope around for the blankets. When my hands continue hitting the mattress and no comforter, I crack open an eye. Declan's next to the bed, propped up on a pair of crutches.

"Where'd those come from?" I mumble.

"Doctor says it's not healing properly." He moves his hand in a "come ahead" gesture. "Time to get out of bed, lass."

It takes far more effort than it should to sit up and locate the blankets, piled at the end of the bed. "Need more sleep."

He grips the covers and wins our brief tug of war, even balanced on crutches. "You've been asleep for the better part of four days. You need to get up, drink, and eat."

I pull my knees to my chest. "I've had water."

The mattress gives as he sits on the edge, and he slides a finger under my chin to tip it up. "Nora."

Why does he care? What harm is it doing anyone if I choose to stay in bed? I know I'll have to get up eventually.

I'm just not ready to.

I'm twitching and shuddering with cold, though. If getting up means I'll be warm again and he'll leave me alone, I'll do it. I scoot out of his reach and swing my legs over the edge.

The problem is the moment I try to stand, my legs buckle and I crash to my knees, wincing as pain sings up my legs. Could I stay on the floor? It would take care of everything. I don't have to move, but I'm not in the bed any longer. I'm still cold, though, and growing colder. Getting to my feet takes some maneuvering, and once I'm upright, I start swaying, the lack of food and water finally catching up with me. Spots dance in front of my eyes, and I screw my lids shut, throwing out a hand to catch myself before I can fall again.

It lands on something warm and hard, covered in denim. Declan's leg. He closes his hand around mine, and as I open my eyes, he's frowning. "Can you walk?"

"Doubtful."

He mutters something unintelligible and reaches for his crutches. "Looks like you're getting your way. Go on. Back in bed. Do *not* lie down. I'll bring you another glass." The one I'd left on the table is empty.

The bed. The wonderful, amazing bed. I climb on and pile the pillows up against the headboard, settling back with the blankets pulled to my chin.

Declan limps in a few minutes later with a glass of water and a plate of what looks like toast. He sets the plate on the bedside table and hands me the glass. "Drink," he growls as I stare at it.

I take a sip, throat constricting, stomach twisting as the liquid hits it. I put it on the table. "I'll drink it later."

"You're likely already dehydrated. If you don't start trying, you'll end up in the hospital." He nods at the glass. "Come on."

Hospitals are full of people. Hospitals are sterile, noisy places that end up bombed. I fumble with the glass and spill the water onto my hand and the table. The simplest tasks seem impossible. I also don't care if I ever complete them. All I want is to go back to sleep.

The glass is slippery in my grip, but I manage to keep from dropping it. Another sip, longer this time, has the same effect, stomach protesting violently. I eye the toast. He's probably going to want me to eat that next.

"Nora." He wraps a hand around mine, steadying the glass. "Try for me."

I meet his eyes, struggling to focus through the numbness encasing my body. Where was this patience and caring before? An ache creeps in and winds around my heart, squeezing it. I could have used this Declan a couple times over the past weeks. Together, we guide the glass to my mouth, and I manage a few more sips before shaking my head. "It's going to come back up if I don't stop."

He pries it from my numb fingers and places it on the table on the other side of the bed. Ignoring his directive, I slip down the bed, head on the pillows, blankets matted around my shoulders. The warmth is a siren's call, beckoning me to the land of sleep and peace, where the world goes on around me and I don't have to think.

"No falling asleep on me." His quick grin doesn't reach his eyes. "You're worrying me."

"Why? I'm okay. Tired. I'll be better after more sleep."

He snorts and shifts so he's lying beside me. "I'm not a doctor or a head shrinker, but if someone sleeps away the better part of a week without waking for water or food, that's more than needing sleep." He curves a hand around the side of my face, thumb stroking my lower lip. "I'm a bastard. I figured you were getting up while I was at work. You weren't, were you?"

It's different here. My nerves are still primed, ready for the next explosion, and when it doesn't come, they start fraying. Sleeping it off is the quickest way to fix it.

"I hate it here," I whisper. "It's *quiet*. I can't think." The lucid moments are few and far between, but what I remember about them is that damn sandbag sitting on my chest. No matter which way I turn, it won't fall off.

His thumb stills, his gaze intent on mine, the gleam in his eyes something I never would have expected from him—desperation. "You scared me. Second time you've done that. Your panic attack on the street," he continues as my brows draw together in confusion. "That was the first time, and once is enough. This time? I can't leave you, and I'll have to. I'm due on assignment as soon as my cast's off."

I bat his hand away. Leaving. I knew he'd be leaving me at some point. I didn't need it thrown in my face quite so soon. "So go. I'll get up. I'll eat. Shower. Do normal stuff. You don't have to worry. Just…let me sleep a while longer."

He doesn't say anything for the longest time, his hand drifting to my shoulder, working its way under the blankets to my hand. Lacing his fingers through mine, he rests our joined hands on my hip. "I can't do that. You're getting up."

* * *

Being awake is as awful as I'd imagined.

I'm cold. The numbness hasn't dissipated, even though he built up the fire and the rest of the house is pleasantly warm. I miss the bed, how it cradled my body, the sheets and blankets a fort that kept out reality. Half the water I drank came up, along with the toast. There's another plate of it in front of me, and Declan expects me to eat it, despite my roiling stomach.

I push it away and huddle deeper into my sweater. It's one of his, the sleeves dangling far past my fingertips, the hem falling almost to my knees. The wool smells like him.

"Do you even know what you're doing?" I ask.

"I know you need fluids and calories. Your other option is the hospital." He nudges the water glass. "Drink."

He keeps me awake for hours, forcing me to swallow most of two full glasses. Surprisingly, they stay down, and the half a piece of toast I manage to eat stays with it. When I scoot my chair away from the table, he follows, grumbling as he scoops up the crutches.

The couch cushion gives easily under my butt. Two years of squirming around to avoid the spots where the springs poked up—over. Over in a matter of hours and a plane ride. I pull the sleeves over my hands and curl into the corner. "Why crutches?"

He leans them against the couch. "Had to check in with the clinic when I got back. Doctor didn't think me leg was healing properly and told me to stay off it as much as possible." He slaps the crutches with a glare. "Fuckin' things."

I shrink back. "How long until you get it off for good?"

"He'll recheck in two weeks."

There's a book sitting on the table, half-buried under mail and newspapers. "You still get the paper delivered?"

"Neighbor's kid needed a job."

I frown. "So?"

He shrugs. "He went around selling subscriptions. Have to pay to read the bloody thing online anyway, might as well get something else out of it."

The confusion clears. Such a Declan thing to do, a kind gesture almost lost in a sea of casually cruel ones. Under the weight of the invisible sandbag, my heart softens and gives, and I shut my burning eyes.

Papers rustle, and he hisses quietly as the cushions squish and jiggle. I open my eyes to see him with the book in his hands, paging through it. It's *Middlemarch*. I'd thought we'd left it in Sarajevo.

"I can't remember exactly where we were." He glances at me, a question on his face.

"I thought I'd left that behind." The book itself doesn't look familiar. The copy I had was battered, notes crowding the margins. I stole it from the university book shop a few months after Ryan was killed, during one of the respites in the fighting around the old campus.

He holds it up so I can see the cover. "You did. We weren't finished, though, and I figured you'd want to know how it ends."

I already know. Dorothea marries Ladislaw. I shut my eyes and rest my head on the back of the couch. "Featherstone had just died."

"No falling asleep on me."

I keep my eyes shut. I'm awake, for all the good it's doing me. "I won't."

The room's silent except for the sound of the fire crackling. Month after month of stillness shattered by a gun, or a shout, and now all I hear is quiet.

"It caught us by surprise, you know?" I say softly. "We heard about the problems in Ukraine, the gossip spreading through Russia. If there were any hints of instability in Bosnia, though, it didn't make it to the States. Ryan never would have allowed me to come with him if he thought there might be problems."

"But he'd go himself?"

I open my eyes to see Declan slouched into the opposite corner, his broken leg propped on the coffee table, *Middlemarch* abandoned in his lap. "He could be damn stubborn when he wanted." He'd been practically giddy when he'd found out he'd be allowed to go.

I pick at the wool pilling on the sleeves. "The first firefight was over by the old Olympic stadium. Quick and dirty, only lasted a few minutes. Two dead. It didn't occur to me until after Ryan was dead that was the real start of the war. A debate over Communism and its place in government turned violent."

It slams into me. Image after memory. Those times I'd been out sneaking around and missed the rebels gathered in the alleys. The building that had blown up a block over as I picked through the meager offerings at the food drop, causing the floor to rumble violently under my feet. Pretending not to see the foot sticking out of the rubble.

Ryan's desk sliding into the flat below. The blood on Danilo's face the night the club was bombed. My chest constricts and my vision greys, nerves on high alert as I wait for the next blast. The longer it takes, the tighter my chest gets, and no matter how hard I fight I can't draw any air in.

"Shit. Nora? Nora. Breathe." He pushes me around and shoves my head between my legs. "In and out. In and out. That's it. *Breathe.*"

Breathe. Fear skitters under my skin. I reach up and grasp his hand, pulling it down, clasping it between both of mine. I'm safe. I'm in Galway. I got out. The grey recedes, my lungs relax, and I gasp in air.

Declan frees his hand and rubs my back, long, soft strokes that calm me further. I straighten and groan as my head spins. "Okay?" he asks.

I nod, sucking in another breath. "Yeah." He resettles himself in his corner and when he lifts his arm, there's a new hesitancy to the familiar move. But it's that bridge I need between the war and now, something to ground me, and I scoot next to him, laying my head on his chest.

The heat of him seeps through the wool, warming me and thawing some of the numbness. "You sure you'll be all right alone, Nora? I won't be around much now that we're home. The equipment I have here isn't as sophisticated as what they've got at the agency. I've got some long hours in the editing suite ahead."

I nod, rubbing my cheek along the worn cotton of his shirt. "I'm okay."

We both know I'm not.

CHAPTER TWENTY THREE

He lied.

Declan's been around more than he led me to believe he would be over the last few days. He's trying to be unobtrusive about it, but he's hanging around and the worry is starting to make him peevish. This morning he practically shoved me out of bed.

For the last three days, he's made sure I've kept busy, drinking plenty of water and tea, eating, and we've finished *Middlemarch* and moved on to his choice, *Catch-22*.

I've thoroughly explored his house. It's as austere as the living room. The appliances in the kitchen are out of date. The cabinets stick when you try to open them. His bedroom contains a bed, an armoire, two small tables, and a chest of drawers. The second room is smaller and littered with photos and cables and various pieces of equipment and baggage. A gorgeous picture of the Mountains of Mourne graces one wall, and the table holding his laptop and printer is buried under old newspapers and mail. Every wall is white, most have small cracks, and the only room in the house that looks like it's been updated sometime in the last twenty years is the bathroom. He doesn't say anything about the marathon showers I take. I can't get enough of the seemingly endless hot water supply and steady pressure, pounding a drumbeat on my shoulders.

Today he wants me to go outside.

"Look, I need to go into the city. Meet with the editor, work. I can't drive meself. I don't want to have to call for a car anymore. You'll have to do it for me." He gestures needlessly at his cast.

"I don't have my driver's license. And everything's on the wrong side." Plus leaving the house isn't high on my list of things to do. Nothing is, really, other than sitting on the couch cocooned in a blanket and taking my turn reading when he hands me the book.

The numbness and the weight lift at opposite times mostly, leaving me burdened with one and not the other. Hiding the inexplicable tears is downright impossible at times, though it's kind of funny having Declan stare at me, terrified. I can almost seeing him wringing his hands.

Hence the pissed-off-ishness. Like now.

"Get up. Get dressed. You'll figure it out," he growls, and, lifting his crutches, swings out of the living room, muttering under his breath. I pull the blanket tighter around me and scrunch myself further into the corner of the couch. If I'm small enough to fade into the background, he'll leave me alone.

"Get your bloody arse off the couch and get fucking dressed!"

Uncoiling slowly, I push to my feet and wait for the wave of dizziness to recede. It does so a lot quicker than it did the day before. I shuffle out of the room, blanket trailing behind me. I exchange my baggy sweats and Declan's sweater for jeans and one of my sweaters, though I'd rather wear one of his. I like how it enfolds me. I manage to tie my shoes without falling over.

Declan swings out of the second room, his study or whatever it is, and scowls as his laptop bag swings forward. "Fucking crutches." He adjusts the strap and leads the way out of the house, digging into his pocket for his keys as I shiver next to him on the front stoop. He passes them to me and I drag my feet all the way to the car. I'm having trouble breathing again. It happens on occasion, when the sandbag on my chest becomes an anvil, shuddering every so often like a hammer's hitting it.

By the time we reach the car, my hands are shaking. I don't want to do this. I don't want to take this step forward. He takes the keys from me, unlocks the door, and hobbles around the hood of the car to the passenger side. He glares at me across the roof. "Get in."

I get in and automatically adjust the seat and the mirrors. I can't do this. Too strange. Driving his car requires more concentration than I'm able to put forth. Key in the ignition, hands on the steering wheel, and I stare blindly out the windshield.

"Nora. Turn the car on."

I turn the car on.

"Put it in reverse."

I put it in reverse.

And on and on, grinding the gears and making him wince. He's impatient, voice gruff with it, though he's careful not to raise it. Twenty minutes later, I pull into a small parking lot in front of a run-down building. "Come on."

I'm a puppy. A puppy who's been kicked and punched yet still follows along, hoping for that one stroke of affection that makes it all worthwhile. My tail's between my legs as I stumble after him, head down as he fumbles with the door.

It's an office of some sort, most of it dark and empty. Desks, chairs, other work-related detritus clutter the rooms, but for the most part, no one's in. We pass through one door, walk down a short hallway and into a small, windowless room full of computer equipment.

"Sit."

I find a chair, remove the stack of photo paper from it, and sit. He sets his crutches aside and pulls out his laptop. After booting up, he hooks it into one of the larger monitors in front of him.

"What is this place?" I ask.

"Editing suite." He shoots me a quick glance. "Everything gets cleaned up here. Photo printer's in the corner, though

181

most times they're JPEGs sent to the editor."

"Do you ever work with film?"

He grunts, hits a few keys. "On occasion. Mostly if I'm shooting for myself. There's a dark room around the corner." Thumbnail images pop up on the screen in front of us, and he scrolls quickly, pictures blurring into indistinguishable blobs. "Here."

My face fills the screen. It's one of the photos he showed me before, one of fear and determination. He substitutes it for another. This time I'm laughing. He clicks through a few more, every single one of them of me.

The last one he brings up is me staring out a window. It's black and white, my face at the forefront. It's not quite blurry, but not quite in focus, either. Like I'm only mostly there.

"Do you know what I saw when I looked at this picture?" He doesn't wait for my answer, simply turns and catches my chin between his thumb and forefinger. "All of them, really. That's a woman who lived a nightmare for two years and didn't break down. I see them and I see you now, and I can't figure out how they're the same person."

Tears sting my eyes. Stopping them is impossible. They come with great, gulping sobs, to the point where I almost hyperventilate. I hunch in my chair, face in my hands, the loud snuffles and aching grunts the only sounds. He doesn't touch me, hold me, comfort me. The only time he comes anywhere near me anymore is in bed, his body curving around mine in a move so automatic I think it's a habit for him rather than a choice. And the one time, the *one time* I want comfort, he stares at me in horror. Maybe disgust.

I get up and fumble my way out of the room, biting on my lip until it bleeds to keep the sobs inside. Sheer luck steers me toward the bathroom. I sink to the floor and let the rest of it come. Hands fisted. Hot saline on my cheeks. A brutal, brutal ache in my throat. Nose so clogged I can't breathe. The tile magnifies everything and throws it back at me.

Minutes bleed together, and the hysterical crying fit slows, then stops. My entire face feels swollen. I blow my nose and splash cold water on my face, but it doesn't help. I'm a mess. In more ways than one.

Declan wants a miracle. The woman in those pictures is gone, possibly never to be seen or heard from again. Whatever it was that kept me alive after Ryan's death is gone or buried so deep I'll never find it. Not without help.

Declan's staring at the screen when I return, and rather than take my seat I stay near the door. "I don't know who she is," I say quietly, "but I don't think I'm her anymore."

He sighs. "Come here, lass." He spins the chair around and pushes it against the desk, holding it in place. He props his foot up on a nearby crate and holds out a hand.

Here's the comfort I wanted. Late, but I'll take it. He surprises an "oomph" out of me when he tugs me down to his lap, chair sliding. I cling to his neck as he puts his good foot on the floor to stop the movement.

We sit for long, long minutes, his hands holding me to him, one on my thigh, the other at my hip, and I turn my face into his neck. His warmth and scent push away the anvil on my chest and the numbness in my brain, and I hate the moment of lucidity I get from his touch.

I'm not ready to move, not when I'm so tired. Not right now.

"I don't want you to be the reason I get better," I whisper. "I don't want to need you. Or want you. I don't want you to hang around to look after me. I don't want you to resent me. I'm getting in your way."

"Shut up," he says wearily. He shifts me closer. "Just shut up for a minute."

* * *

Things are…different, after the day in the editing suite. Not hugely different. Just that the two of us seem to realize touch and affection have previously unknown healing properties, and Declan isn't as stingy. I'm not as gun-shy. Still no sex. My libido has been less than nil.

He rolls his shoulders and winces as he sits at the kitchen table, almost a week after my epic breakdown. The weight is mostly gone from my chest, but the numb feeling is relentless. The tears still threaten, though at least now Declan doesn't ignore them or stare at me like I'm an alien.

"Problem?" I put a cup of tea in front of him, and turn back to get a spoon.

"Slept wrong."

I set my own mug on the table and step behind him, the move ingrained from years of coaxing Ryan away from his desk when he'd slumped over it for too long. Declan's low groan of appreciation as I dig my knuckles into his neck is oddly gratifying. "How'd you pull that one off?"

"Couldn't sleep last night, didn't want to wake you. No, no, don't stop, it was good," he protests.

I come around to face him anyway. "Why didn't you say something?" If I'm going to put myself back together, he has to let me go at some point. Might as well start with sleep. "You don't have to hold me every fucking night. I'm not a child."

"It's my choice." The impatience in his voice cracks out like a whip. "Now will you go back to what you were doing?"

"We need to talk about this."

"No."

"Declan—"

He holds up a hand. "When I don't, you start twitching. Whimpering. Makes it harder for me to get any sleep at all."

I blow out a breath and glare at him. Of course he'd say something like that. It's a little sick that I gain comfort from it. I step behind him and resume the massage. "Then I'll sleep on the couch."

He reaches up and captures one of my hands. "You'll stay in the damn bed." On a growl, he nips into a fingertip and releases my hand. The tiny sting crashes through my lethargy like a camera flash, there and gone. "I'm not going to kick you out of it." He hisses as my thumb punches down on a knot at the curve of his neck. "Doctor wants to see how my leg's doing. Think you can drive me in this afternoon?"

"Yes." He sips his tea in between grunts, and I smooth my hands along his neck, threading them into his hair. "I think I should talk to someone. About…all this." I need to. The numbness is troubling, the meltdown more so. And I won't use Declan as a crutch.

"I've the name of a solicitor in my study. I'll get it for you."

I shake my head before I remember he can't see me. "Not an attorney. I'm not ready for that. No, I mean like a shrink. Psychiatrist. Counselor." I sit across from him and pick up my mug. "I'm not getting better. Not really. Sitting here, drinking tea, trying to pretend I *do* feel better…it's exhausting. I'm tired. So fucking tired. And every day it's an effort to stay out of bed." His eyes widen in alarm. "Couldn't you tell?"

"No. Yes. Fuck. I don't know. I don't know what I'm doing here. I don't know what to do with you. You're fragile. I can see that. One wrong move and you'll break." He passes a hand over his face, and for the first time I see the lines of fatigue and worry, the shadows of it in his eyes.

It's gone in the next heartbeat, and he pushes back from the table. "I'm going to take a shower. Appointment's in two hours." He hesitates, then comes around the table and stops next to my chair. He draws me out of the chair and tips up my chin. "That woman in the photos. Is she still in there?"

He searches my face for an answer I don't have, and I shut my eyes so I can't see the disappointment in his. They fly open again as his lips brush over my forehead, something he hasn't done in weeks. I missed it, missed the sweetness of it, missed the Declan it represented.

My heart sputters once, twice, three times as he eases away and limps out of the room.

CHAPTER TWENTY FOUR

We talk more now. We have actual conversations lasting longer than a few sentences. We usually have them in bed, strangely enough. The story comes out fragmented, how I ended up in Sarajevo, what happened after Ryan's death. The shrink said talking about it would be good for me. I'm not convinced, but Declan's a willing audience, so I've been trying.

"My brother stayed in touch." I prop my head up on my hand. "That first year, we'd exchange emails. It was pretty sporadic, given how poor the internet connections could be. I spoke to him a few times, but that stopped after the cell towers were blown. I didn't have a landline number for him to call."

Declan covers my free hand with his own, lacing our fingers together. "They didn't cut all communications out of the city."

"No," I admit. "After I snuck out of the embassy, I called my parents. That conversation did not go well. Our relationship was always very civil. We're not close. It's not filled with animosity and drama, but I always got the impression my parents had kids because that was what was expected. And they really didn't like the idea of me going off with Ryan for a year.

"So I limited contact to Tim after that. When the cell towers went out for the first time, I stopped emailing, too.

Stopped trying to get in touch with anyone, really. I don't know anything about these terrorist watch lists. Tim could be on one, too, for collusion or some such crap. I've been out of touch with just about everyone for so long it wouldn't surprise me if they believed I'd died there. Not to mention I stole pretty much everything I needed after Ryan died." Including the flat I'd been living in when I found Declan.

"I doubt they'll hold you for larceny," Declan says dryly. "Why did you leave the first flat?"

To escape the memories. I keep my gaze trained on our hands. "I didn't right away. It hurt too much to stay there. We'd been happy. Ecstatic. All I saw were memories of what I didn't have any more. I got caught stealing by one of the government soldiers once. He got it in his head I'd make a good spy, and all I wanted was to be left alone. He made me paranoid I was being followed every time I went out because he had this creepy ability to find me when I wasn't expecting him. I broke into the flat I ended up living in on a whim. Used a credit card on the lock." I grinned. "I wasn't going to take anything or stay, but it looked like no one had been there for some time. I took a chance and made it my new home and started covering my tracks every time I went out."

His thumb drifts back and forth, back and forth, over the back of my hand. "Have you called the solicitor yet?"

"Trying to get rid of me?" The question comes out lightly, belying my sinking stomach.

His smile is quiet and small. "You don't belong here." He withdraws his hand. "You can stay as long as you need. I don't want you leaving until you're stronger. I do think this will take a while though, and talking to a solicitor wouldn't do any harm."

I flop onto my back, swallowing the lump in my throat. "They'll be able to find out I entered with my fiancé, Declan. Then I leave the country married to another man? This won't work. I need more of a paper trail to fool the US government."

"The marriage certificate will be enough."

I snort. "No, it won't. Some analyst with too much time on

their hands will put two and two together and figure out that Nora Eddington married Declan Moran in an attempt to save her ass from prosecution."

"You can't hide from it forever."

"Can't I?" He's right, unfortunately. He has a life to get back to, and I have a new one to create. "Fine. I'll call him in the morning."

Declan's quiet long after I stop talking, and I'm about to roll onto my side, away from him, when he looms over me. He kisses me—a soft, hesitant kiss, a feather touch over my mouth—and I want more. "She's coming back," he whispers. "I see her. She's still in there."

Before I can reach for him, he nudges me onto my side and wraps himself around me. Simple cuddling. We fit together like we were born for this, and his hand worms its way under my t-shirt and splays across my belly, our legs tangled together. Something's different. I run my foot up his leg. His cast. His cast is finally gone. He must have taken it off earlier today. I've gotten so used to seeing it.

It reminds me of something he said weeks ago, how once he'd healed he'd leave again. "When are you leaving?" I ask, the question loud in the otherwise quiet room.

He stops nuzzling my neck to answer. "Two days. Mexico. The borderlands."

The most dangerous part of the country. Cartels shooting at will, fighting for dominance. Bodies left in the street as a message, usually minus their heads. I don't want to think about him in one of those streets, his hands behind his head as a pistol's pointed at it, waiting for his executioner to take the shot.

He shifts me onto my back and cups my jaw with a tenderness that shocks me into stillness, his mouth soft and gentle over mine. He does it again, a sweet, soft kiss, and my hands curl around his wrists.

He comes back for more, and the kiss is deeper. Hotter. Potent. Sparks ignite and flame, the embers of desire flaring to life with nothing more than these few kisses. Our tongues thrust and parry, stroking, curling, dancing, chasing each other.

I tear my mouth away from his to trail my lips along his jaw, reveling in his hisses as I scrape my teeth over his skin. Tonight. Tonight I want to touch him. I want to touch him the way he's touched me. I want to drive him crazy. I want to watch him break apart under my hands.

"Ah, Christ." He takes my mouth again in a fury, the kiss so powerful it almost hurts. "Let me have you, Nora. Let me have you tonight." He whispers the words into my ear, and the rough desperation in them has heat surging and spreading.

I remember what it's like to be had by him. Delirium. Glorious insanity. Losing myself in his touch, yearning for *more*.

I want that *more*.

"No," I gasp, wrenching my mouth away from his. "Let me have *you*."

He tugs at my lower lip with his teeth. "Same thing."

Wriggling free of his hold, I put some distance between us and sit up. "No, it isn't. Don't," I warn, holding up my hands. "Don't come any closer unless you're ready to give me what I want." *Need.* I need this like burning. It's insane, how badly this is spiraling through me.

"You never let me touch you. Not enough. Not enough to know what turns you on, what you hate. You don't need a map for my body anymore. *You know me.* You haven't given me that same luxury. I need to touch you, Declan," I whisper. If he says no, if he backs away, I'll know this will never be a two-way street.

Wariness shadows his face. Slowly, painfully, achingly slow, he sits up. So cautious. Is he...scared? Scared of what will happen when I ask him to hold still? When was the last time a lover ran her hands over him? When was the last time he let her do it? Found every secret place on his body, lighting him up? The challenge of it races through my blood, and I mirror him, cupping his face and bringing our mouths back together. Where they belong.

His hands clamp on my hips, and I force myself to ease off. The first shudder ripples through him as I nibble at his ear.

The second one hits as I work my way down his throat. He's all but vibrating when I stroke my hands over his chest, scratch my nails along his abdomen. That wariness won't leave his face, the expression so close to panic I want to laugh. I press my lips to his, unable to stop my smile. "I'm not going to hurt you," I murmur.

I push at him, to get him to lie down. *Oh.* His chest is hot to the touch, hot and so different from Ryan's. Mine. My playground. Mine for the night. He acquiesces and I kneel at his hip, licking my lips in anticipation. Where do I start?

He chuckles softly. "You're looking at me like a starving man at a buffet." He sobers, face strained with lust. "Take off your shirt and come here, lass." He grasps the hem and pulls it up, dragging it over my head.

I trace patterns over his stomach, watching the muscles twitch under my fingers. Then I give him what we both want and sprawl on top of him. Skin to skin, and our groans are embarrassing. Rubbing against him, I stretch up and attack his mouth, lacing my fingers through his hair and anchoring his head in place.

Why haven't we ever taken our time like this? Why was he always in such a hurry to have me limp and pliant beneath him, over him, beside him? Now I have him laid out before me, and all I want is his mouth on mine. Hard and more than a little possessive.

I nip into his chin and slither down, licking and sucking wherever I feel like, gauging his reaction and going back for seconds, sometimes thirds. A flick of my tongue against a nipple gets me a hiss. A scrape of teeth in the same spot gets a hand, huge and strong, cradling the back of my head. But I'm not done yet. I'm just getting to my favorite part.

The muscle of his hip running down to his groin is partially obscured by the waistband of his boxers. If my hands tremble a little too much, he doesn't seem to notice. His hips come up as I tug at his shorts.

Oh. Yum. *Mine.* I can't breathe.

"All right there?" He lifts his head, brow cocked.

I scratch the inside of his thigh lightly, smiling when he hisses. "Now I am." I run my hands up his legs, following with my mouth.

I can't reach my destination fast enough. I'm greedy. His skin is hot under my tongue, and he jerks as I bite gently, stroking my hand over his cock at the same time. Palming him. Testing him as I move from hip to hip.

His groan is a harsh, guttural thing as I take his cock in my mouth. I love this, love this power, love how he squirms for more. Love that tantalizing combination of silk and steel, tempered with a salty tang. It's so completely, uniquely *him*. The thick, heavy weight of him on my tongue, feeling it pulse and twitch, sends a jolt of smug satisfaction through me.

He tears a squeak from my lungs as he yanks me up and flips me onto my back, tearing my panties off.

There's no preamble. He arrows in on the good stuff, taking a nipple into his mouth and laving it until it's hard almost to the point of pain. Switching his attentions to my neglected breast, his fingers don't allow all his hard work to go to waste, keeping me on edge.

He licks his way lower, lower, dipping into my belly button, his fingers blazing a trail for his tongue to follow. Thumb manipulating my clit, it gets harder to breathe as the pressure builds.

"Stop," I gasp, tugging at his shoulders. I'll be done as soon as he puts his mouth on me, and I want him with me when I fall.

He's as eager to get to the main event as I am. Lifting my hips, he plunges forward. His jaw tightens as he stills. "Jesus, lass. You feel too damn good."

How could I forgotten how this feels? Full. Satisfied, yet hungry for more. Stroking my hands over his back, I hook them over his shoulders and pull him down to me, tilting my hips and meeting his long, slow thrusts.

It's maddening. It's a relentless, agonizing chase, and I'm quickly dissolving to nothing beneath him. "Declan," I plead. The heat's unbearable. I dig my nails into his skin, and he reaches back and grabs my hands, raising them above my head and pinning them with his own. And still his hips rock in that interminable rhythm.

He broke me before, on the night of the bombing, and again on our wedding night. He's doing it again, his gaze intent, his hips rolling against mine with purpose. The spring inside coils tighter, tighter, cracking with the pressure, until my legs tighten around his waist and I bow up, fingers clenched in his, the scream of release dying in my throat. He follows me down, grunting out his own release, hips jerking erratically.

I'm scorched. I am stripped and barren.

His breathing is harsh in my ear. When he releases my hands I wrap my arms around him. "Cheater," I murmur.

"How you figure?"

I whimper as he props himself up on his elbows, pulling out of my hold. "You interrupted me."

He brushes a kiss over my mouth. "If I'd let you keep going, it would have been over way too soon." He shifts to the side and rolls off the bed. He scares another squeak from me as he scoops me up. "The edge is off. You can continue in the shower."

He keeps his word, and I bruise my knees on the hard porcelain of the tub, loving how he trembles under my hands. We cocoon ourselves in the bed. Night gives way to dawn, and we collapse in a heap, finally too tired to keep going.

It's only a few hours later that I'm woken by his tongue. When he allows me to stumble out of bed in search of a shower and food, he follows me. We try out the couch and the table in his office. He perches me on the edge of the kitchen counter and chuckles when I bang my head on the cabinets as I'm consumed by pleasure.

We are starved for each other. We have wasted so much time.

All too soon he has to pack for Mexico. I'm sitting cross-legged on the bed, ensconced in one of Declan's sweaters and nothing else. "You're not going to worry about me, are you?" He stretches across the bed and grabs the jeans next to my knee.

"Nah." Of course I will. I'll worry about him every minute until he's back home. I can't tell him, of course. It'll just launch another "Don't get attached to me" speech, and I don't particularly want to hear it. His words and his actions are at war with one another, and in the hours leading up to this, his departure, I've made another discovery, one that makes me uncomfortable. I've become very attached to him. I don't know what I want from him, but I do know I don't want him to go.

I don't want him to leave me.

He keeps tucking items into his damn duffle bag, muttering to himself like he's got a mental checklist.

"Sunscreen. Don't forget the sunscreen. What?" I protest when he gives me a bland look. "It's Mexico. They have sun. You're in the borderlands. It's desert. Ergo, more sun. You're Irish. Do you need me to keep going?"

He doesn't quite manage to hide his smile, though his next words are sober enough. "You'll be all right here?"

"Yes." No. "You're not going to be gone that long anyway." A month. A month is forever.

I could be gone by the time he gets home.

During one of our respites, Declan handed me the phone and the phone number for the attorney he'd found. The conversation took some time, and he sat by my side, his touch grounding me when panic and fear wanted to drown me. After, he dragged me back to bed and fucked me until I couldn't remember what I'd been so worried about. It was the call I received this morning that has me in turmoil.

If I'd stuck around the embassy a few minutes longer, I would have gotten out of the country. They weren't talking about me. I was never on a watch list. I didn't have to marry Declan. I could have avoided all of this, been home with my family months ago.

I never would have met him. Never would have insisted he get out of the street and save himself. Never would have grown to crave those gentle, sweet touches he gave without thought or the enthusiastic arguments over the state of modern literature.

I know I ought to tell Declan, tell him that I'm free, but that means I'll have to leave and I have nowhere to go. I have little desire to see my friends, and less to see my parents. I want to see Tim. Eventually I'd like to see Ryan's parents and his brother. I'd like to find a better resting place for Ryan's ashes than a battered metal box stuffed in a duffle bag.

The new life I'd wished for is happening, whether I'm ready for it or not.

The news brings me a little reprieve. I can't go anywhere without my passport, and there's some things to clear up with the Irish government regarding my entry into the country. I've got a little time. Time enough to drive Declan to the airport and watch him leave.

He ignores me as he goes about the rest of his packing, and I slide off the bed, pull on my jeans, and decide to wait for him in the living room.

The car ride is icy in its silence, Declan slipping away before he even gets on the plane. The words are on the tip of my tongue, begging to be set free. Tell him. Tell him he'll have his life back. Then we're pulling onto the airport drive and it's too late.

"I've been cleared," I blurt.

I'm surprised I managed to get that out around the pressure in my chest. The already tense quiet magnifies, becoming a whooshing sound in my ears. There's no sound. There's only Declan staring at me with anger flickering in his eyes, cooling to resignation, flattening to nothing. Nothing.

He nods, climbs out of the car, and retrieves his bags from the trunk. The slam reverberates through the small car, and I wait. I wait and wait and wait, wait for his retreating back to turn around. I get nothing. He disappears through the doors of the airport without a word or glance for me.

His reaction is the fracture that finally breaks me to the tiny pieces he said it would. Shattered, I sit in the car, staring at the doors, knowing he won't walk back out of them and hoping he will anyway.

CHAPTER TWENTY FIVE

"You have terrible timing, lass."

I roll my eyes and remind myself I'm relieved he called in the first place. "I just found out myself, okay? Cut me some slack, it's a lot to process." I push through the small pile of mail on the kitchen table and find my notes from my most recent call to the attorney. "There's still red tape to cut through. I'm waiting on checks and shit. Once I get them, I can pay you back."

Static crackles in my ear, and Declan's response cuts out. "The phone's breaking up. What did you say?"

"You don't owe me any money. Just forget that right now. Anything else I need to know?" More static, but at least this time I heard the question.

"Not really. I can't do anything until my new passport arrives, and there's a few things Mr. O'Rourke is handling. Once that's done, I'm cleared to enter the US. Given that we're dealing with the government, it'll probably take a while. And I do too owe you money. I didn't ask you to buy me anything." Ask me to stay. Tell me to stay. Don't let me leave. Tell me I have a place. Anywhere. Tell me where I'm supposed to belong.

"You were complaining about not having enough sweaters. I bought them. Deal with it. You'll tell me when you're leaving?" Static, followed by shouts. A car rumbles by.

"Yes." I might. I might not. I may end up on my knees, begging him to let me stay, for some indication of what I'm supposed to do now. I might run as fast as I can, especially if he doesn't give me an explanation for why he left the way he did. "How's everything over there? You drink the water yet?"

He snorts. "It would have added some excitement. Nothing much happening. Locals say things have been quiet lately, which doesn't bode well."

If 'boding well' means he'll be safe because the violence has died down, I'm going to have a hard time agreeing with him. "They think something's going to happen?"

"They aren't sure." A flash of static. "I..." White noise. "...opportunity..." Hissing.

"Declan?" The line's dead. I pull the phone away from my ear, as though staring at it will make him call back.

He doesn't.

A week goes by before I hear from him again, and the same thing happens. The static is worse than before, competing with road noise. I'm able to understand he's moved farther out into the desert before the call drops.

It's nothing but radio silence after that. He left his cell number, and I'm tempted to use it but decide against it. He hasn't apologized for how he left and as the days bleed into weeks, I realize he won't. Once I do, the last thread tying me to him snaps.

I miss him. I miss him and worry about him and wish he was here far more than I'd expected. It pisses me off, considering how he left, walking away and not bothering to apologize for it. The shrink asks me to examine those feelings. Every time I do, the irrational part of me feels guilty and disloyal to Ryan. The rational part says to tell him to fuck off and walk away.

I choose to ignore it instead. Hence the reason I'm not calling him, no matter how many times I start to punch in the number, no matter how itchy my fingers get.

The end of week three comes and goes without any word

from Declan. I can't call him. I won't. If I call him, I'll be acknowledging how worried and panicked I'm getting. I'll spend hours on the couch in a ball, picturing him on his knees with a gun pointed at the back of his head, or tied up and gagged in a dimly lit hut, some guy with gold teeth smiling broadly as he taunts him.

The longer the silence stretches, the more I realize I *care*. I want him home. I want his arms around me, the gesture so automatic I'm not sure he even realizes it. I want him muttering over his laptop or pointing his damn camera at me or sitting on the couch, trying to convince me to read *Helter Skelter* instead of *House of the Seven Gables*.

I want *him*, charming, casually cruel Declan, the man who'd rather walk away than admit he has feelings for me. It disgusts me.

It also scares me to the point I break down and call my brother to prevent me from breaking down and calling Declan. Once I do, a wave of homesickness hits. We talk for a few hours, and I find myself promising I'll see him in a week. The small college he's attending in upstate New York is an easy bus ride from the city. I book my ticket for two days from now and hope Declan doesn't come home unexpectedly.

Because I won't be coming back.

This is not my place; this is what I've learned in the three weeks Declan's been gone. I do not belong here, waiting for a man I'm not even sure wants me around. I do not belong where I know no one and can't work to support myself. I do not belong in this mostly empty but somehow charming little house. I'll never find my new life holed up here. The starkness of the walls is starting to get to me anyway.

This is not my place. It's time for me to find where my place *is*.

* * *

Sean's brows come together. "Sure, I can get you to the airport tomorrow. You know Declan's not due in for another week, though, right? He's checked in, on schedule. No pull out needed."

Oh, so he's checked in with *Sean*, but not me. His wife. Anger simmers in my blood, and I shake my head. "Can you get me to the airport or not?"

He narrows his eyes, but all he says is, "What time's your flight?"

"Two." An hour for check-in and security, and the drive to Shannon is several hours. "You'll pick me up around ten, I'm assuming? I don't want to be late. Racing through the airport isn't fun."

He scrapes back his chair and puts his mug in the sink. "Ten it is."

I lock the door behind him and return to the bedroom to pack. I've more clothes than what I came with, and fitting them in has been interesting.

The small duffle bag I brought from Sarajevo is overflowing. I dump it out on the bed and start over, refolding shirts and sweaters to make them smaller. A gorgeous royal blue sweater distracts me momentarily. It's one of the ones Declan bought me shortly after we arrived. The sweater was one of the first things that shocked me out of my stupor, the color so vibrant it dazzled.

The metal box next to it is completely out of place. I abandon the clothing and reach for it, the metal grubby with old dirt and scratches. Ryan's ashes. Declan, Murat, and Ismael committed what would be a crime in the States to retrieve the only thing that mattered to me in the entire city. The last piece of my old life. The piece that needs a final resting place.

I never took Declan to the cemetery. I have no idea how he found the gravesite or what possessed him to dig it up in the first place. But he did, and if I needed any sort of evidence the man isn't as careless with other people as I'd thought, it's staring me in the face.

Somehow that's more terrifying, knowing that he does care for me. It's no longer enough. He can't rely on actions alone anymore. Hands shaking, vision blurring, I bury the box at the bottom of the bag and stuff sweaters and jeans and shirts on top of it.

I don't sleep. The bed is haunted by our last nights together, and every time I shut my eyes, I see Declan stalking away, into the airport, leaving me to pick up the pieces and glue them back together.

My head aches and my eyes are gritty from lack of sleep when Sean pulls up at ten on the dot, and I haul my bag out to the car before he can open the door. He keeps his mouth shut as I snap on my seatbelt and stare through the windshield, waiting for him to put the car in gear and go.

We're halfway to the airport when he speaks. "You have everything? Passport, marriage certificate?"

"Yes." Shut up. Shut up, Sean, and drive.

More hills roll past, dotted with sheep. He opens his mouth again a few minutes later. "Look—"

"You know, you don't strike me as the kind of man who sticks his nose in other people's business, mostly because you don't strike me as the kind of man who cares. Is there something you want to ask me? If there is, ask."

He blows out a breath and glares at me. "I'm sayin' something because you've not mentioned Declan once. He doesn't form attachments to his women, but he's attached to you. He's not going to take it well, you sneaking out this way."

His feelings aren't my concern anymore. If he gets angry, he's got no one to blame but himself.

After that, Sean keeps his own counsel and doesn't try to talk to me for the rest of the drive. He gets my bag out of the back and sets it on the sidewalk next to me, and I stuff my hands in my pockets. "I have to go," I say quietly. "I can't think about anyone else right now. I have to fix myself first before I can think of including another person in that equation." I've put this off for too long.

I pick up my bag and glance at Sean. His face is devoid of expression, almost like he's bored. Stifling a sigh, I head into the terminal.

The flight to London is short and bumpy with turbulence, the flight to New York long and not long enough. I sleep in snatches, the drone of the engines alternately lulling and aggravating. We land, and I drag myself through the airport to baggage claim and out to a cab, ready to be done with traveling. I need a shower. A bed. Food will come later.

The city's a shock; Sarajevo was a ghost town, Galway miniscule compared to the crush of noise and movement and life that is New York. I lock myself in my hotel room and sleep for hours, haunted by dreams of Declan, a thunderous gleam in his eye as he stands over me, furious I left without saying a word.

I shoot up in bed, clutching the sheets to my chest. The room is wreathed in shadows, the lights of the city filtering through the cheap curtains. He's not here. For the first time in months, I'm in a place where he is not and has never been.

I miss him. I miss him more than when I was lying by myself in his bed, waiting for the phone to ring. I miss him more than I want, more than I can handle, the weight of it squeezing the last of the air from my lungs.

I'm alone. I am well and truly alone, with my poisonous thoughts for company. Thoughts that say I'm a coward and possibly an idiot, leaving without demanding an explanation.

I tell them to shut up, then I flop back down and shut my eyes.

Sleep's a long time coming.

CHAPTER TWENTY SIX

Tim gives me a funny look. "Aren't you going to answer that?"

I shake my head. "I'll call them back later." It's probably Declan. Aside from Tim, he's the only one who has my new cell number. I'd texted him once my service was set up and ignored his responding text. I wasn't ready to talk to him then, and I'm not ready to talk to him now. I'm not sure I'll ever be ready.

Tim lets it go, and we continue down the sun-dappled sidewalk toward the cafe he's chosen for breakfast.

I've been in the States for a month. We spent a few days in New York City, and I felt like I was suffocating, so I followed him back to his college town in upstate New York. It's a pretty one, surrounded by hills, one of the Finger Lakes glistening in the distance, orderly streets splitting off and snaking around the tip. I found a part-time job and a cheap room for rent. Finding a new therapist was tougher. I'd dipped into the bank accounts I hadn't touched for two years and spoken with three different counselors. None felt right.

There's no view of Galway Bay from any of the hills. No scent of the sea carried on the wind. I haven't been sleeping. My bed is horribly empty and cold.

It'll get better. I just have to wait it out.

Inside, we find a table and sit, scanning the menus tucked in between the salt and pepper shakers. Tim tells me about his classes, and I half-listen, the temptation to pull my phone out and listen to my voicemail growing stronger.

"Nora?"

I flinch. "What? Sorry. I wasn't paying attention."

"I could tell," he says dryly. "You talk to Mom and Dad yet?" He nods to the waitress and turns over his coffee mug.

"No. I've been putting it off. They weren't exactly supportive to begin with when I left. They know I'm alive. I sent them an email. I'll see them eventually." When I'm sure I can handle their displeasure.

The phone's burning a hole in my pocket. It has to be Declan. But hearing that whiskey-rough voice with its charming accent would send the tiny bit I've struggled to rebuild crumbling into dust.

It rings again as the waitress leaves with our orders, and at Tim's exasperated look, I dig for my phone. "I'll just shut it off if it annoys you so much."

Declan's number flashes on the read-out. I send the call the voicemail and shut it off.

I might as well have sliced open my chest. My attempts to remain engaged in the conversation with my brother fall miserably flat, my thoughts circling around to Declan's call. He has to have received the papers by now. It's the only reason I can think of he'd be calling, though it isn't much of a reason. The divorce should be simple. We have no joint assets.

Filing was surprisingly easy. I'd signed the papers in front of the notary and paid extra to have them express mailed to Galway. The sooner this was over, the better.

We finish breakfast and walk out into the warm April sunshine. "Looks like you're sticking around," he says, glancing over. "You sure you want to? There's shit to do. We're in the middle of fucking nowhere. Honestly, I'm surprised you haven't headed to Pittsburgh yet."

I sidestep a group of chattering girls. "I can't think of a good enough reason to go. I haven't been in touch with my friends there since Ryan died." I'm not ready to face another city where we'd made so many memories. Someday I will be.

That day isn't coming any time soon. "I dunno. Here seems as good a place as any. The bookstore's not so bad, and it keeps me busy. I didn't really know what I wanted to do with my life before we left for Sarajevo anyway." My job as a receptionist for an interior design firm hadn't been terribly exciting.

He walks with me through quieter streets and stops when we reach the block where I'm staying. "Seriously. You might want to call Mom and Dad. I think they're actually worried about you."

I make a face. "I'll think about it." He waves and walks back the way we came, and I cover the rest of the block to the house, head down as I dig for my key.

"Lass."

I snap my head up so fast something cracks in my neck. What the *hell* is he doing here? "Declan?"

He stalks down the porch steps, and my muscles tense as he approaches. Black hair in casual disarray. Blue eyes crackling with anger. He shouldn't look this good. "We need to talk."

Well, he did come all this way. I suppose we can talk.

I unlock the front door and lead him inside and up the stairs to the second floor. His steps are thunderous in the short hallway, his presence disconcerting and intimidating.

As soon as we're inside my room, he digs into his bag and comes out with a fistful of papers. "What the fuck is this?"

It's hard to make out the print on the scrunched papers in his hand. "I see you got the paperwork." I struggle to hold on to my cool as he growls. "What? I did what you told me to do. I filed for divorce. That's what those are. Divorce papers. You sign them and the attorney files them and we're good. You can go gallivanting off to wherever the hell it is you're supposed to go to next without worrying about some woman waiting for you."

He glares at the papers, then at me. "You could have called."

Fuck cool. I dig down for my anger. "Like you could have while you were in Mexico?" I level my gaze at him. "You call Sean to check in, but not your wife? You keep fucking up,

Declan. I'm running out of reasons to forgive you." I turn away and drop my purse on the bed. "Besides, from the way you walked away from me at the airport, I thought you'd expect this." I glance at him. "Why are you here?"

He drops his gaze to the papers and smooths them out before folding them carefully and tucking them in his bag. Then he wanders over to the window. "If I don't sign those, we're still married."

"Yes." He'd better damn well sign them. I will not be tethered to a man who has made it perfectly clear women are temporary in his life.

"As my wife, you'd be able to stay in Ireland."

If that was what I'd wanted, I'd have headed for Dublin. Shannon. Kilkenny or any of the other towns and villages on the island. "Yes."

He's quiet a while, staring out at the street like it'll give him the words to voice what's going on in his head. The longer he's silent, the more annoyed I get. I kick off my shoes and scoot farther onto the bed, and he finally glances over.

"Come back with me."

I'm sorry, did he just ask me to come to Ireland? With him? I'm sure my mouth hanging open makes an attractive picture, but I can't process what he's just said.

He sits on the edge of the bed near my feet. "You took me by surprise when you said you were clear. The first thought in my head was you didn't have a reason to stay with me anymore, and I didn't handle it well."

No shit. I cross my arms over my chest.

"I wanted more time."

I frown. "Time for what?"

He slides over so he's at my hip, reaching out to curve a hand around my jaw. "Christ, I've forgotten what your skin feels like under my hand." He strokes along my cheek, down to my mouth, his eyes locked on mine. "You wanted to know what you are to me."

I did? I do.

"You're the first woman I've wanted to come home to.

You'd distract me at the worst times out there in the desert, when I should have been thinking about who might attack our truck. I'd reach for you in the middle of the night and find empty space. I'd come home and expect to find you curled up on my couch or cursing in the kitchen because the stove wouldn't light, and you weren't there." He inches closer. "It's not love. I don't know that I'd know what it is even if it sat up and shouted at me."

Oh. Oh, *god.* I let out a shaky breath. "If you'd said something before, I wouldn't have left."

"And I'm an ass for not figuring that out sooner." He gives me a small, self-deprecating grin. "I got home after weeks worrying what would happen to you if I'd gotten my head blown off, and when you weren't there, I thought I'd lost the one thing that made that house a home. So I'm not signing those papers. If I don't sign," he says slowly, "I have time to figure this out. Without it, I don't have time, and this isn't something you'd rush. Am I right?" I shake my head. "Will you give it to me?"

Can I? Part of this feels like too little, too late. I drop my gaze. "I don't know if I can." I pull his hand away and wrap it in both of mine. "I'm a mess, Declan. Relationships for me are about putting the other person first, and I have to put myself first this time. I need to fix myself." My chest tightens. The reason I left, the one buried under the pain of how he'd treated me, is still true. It hasn't magically gone away because he's admitted his mistake, and that he wants me with him. I have work to do. I didn't expect it to hurt this much. "I need you to sign."

He frees his hand and slips it around the back of my neck. "No."

"No?"

He scoots me across the bed, lifts me to straddle his lap, his hands coming up to frame my face. "No. I made a mistake, not saying something before I left for Mexico. I kept making it by not coming after you sooner. I'm not signing," he repeats. "I've never tried this before. I didn't want the guilt on my head, the possibility that someone I care for, who cares for me, would have to live with the grief I cause them by getting killed on an assignment. Then you pulled me out of the street. Take a chance on me, lass. I'm taking a chance on you."

The band constricting my chest breaks, and I tip my forehead to rest against his. For the first time since I left him, I feel I'm finally where I'm supposed to be. "You want to make this work?"

"I want *you*."

I lift my head and find his mouth is inches away. "You gonna kiss me if I say yes?"

He smiles. "Only if you mean it."

Of course I mean it. "You gonna take me home?"

He tips back, making me sprawl over him. "I will. After you say yes and we take advantage of this bed." His hands work their way under my shirt, fingertips brushing along my spine.

I splay my hands across his chest, rubbing my fingers along the worn fabric of his t-shirt. "Sex doesn't make everything better, you know. You're going to have to talk to me." His eyes darken and he looks away. "Declan, I'm not leaving without a promise you'll talk to me instead of stalking off all broody. You seem to have a problem talking about things that bother you. That shit won't fly with me."

The intensity of his gaze causes my heart to stumble and trip. "I'm not walking away from you anymore, Nora. But if I'm promising something, I want one from you as well. Be patient with me. And for Chrissake, if I'm fucking up, call me on it."

"Don't I already do that?" I stretch up and tease his mouth with mine. I wonder if he knows how much he's already told me, with his touch and his kisses and his words. This man may never tell me he loves me. And I won't need it. Not as long as he shows me like he has today. I sink into the kiss, joy surging through my veins. "Okay," I whisper against his mouth.

I am not okay. Not yet. But I will be.

EPILOGUE

"I really have to go, Declan. I'll call you when I get home." I cradle the phone between my ear and my shoulder and shuffle some of the books around. Is it really so hard to put something back where you found it? I pluck a stray copy of *The Long Kiss Goodnight* from the shelf and tuck it under my arm.

"A text will be fine, lass." When Declan found out I'd been staying well past closing to complete inventory counts, he insisted I call or text him once I got home. The streets of Galway might look safe, he said, but I shouldn't take chances.

Never mind he's not even in the country anyway.

He got the jump on me tonight, though, calling shortly before closing. "Better yet, just go on home now. Inventory counts aren't part of your duties, are they? Take a night off," he says.

I roll my eyes and pluck another book from the wrong shelf, dropping the one under my arm on the floor. I should have moved the cart. "No, staying to help with inventory isn't part of my duties. I've got nothing better to do, though, so I might as well."

Our house feels so empty. When he first told me he'd taken a two month assignment in Jordan, I'd been furious. Him pointing out his assignments regularly lasted that long didn't help. Two months apart and him in a country losing ground to militant extremists every day? It was worse than Sarajevo.

I won't say I became okay with it when he showed me the house he was trying to buy, but I understood. The amount of money he'd make from the sale of those photos and the possibility of a solo show at the London Photographic Society meant the charming house near the cliffs could be ours.

It was bigger, as he'd said. Much bigger. Enough space for a dog and a couple of kids. It was the first time he'd said anything about wanting children. I wanted them eventually. When I was ready for them, I'd planned to talk to Declan. The man beat me to it.

He growls. "Don't stay too late. And text me when you get home." I promise to do so and hang up, then hunt up a cart.

"Nora?" Molly, my boss, pokes her head into the aisle. "Finish up with the shelves and go on home. The computer's blinking at me again, and Andrew can't get in to fix it until the morning."

Looks like Declan's getting his wish after all.

I finish up, wondering how hard could it be to remember that H came after G, not M. Books ended up in the strangest places. Molly shoos me out the door and locks it behind me, the soft glow of the display lights casting shadows onto the sidewalk. The gentle August warmth faded as the sun went down, and I shiver in my thin sweater, hurrying to the car park.

The streets are crowded with tourists and locals alike, enjoying the clear summer night, so it takes longer than usual to reach our house on the outskirts of the city. Lights shine through the living room windows as I pull into our street, and I let the car idle a moment as I try to remember if I'd left them on. Maybe Sean had been by? He had a key, though Declan wasn't due home for another week; there was no reason for him to come around.

I fish my phone out of my purse and prepare to call the Garda, creeping up to the front door. It's shut, and before I can hit the Call button on my phone, the door swings open and Declan's standing in front of me.

I blink. It's not real. He's supposed to be in Jordan until

next week, possibly longer. I poke him with a finger, surprised when he grunts and catches my hand, dragging me against him and into the house.

Then his mouth is on mine, and yes, he is very, very real. Hot and demanding and possessive, everything I've come to expect his kisses to be over the past five months. I sigh into his mouth and loop my arms around his neck, wrapping my legs around his waist as he braces me against the door.

"You're home," I murmur when he lets me breathe.

"Missed you," he growls. He slicks his tongue over my lower lip, slipping it inside to glide along mine when I whimper. He stumbles away from the door and over to the couch, thumping onto it with a groan. "Christ, Nora. You feel too good." His exhalation is shaky, and he tips his forehead against mine.

He's *home*. The days and weeks he'd spend thousands of miles away are worth it now, feeling his arms around me, his hands warm on my skin. I kiss the tip of his nose. "You better not be going anywhere soon. I picked up a new book for us." We'd kept up the habit of reading aloud to each other. Old-fashioned, yes, but there was little I loved more than hearing Declan speak.

"What'd you get?"

I grin, lips spreading farther as he groans. "Ah, ah, no complaining, it was my pick this time. *The Maltese Falcon*," I say. "What, did you *want* to read more smut?" He'd chosen an immensely popular erotic romance just before he'd left, for some reason thinking I wanted to read it. I'd thrown the book at his head.

"No," he says firmly and moves his head back so he can look at me. "I have something for you."

I clasp my hands behind his neck, rubbing a thumb along his skin. "You mean coming home early wasn't enough of a present?"

He grins, that brilliant, charming grin that never fails to get me wet. "Oh, you'll be calling in sick tomorrow. I've a mind not to let you out of bed for a long while."

I lift a brow. "And if I told you to fuck off?"

"Only foolin', lass. I know how much you like your job." He kisses my forehead and reaches over to the table next to the couch, his breath stuttering as he palms a small box. Suddenly wary, I watch as he thumbs it open, the box shaking as his hand trembles. "I thought we should make this a little more official."

Inside is a silver ring, covered in delicate scrollwork. He works it free of its velvet cushion and sets the box aside, grasping my left wrist and guiding my hand down. "It's a traditional Irish wedding band," he says gruffly. The metal's cool as it slides onto my finger, the band a little loose. I suck in a breath and stare at it. Such a slight weight, a small change, and it breaks everything wide open and I know with dead certainty Declan will continue to take a chance on me for the rest of our lives.

He's amazing. Amazing, stubborn, and mine, tactlessness and all. Forever. I cup his jaw. "Thank you," I whisper. Tomorrow, I'm going through every jewelry shop in town until I find the perfect ring for him. Titanium. Something almost impossible to break. I kiss him softly. "Take me to bed."

He cups my ass and surges to his feet, striding out of the living room and into the bedroom. Hands and mouths crazed with need, we're naked in less than a minute, reacquainting ourselves with all our favorite parts.

"*Move.*" I scrape my nails down his back when he pauses, the head of his cock pressed against me. Tormenting me.

"Spent the last two months dreaming of this. I'm damn well taking my time." The chords of his neck stand out from the strain of going slow, and I rear up and bite one, surprising him into pushing forward with a long, broken groan.

I don't want slow. *Slow* is for later. He gives in and gives me fast, sweat and fire and a pleasure so fierce it threatens to pull me under. Afterward, curled up against him, my head on his chest, I ask the question I'd been fighting with ever since he showed me the house. "Do you want kids?"

His hand rests at my lower back. "Wouldn't mind a couple.

Think they'd be fun." He shifts his hand to hip and moves me to straddle him. "Not ready to share you yet, though."

I nip into his chin, relieved at the answer. "So lots of practicing, huh?" A shudder slips down my spine as his mouth finds the sensitive spot under my ear.

"Absolutely." He flips me onto my back and sits back on his knees. "Why don't I show you what I've got in mind?"

It's easy to return his sly smile. I stretch my arms above my head, lips widening to a grin as his gaze heats. "I believe you said something about not letting me out of this bed for a few days? Perhaps we should start there?"

His mouth twists in a smirk. "Perhaps." And he bends down to kiss me.

Author's Note

While the Siege of Sarajevo was real, the events in this book
are a work of fiction. Any errors, geographical or otherwise, are
mine.

Fracture playlist

This playlist is available on Spotify! Just search for AmandaKByrne.

"Hell" Squirrel Nut Zippers
"Castle of Glass" Linkin Park
"Ping Pong" Bassnectar
"Gorecki" Lamb
"I Stay Away" Alice in Chains
"Metal Heart" Garbage
"Switchblade Smiles" Kasabian
"O Nata Lux" Morten Lauridsen
"The Funeral" Band of Horses
"Bullet the Blue Sky" U2
"Gimme Shelter" Merry Clayton
"Long Way Back Home" Barenaked Ladies
"Central Reservation" Beth Orton
"Turn Me On" David Guetta feat. Nicki Minaj
"Why We Fight" The Decemberists
"Zombie (Acoustic)" The Cranberries
"Sleep Now in the Fire" Rage Against the Machine

Here's a sneak peek at *Hidden Scars*, available September 2015.

Snow flew with such force, Sara couldn't see the plane. Hell, she couldn't see the gangplank. This could not be good. There was no way they would be able to take off.

Only her boss would make her fly to Chicago on a sales presentation knowing a massive storm was on track to barrel through the Great Lakes and hit the city before they could return to Portland. Turning from the window, she wheeled her roll aboard to the ticket desk.

Canceled.

She blinked. The sign could not be right. She blinked again. Yup. Flight 246, Chicago to Portland, was canceled. Fantastic. One thing was certain. She was not spending the night in the airport. Her narrow skirt was too uncomfortable.

Taylor had to be around somewhere. Scanning the gate area, she skipped right past her partner in crime for this trip before she spotted him leaning against a support pillar. She marched over. "I'm going to see about booking a flight out tomorrow, and then I'm heading to the nearest hotel with a free room. You staying or coming with?"

He straightened. "Coming with. I'm not keen on sleeping on the floor." He followed her over to the ticket desk line, and then promptly ignored her.

Standing next to him, she did her best to ignore him as well, running through the report they'd have to give when they arrived home, ticking off errands she'd need to run, stifling a groan when she remembered she hadn't gotten a birthday present for her mother.

Her gaze slid sideways. Taylor was an attractive man. Tall, slimly built, his dark brown hair edged toward red and his hazel eyes cornered the intensity market. He was just so damn quiet, so good at blending into the woodwork, she honestly didn't remember he worked down the hall from her until Larry had announced they'd be working up the presentation together.

He'd proven to be the perfect partner, efficient, calm, and willing to wait out long outbursts by the potential client. The late nights she'd come to expect with her usual work partner never happened, and he didn't crowd into her space. Though she found herself wishing he would sometimes. He didn't wear cologne, so it was only when he'd bend in close to her desk that she'd catch the hint of juniper from his aftershave.

No, Taylor was all about the job, and that was all that mattered. Nailing the presentation was the big, glossy cherry on top.

The line inched forward, and her feet started to cramp. She shifted from foot to foot, trying not to grimace.

"What are you doing?"

She didn't jump, though it was a near thing. Damn ninja skills. She smiled up at him. "Feet hurt." *Don't say it. Don't say I shouldn't have worn heels.* The four inch, round toe pumps were actually some of the most comfortable heels she owned. They were, however, still high heels, and the balls of her feet were beginning to protest.

He made a noise that sounded like a snort. *Typical male response.* Her shoulders set into a hard line.

They finally made it to the desk and were assured if the storm blew through tonight like the forecast predicted, the runways would be operational and tomorrow's midday flight to PDX would leave as scheduled. Maybe not on time, but it would leave.

Grateful to have one part of the evening over, Sara headed for the baggage claim. She'd flown through Midway often enough to know which end of the baggage claim to go to for the airport hotels. Taylor resumed his strong, silent type impression and followed her.

Digging out her Blackberry, she pulled up an app and started checking for hotels. The search returned a couple options, and she blew out a breath, some of the tension leaving her back. "Hey, can you see if there's a Red Lion shuttle? Supposedly they've still got rooms available."

"You could call them."

"About to. But if the shuttle's already here, we might as well get on it. It's way too cold out to keep standing around."

She jerked at the hand on her elbow, the warmth from his touch zinging through her. She glanced up at Taylor's impassive face. "Shuttle's over there. Just pulled in."

Good. Great. She nodded rather than speak, certain her voice would crack.

The air froze in her lungs as they stepped out of the terminal. Snow swirled under the overhang, piling on the roadway. Would the shuttle even be able to leave? They didn't get storms like this in Portland. The driver stood next to the shuttle door, waving people on, so she tightened her grip on her roll aboard.

They climbed aboard, and after she found a seat, she dialed the hotel. The call dropped. She tried again. No signal. Technology sucked balls. It never worked when you needed it most. She crossed her fingers the website wasn't lying and they'd have rooms available. With the number of travelers stuck in the airport this evening, she'd take all the luck she could get.

The damn heels were choking her feet. She couldn't wait to get the shoes off and stick her feet in some cool water. She imagined a nice, long, relaxing shower, followed by a horrendously expensive glass of wine. It would be worth it.

Twenty snow covered minutes later, the shuttle crawled to a stop at the entrance to the hotel. Biting back a moan, she did her best not to limp to the front desk and pasted on a cheery smile. "Hi. I'm really hoping you've got a couple of rooms available."

The front desk clerk was already engrossed in her screen. "You're in luck. I've got a single available. Queen sized, non-smoking."

Her nerves went on high alert, telling her feet to turn right around and walk out the door, find another hotel. Silly. She shook it off. No reason to panic. If there was one room left, they'd get one of those cot things. "I'll take it. Do you have a rollaway?"

The clerk's smile was apologetic and did nothing to quell the anxiety rising once more in Sara's stomach. "No, I'm sorry. That is, literally, the last bed we have."

Her stomach twisted at the thought of spending the night with a man for the first time in seven years. One of them would sleep on the floor. Easy. Her hands were steady as she pulled out her corporate Amex, and she gave herself a mental pat on the back. Her therapist would be proud. Once she'd received the room key, she discovered Taylor had been behind her the entire time. She held up the key. "Room 505. I promise I don't snore." Her grin felt brittle. She kept it in place, letting it fall only after Taylor nodded and walked off toward the elevators.

She could handle one night with a stranger.

Since he couldn't see her, she limped her way to the elevator, and once inside, gave up and pried off her shoes. "Don't say it," she muttered, anticipating Taylor's retort. She yawned, fatigue overriding everything else. Her fantasy of a hot shower and a glass of wine died a quiet death. All she wanted to do was undress and fall into bed.

"Wouldn't dream of it." Was she crazy, or was there a hint of a smile in his voice? She risked a glance at his face. Perfectly blank. The man was a frickin' safe.

They found room 505, and she swiped the card key through the reader. She fumbled for the switch on the wall, and the dim light didn't do much to chase the shadows from the room. Her gaze immediately fell on the bed. Definitely not big enough for two. Hell, even if it was a king size it wouldn't be big enough. "I'll take the floor. I'm sure there's extra blankets and stuff in the closet." Most hotels had them. Right?

"Take the bed. I can sleep on the floor." He set his laptop case next to the closet.

"No, I'll take it." Despite her tiredness, she doubted she'd get much sleep anyway, and she didn't want to keep him awake with her tossing and turning.

Now he did snort. "Fine."

Hitching up her skirt, she knelt in front of her roll aboard and found her toiletry kit and the boxers and oversized t-shirt she'd been sleeping in. Taylor was working at the knot in his tie when she shut the door to the bathroom.

Deep breaths. He hadn't shown any signs of being attracted to her, either tonight or in the past. He hadn't put up much of a fight over the bed versus floor thing. She could do this. She could think of it as a practice run for when she *did* want a man in her bed, and, well, being in the room was safer than trying to sleep in the concourse.

Drawing her brown hair into a ponytail, she washed her face, then pulled on her sleep gear. After one last check in the mirror showed she'd gotten rid of the mascara rings under her eyes, she opened the door.

"Taylor, did you—" She stepped out and the words dammed up in her mouth.

The tattoo covering his back was more than ink. It was art. It belonged on full display, where it could be admired, studied, envied.

Black shaded to grey, the edges of the frame bleeding out rather than squaring off. A lone figure was stretched along his spine, and she could feel the pain of the needles as they worked over the thin skin, so close to bone. Stuck in the middle of a desolate wasteland, it conveyed a bitter, suffocating loneliness, the figure hunched over as it walked.

His muscles rippled, and she balled her hands into fists, shocked at the impulses twitching under her skin. She wanted to trace every line with her fingertips, then do it all over again with her tongue. It was a slim back, broader at the shoulder, tapered at the waist, fit and lean. A back that would hide well under a tailored suit.

It had her considering Taylor Smith in a whole new light. The unassuming sales executive with his quiet good looks took on a sleek and sensuous edge.

Her mouth snapped shut when he glanced over his shoulder. "Um. Blankets? Were there any?" Swallowing became very difficult as she watched him walk to the closet, muscles bunching as he reached up.

He tossed the blanket on the bed. "Thanks." She grabbed the pillow nearest to her and hugged it to her chest.

There were scars. Faint ones, thick ones, running over the ridges of his abdomen, up on his biceps, and a long, jagged one trailing down his sternum. There had to be a story behind those, too, and the questions whispered in the back her mind.

She wasn't staring. She just couldn't bring herself to meet his gaze. She shifted it to the floor, the pillow falling from her hands.

"Sara."

Her head snapped up.

He reminded her of a hunting cat, all patience and stealth. His expression gave nothing away, although he had to be annoyed by her staring. If her scars were visible, she'd be annoyed, too.

She brushed the guilty thought aside. "Yes?"

"Room service? We didn't get a chance to eat." He handed her a paper menu. "You done in the bathroom?"

She nodded absently, studying the menu. Better to study the menu than the man in front of her.

When the bathroom door clicked shut, air rushed from her lungs. She had to get a handle on this. This was Taylor. Boring old Taylor. Who cared if his body made him a little more interesting? Under it, he was still the same person who ignored her unless he needed something for work. It was probably her mind's way of telling her she was ready to take the next step. There were other men out there if she wanted an entanglement. Men who talked. Unlike Taylor.

Sitting on the edge of the bed, she switched on the TV, flipping channels while she waited for him to come out. Russell Crowe's face flashed over the screen, and she paused. *LA Confidential.* Sweet. Scooting toward the headboard, she grabbed the remaining pillow and tucked it behind her.

Guy Pearce was interrogating the three punks they'd picked up on suspicion of committing the Nite Owl murders when Taylor emerged from the bathroom. He'd exchanged his suit pants for a pair of ratty grey sweats, and covered his scars and tattoo with a worn t-shirt. Good. He'd be less distracting.

He sat on the bed and reached for the phone. "You know what you want?"

"Mmm." Sara kept her eyes on the screen. *Ignore him.* "Club sandwich. Fries. And wine. I think there's a merlot on there."

Her mind trick worked, and by the time the food arrived, he was back to being Taylor, quiet Taylor, and she picked at her food, the film sucking her in. God, she loved this film, the intricacies, the performances, the *costumes.* The women of that era knew how to dress. They didn't starve away their curves. They played them up, skirts slim and molding over hips, waists nipping in, colors popping.

"What are we watching?"

She almost jumped at the question. He'd melted into the woodwork, as usual. She bit a fry in half. "*LA Confidential.* One of my favorites."

"Never heard of it."

She flapped a hand at him. "Now you have."

There may have been a soft chuckle, but as Vincennes was about to get his brains blown out, she wasn't paying attention.

Reality returned as the end credits rolled, and she stretched, noting with surprise her plate was gone. She smothered a yawn. She was wiped, and even though it was only half past ten, she needed to pass out. "Um. D'you mind if I turn in now? The light on the bedside table won't bother me."

He shrugged, hazel eyes inscrutable. "Probably a good idea. I might catch up on some work."

Was that all he did? Work? Normally at this time of night, she'd be curled up in bed with a book. He had to have hobbies. Things he did outside of work.

And it *so* wasn't any of her business. "Whatever." She climbed off the bed, taking the pillow with her and dropping it on the floor.

"You don't really need to do that."

She glanced up. "Do what?"

He lifted a brow. "Sleep on the floor. I'll do it."

"I don't mind." She wasn't going to let him take the floor for her any more than she was going to share the bed. He could have it. The hard floor would help keep her from sleeping too deeply.

She padded into the bathroom and brushed her teeth, lecturing herself. Everything would be fine. Taylor was a co-worker. Not all men were horrible assholes. It was one night, and she was on the floor, he was in the bed, and everything would be fine.

He was stretched out on the bed, reading through some papers when she came out of the bathroom. He didn't look up as she picked up the blanket from the end of the bed. Spreading it over the floor, she lay down, pulled half of it over her, and shut her eyes.

She was asleep within seconds.

* * *

Taylor sat in the semi-darkness, listening to Sara's steady breathing. He'd seen her reaction to his tattoo, his scars. He was used to it. It was a typical female reaction. Everything else about her was off. The outgoing, friendly Sara had secrets in her eyes.

Curvy little thing. The shirt she slept in covered it well. Her suit was a different story. It had followed those curves like a sports car hugging the road. His fingers twitched with the urge to peel it off her, piece by piece, find all her sweet spots with his tongue as her clothing fell away.

The contrasts sparked his curiosity. So he'd sat back and watched the movie, picking up what he could without asking questions. The longer he stayed quiet, the more comfortable she seemed, at least until the end of the movie. She'd tightened up again as she'd gotten ready for sleep.

A soft snuffling noise drew his attention to the floor on the opposite side of the bed, and he eased over. She'd curled into a tight ball and was huddled under the blanket. He shook his head. Stupid. It was snowing outside, and she was sleeping on the floor with nothing more than a blanket. She needed a quilt.

He watched a shudder work through her. Fuck this, fuck

the chivalry. It was too damn cold, and she'd looked completely worn out by the time the movie ended. They both needed a good night's sleep. He slid off the bed and stalked around the end of it.

She jerked, then stilled, as he placed a hand on her shoulder. One eye cracked open, and he swallowed a sigh. "It's too cold for this shit, Sara," he said quietly. "Get in the bed. I won't bite."

Both eyes open, she stared at him a while longer, watching him with a weariness he felt echoing in his bones. She struggled to sit up, kicking aside the blanket. The pillow went back on the bed, and she crawled under the covers, curling into a ball once more as she shivered with cold. "Thanks," she mumbled.

"Nothing to thank me for." He wasn't some kind of monster. He circled the bed and slid in, listening for her breathing to go deep before he lifted his hips and pushed his sweats down, then eased into a sitting position and yanked off his t-shirt. He wasn't going to touch her, but he wasn't going to make himself uncomfortable, either. She'd have to deal with his boxers.

As he waited for sleep to come, he wondered who'd made her so afraid.

ABOUT THE AUTHOR

When she's not plotting ways to sneak her latest shoe purchase past her partner, Amanda writes sexy, snarky romance and urban fantasy. She likes her heroines smart and unafraid to make mistakes, and her heroes strong enough to take them on.

If she's not writing, she's reading, drinking hot chocolate, and trying not to destroy her house with her newest DIY project. She lives in the beautiful Pacific Northwest, and no, it really doesn't rain that much.

You can connect with her online at amandakbyrne.com